MONA LISA'S SECRET

PHIL PHILIPS

A cataloguing-in-publication entry is available from the catalogue of National Library of Australia at www.nla.gov.au.

Requests to publish work from this book should be sent to:
admin@philphilips.com

Philips, Phil, 1978-

ISBN-13: 978-0-9925345-5-4
ISBN-10: 0-9925345-5-0

Typeset in 11pt Sabon

For more information visit
www.philphilips.com

Dedicated to my cousin Stefano.
Close to our hearts you will stay loved
and remembered forever.

The Mona Lisa painted by Leonardo da Vinci.

Fact:

Vincenzo Peruggia was the man who stole
the Mona Lisa in 1911 and kept it hidden away
in his Paris apartment for two years.

Chapter 1

In the heat of summer, renaissance restorer Bernard Martino entered the Louvre and forced his way down the seemingly endless corridor of vaulted archways in a hurry. His loose white shirt clung to his back in places as he pushed through the masses of sweaty tourists that flowed like a sluggish river through the galleries.

In the distance of the Denon Wing loomed the gateway to the Louvre's most popular section – *La Grande Galerie* – which housed the most valuable Italian masterpieces of all time. Bernard panted with the effort of forcing his unfit, slightly overweight forty-year-old frame through the crowds.

'Hey, slow down!' shouted an American who was shoved to one side as Bernard charged past. 'What's the hurry?'

Bernard ignored the man's outburst and continued clearing a path for himself. His round face was now drenched in sweat and his breathing became more ragged with each stride as he reached the *Winged Victory of Samothrace*, a Greek marble statue which

1

dated back to 190 BC and connected the Denon Wing with the Sully Wing.

He stopped to take a breath, his eyes darting upward to the security cameras mounted high on the walls, turning to capture his every move.

'Fuck you,' he muttered with a rude hand gesture to the nearest camera, his tone filled with menace. 'You destroyed my life today. And that's why I'm going to destroy yours.'

All of a sudden, a message was played over the Louvre's PA system in French.

'This is an announcement for Mr. Bernard Martino. Stay where you are and we will come to collect you. I repeat, stay where you are. Thank you.'

Bernard sighed, glancing back down the hallway to see three of the Louvre's personal guards in their blue uniforms fast approaching from the reception area. Their boots thumped the marble floor as they ran toward him.

Bernard knew their orders would have been simple: to stop him at any cost.

A whistle was blown and the throng of people moved over to one side to create a rift for the guards to pass through. They looked like marines, all with clipped hair, over six feet tall and armed with Glock nine-millimeter semi-automatic pistols in their holsters. They were dressed in navy from head to toe and had a large white police insignia emblazoned on their backs. Also in view were white communications earpieces that hung down from their left ears and disappeared into their jackets.

Bernard took stock and then began to race up the

stairs to a blur of beautiful ceilings. 'Today I will reveal the lie ...' he shouted. 'No more lies!'

In his left gloved hand he held a bottle of San Pellegrino mineral water and in his right a set of keys that dangled down from a circular key chain. One particular key hung lower than the others due to its longer neck. Its shiny rich gold surface looked like it belonged in a keyhole of grave importance.

'Stop, Martino! Or we'll be forced to take further measures,' shouted the senior guard in French, who sported a five-o'clock shadow on his chiseled face. He led the two other men as they passed the *Winged Victory of Samothrace* and hit the stairs, his hand hovering near his holster.

'I can't see him,' the French guard said into his radio mouthpiece. 'There're too many people. He must be heading for the *Salle des Etats*. We have a code red situation. I repeat, code red.'

At the end of the hall Bernard turned right through the wooden-framed doors of the *Salle des Etats* – the large rectangular chamber that housed the *Mona Lisa*. He turned to the northwestern wall. A cluster of tourists were lined up to see Leonardo da Vinci's most famous work, what the French like to call *La Joconde*. He sprinted forward, pushing through the people like Moses parting the Red Sea.

'Hey, wait your turn,' shouted an elderly lady with thick-framed glasses in English.

'*Ta zài tui*,' spoke a Chinese man, shaking his head, clearly not happy.

But Bernard didn't care. Today, he needed to do something. As he reached the front of the queue he saw the *Mona Lisa* in all its glory, set into a raw sandy wall six feet from where he stood. It sat behind two wooden barriers inside a vitrine. Facing the painting, Bernard ducked under the first curved wooden barrier, then slid under the wooden benchtop that sat beneath the *Mona Lisa*.

He could hear the puzzled murmurs coming from the crowd of people around him.

'*Was macht er?*'

'He can't go over there!'

Concealed in front of him on the wall was a cream cover plate; he flipped it open to reveal a unique keyhole. With shaking fingers, he took out the gold key and slid it into the hole, turning it clockwise.

Instantly, the bulletproof glass panel protecting the priceless *Mona Lisa* tilted upward. Following the grooves in the wall and the high ceiling, it ascended smoothly, exposing the oil painting.

There were gasps of astonishment from the crowd as they noticed the moving glass. For security reasons, only a handful of people were privileged to see how the *Mona Lisa* was extracted to be restored and cleaned before being placed back on display, and now hundreds of people had witnessed it.

Bernardo quickly slid out from under the wooden bench and began to unscrew the lid on his water bottle using his gloved hand, careful not to spill the contents.

'What's he doing?' asked a young female tourist with a Canon DSLR camera strapped around her neck.

At that moment the three guards entered the room

with their weapons raised and ready to fire. Bernard turned to see their widening eyes as they saw that the precious *Mona Lisa* was exposed and vulnerable.

'Stop!' shouted the senior guard in French, his gun aimed at Bernard's chest. 'Put the bottle down now!'

Screams of panic erupted from the hundred-odd tourists jostling for position. Most of them dropped to the famous parquet floor while the tourists near the entrance sprinted down the hallway, causing panic along the Denon Wing. People outside the *Salle des Etats* who had heard the screams must have thought it was some kind of terrorist attack, as they began bolting for their lives to safety outside the glass pyramid. There was chaos as men and women tripped over each other trying to escape. Bernard took this in dispassionately. He no longer cared.

'Behold the famous painting,' he said, pointing to it, and felt a wave of pride wash over him at what he had achieved over the years. It was truly his best work. And yet the *Mona Lisa's* enigmatic smile now hung unprotected, laid bare by a man who wanted to destroy it.

'Don't do it,' said the lead guard.

Bernard continued to speak, his voice booming across the room. 'Painted by the famous Leonardo – da Vinci ...' he said theatrically.

'Stop!' the guard warned once more, his voice strong and direct. 'We'll be forced to shoot you.'

'You have all been deceived,' said Bernard, motioning his arm backwards while holding the bottle tightly, ready to move it forward and splash the contents all over the masterpiece in front of him.

'No! Put the bottle down. You move again and we will shoot.'

Bernard began to weep. He knew there was no going back from this. 'I will show you the truth,' he cried. 'Your Louvre curator Pierre Savard, a man I thought was my friend, has betrayed you ... just as he has betrayed me.'

'Hand the bottle over,' said the guard again.

'He doesn't want you to know,' said Bernard.

The guard touched his ear as if someone on the other end had given him instructions. His eyes burned into Bernard's. 'I have been ordered to shoot you if you continue.'

Bernard smiled sarcastically at the guard. 'Pierre Savard, the man in your ear, wants to keep me quiet, because he doesn't want the world to know that the *Mona Lisa* is a —'

Bernard didn't finish that sentence.

A single bullet was fired into his abdomen, causing him to drop to his knees before he had a chance to fling the contents of the bottle onto the exposed painting.

The water bottle fell out of his hand and rolled onto the freshly waxed timber floor. A sharp, strong smell was suddenly present in the room.

'*Acide*,' said the senior guard, who positioned himself above the injured man's body with his weapon trained on him. 'Target is down.'

Bernard's bloody hands held tight onto his torn torso as he fell to one side like a heavy bag of potatoes. He could feel his life slowly draining away. Little by little his eyelids began to close as the urge to go on faded. He was going to die beneath the painting he had spent most of his life restoring. The painting he'd tried so hard to protect. Perhaps that was only right.

With one last whimper, Bernard mumbled something. His lips struggled to move as his eyes closed, but his final words came out in a whisper not loud enough for anyone to hear: 'It's a fake …'

Chapter 2

Los Angeles, Santa Monica
October 17th 2016 (35 years later)

Joey Peruggia opened up the large bi-fold doors to his penthouse suite wearing nothing but an early-morning erection. The soft amber glow of the sunrise poured through his fingers and onto his upturned face, hitting his naked body. It flooded the open-plan room and kissed his girlfriend's exposed curves as she lay on top of the white bedsheets. The smell of the Californian ocean breeze brought a smile to his face as he grabbed hold of the glass balustrade and took in the view. He felt like a king in his castle, looking down at the ant-sized people walking, exercising and swimming on his beach.

As the last living member of the Peruggia family, Joey had inherited it all at the tender age of twenty-six. The sports cars, the boats, and his father's most prized possession: the Beach Club. This, he had renamed Joey's Beach Club in order to break away from the shadow cast by his father, a man so many people had feared. Joey was rich. He was young and free to do as he pleased. Standing there in the sunlight, his eyes glistened a dominant blue and his sun-bleached hair ruffled in the breeze. The Vitruvian Man tattoo on his wrist was a reminder of where he came from and who he was.

Deep in thought, he scanned the south side of the sandy beach. The place where it had all gone down. The memory of his deceased father and brother was still fresh in his mind: the heist. The murders. The betrayal. It had all gone to shit in the very end.

A year had passed, but somehow it seemed like only yesterday. After avenging their deaths, something inside Joey had awoken, making him feel alive. He felt he had lost all trace of his boyhood and innocence.

He thought about his first kill, FBI agent Monica Anton, who had deserved to die. His father had been right all along; she had been toxic. She'd brought nothing into his life but pain and death. The day he had flicked the switch on the detonator that had caused her car to explode was a day that was now burned into his brain.

Joey had grown up with criminal figures for role models, but he was always loved and treated like the baby in the family. Now that everyone in the gang, including his father and brother, were gone, Joey knew he needed to move on and make a new start. He now had the opportunity to shape his own life, one which he hoped to face with a new emotional maturity, and one that he could fill with happiness and fulfillment.

Looking back at the past year, Joey could see he was not the same old stupid surfer kid everyone had once known. He had seen that crime may lead to riches, but it also leads to death and heartbreak, so he'd turned his back on it. He was a changed man with a desire to learn and a thirst for knowledge. He scoured the books and poured himself into the pages. It was through his newfound interest in the arts and literature, in fact, that he'd met the girl of his dreams, Marie.

'Hey, sexy,' said a soothing voice from the king-sized bed inside, interrupting his train of thought.

Joey turned to see his gorgeous girlfriend, whose taut legs straddled the sheets. Marie, a recently sworn-in American citizen with a culturally diverse background of British, Swiss and French, was ten years older than Joey, though her baby face belied her age. Her long, honey-brown hair and hazel eyes complimented her olive complexion, but her sexy legs were what caught his attention now, and he wanted nothing more than to join her for a morning cuddle.

A smile played on his face as he walked back inside what had once been his father's luxury penthouse suite, built with bulletproof windows. In the center of the room was a sunken lounge area featuring four custom-built white leather lounges, all facing each other around a marbled mosaic floor and a billiard table, which backed onto a custom-built dark-mahogany floor-to-ceiling bookcase.

Walking past the billiard table and running the fingers of his left hand along the green baize, he was stopped by a peculiar jarring noise. It sounded like two pieces of metal scraping against each other.

'What is that?' said Joey to Marie, who sat up on the bed. The sound was coming from behind his father's bookcase. He moved closer to listen. The bookcase was twenty feet wide and completely filled with books. The intricately molded carvings were all handmade, and a moveable slide ladder sat to the far left-hand side.

Moving so that his ear was right up against the bookshelf, Joey heard a different noise this time.

Whop ... *Whop* ... Then Joey heard two distinctive *bips* that came to a sudden stop.

'Did you hear that?' said Joey, pointing to the books.

'What is it?' asked Marie, cocking her head to one side.

'I think there's something behind this wall. Maybe there's a secret room in here.' Joey was only half joking. Now that he thought about it, it seemed like exactly the sort of thing his father might have done.

'What? Like a Harry Potter bookcase thing?' asked Marie curiously. 'See if you can find an opening.'

'My dad spent millions on this place. It wouldn't surprise me if he had built a secret room or panic room in here somewhere. The question is how to get inside?'

Marie stood up, threw on her white summery dressing-gown and picked up Joey's ripped jeans off the tiled floor. She sauntered over to her man, who was kneeling on the ground searching for any evidence of a door or entry point.

'Hey, put this on,' said Marie, throwing him his pants. 'No one wants to see your butt crack.'

Joey quickly dressed himself and went back to the bookcase. He tried pushing and pulling the bookshelves, hoping to find a moveable part, but there was nothing. The carefully constructed unit was as solid as a rock.

'Maybe check to see if there's a lever somewhere?'

'Marie, I think you've seen too many movies.'

'Look ... if there's a door, there has to be some kind of access point like a lever, a handle or a button that opens it.'

Joey took Marie's advice and started moving books off the middle shelf and piling them on top of each other on the tiled floor beside the billiard table. The musty smell of unopened books and old paper flew up in the air, causing Marie to sneeze, so she took a step back as he continued his search. One complete row of Encyclopedia Britannica volumes soon covered the penthouse floor. Joey moved on to the next shelf up. Halfway through the third shelf he froze. Something had caught his eye. In the upper right-hand corner, he had spotted an old-looking Bible. A flood of memories came crashing in.

The Bible, with its thick dark-brown spine, was much larger and wider than the books sitting beside it. It seemed like it didn't belong next to a row of bright-blue, glossy books on high-powered boats, yachts and jetskis.

'Hang on,' Joey said.

'What is it?' asked Marie.

'Could it be?' he whispered to himself. 'It all makes sense now.'

'What does?'

Joey turned excitedly to Marie. 'Before my father died, he told me I'd find the answers I seek in the Bible. At first I thought he meant I should turn to religion. He was always a staunch Catholic. But now, I wonder?'

Joey slid the purpose-built ladder along its tracks to the far right-hand side of the bookcase. It locked in place and he used it to climb up three steps to face the book in question. With his right hand he tried to retrieve it, but the book wouldn't budge. He tried to jiggle it out, but it still wouldn't move.

He then took out the books sitting to its left, and

gasped. Behind them was a hinged metal device, inbuilt into the center of the Bible, that disappeared somewhere in the back wall. It was a lever, just like Marie had predicted. Joey quickly described it for Marie.

'The book only tilts back and forth,' said Joey.

'Then try moving it all the way down,' suggested Marie.

Joey acknowledged her advice with a nod.

His anticipation was a nervous kind of energy. He tilted the book as far forward as it could go, and heard it click into place. Then came the muffled sound of some sort of mechanism behind the wall, and part of the bookcase opened slightly outward. Dust particles from within exited the small slit that showed the entrance.

'Shit, you found it,' said Marie, standing beside Joey.

A grin flashed across Joey's face. He loved the fact that he was going to enter into a part of his father's world. There was no telling what he was going to find. 'I wonder what my dad has stashed inside?'

'There's only one way to find out,' said Marie.

She helped Joey pull back part of the bookshelf that was weighted by books. It was a struggle; the door alone must have weighed two hundred pounds. More dust motes floated in the air as it opened up. Apart from the light filtering through the open door, it was dark inside.

Joey went first, Marie behind him. After a couple of steps, an automatic sensor light fluttered on from above.

'Shit ...' breathed Joey, looking slowly around the illuminated space. The room was uncomfortably large and cold, with no windows and no air-conditioning. The ceiling and walls were reinforced with solid sheets of steel to form a boxed room.

'Looks like he built himself a panic room,' said Joey.

'It feels like a vault in here,' said Marie, shivering.

In front of the solid steel walls, a dark-mahogany bookcase unit with wood panelling wrapped around the room. It was in the same style as the bookcase from the outside. Joey could tell from the craftsmanship and the intricate carvings that no expense had been spared. A matching desk with a high-backed leather chair sat to one side. The desktop was covered in what appeared to be architectural plans.

Looking at the desk, Joey's eyes instantly found a framed picture of his older brother, Phil. Next to the picture lay an empty bottle of tequila and a nine-millimeter pistol. He thought about the days after Phil's passing and how his father had dealt with the loss. He remembered how his father had disappeared from the world to grieve, and nobody knew where he'd gone. As Joey faced this setting, he finally knew where his father's place of solace had been.

Above the desk, high up on the wall, rested a poster of the Louvre's famous glass pyramid. Joey's father, Alexander, was the grandson of Vincenzo Peruggia, the man who stole the original *Mona Lisa* back in 1911. Paris and Leonardo da Vinci had always had a special place in his father's heart. On countless occasions Joey had rejected his father's requests that his son join him when he traveled overseas. Joey had been far more interested in surfing and picking up girls. Looking back on it now, he realized he had been immature and stupid to have passed up those opportunities.

Joey moved in further, his eyes scanning the space to find something, anything, unusual. It must have been over a year since the door had been opened, and the smell inside was like being in a second-hand bookstore. Even though fresh air from outside now entered the secret room, the smell was pervasive.

He glanced over at the desk where the architectural plans were lying atop each other. The California Bank and Trust was one of them. 'I told you about what happened there, didn't I?' said Joey, looking into his girlfriend's eyes. 'Imagine what information the police would have discovered if they'd found this room back then.'

'That's not your life now, Joey, you've moved on,' said Marie, lowering her eyes. Then she gave a start. 'Hang on … there's a safe on the floor,' she said in an enthusiastic tone. 'It's open.'

'What's in it?' Joey asked.

Marie kneeled down and dug her right hand inside. She pulled out two folded pieces of paper and opened them, scanning them quickly. 'I don't think these are valuable, but they look interesting. Two old letters, dating back to the early nineteen hundreds.'

'That's weird.'

Marie left the letters where she'd found them and moved to sit on the leather chair behind the desk.

Joey circled the room in wonder, glancing at an array of old art books that lined the top bookshelf.

'Da Vinci … Michelangelo … Botticelli …' read Joey.

Marie had leaned back in the leather chair and was concentrating on something underneath the edge of the desk. 'What does this do?' she mumbled.

'What did you say?' asked Joey, coming over to look. Marie pointed out a brown button under the desktop, like one from an old pinball machine. She pushed it.

What took place next made their jaws drop. Out of nowhere, on one of the wood-panelled walls that didn't have a bookcase on it, a hidden wall slid open and an item moved forward, revealing itself. It sat on a retractable ledge that looked like it was floating in midair. Its function was to move back and forth, like an open hand presenting something as a gift. The ledge held a painting that was encased in an extremely thin glass chamber. A single LED light strategically placed on the ceiling angled down upon it and switched on. The way it was presented was worthy of a James Bond movie.

'What the —' said Joey, all of a sudden lost for words.

Marie stood up, her expression one of deep shock. 'I can't believe what I'm seeing.'

'Isn't that the —?'

'It looks like it … the colors are amazing.'

'Could it be real? But it can't be real. I don't understand,' said Joey, feeling completely at a loss.

'Your dad sure has gone to a lot of trouble to keep it preserved. It seems like it's been kept sealed inside a temperature- and humidity-controlled environment within the glass. Well … that explains the noise you heard earlier. Look, the temperature gauge seems to be broken.'

Joey watched Marie continue to study the oil painting like she had seen a ghost; she ran her fingers across the thin glass in awe. The way the light bounced off the painting was ethereal.

'You're the art expert, what do you think?' Joey asked, searching her eyes, which were filled with so much excitement they did not even blink.

Marie was regarded as one of the best, most respected

connoisseurs in the art world, having worked all over the globe, including at the Louvre. She was now the proud owner of her own art studio in Santa Monica. Author of two novels entitled *Art of the Renaissance* and *The Great Italian Masters of All Time*, she had seen and studied up close many renaissance paintings in her career, but Joey knew this particular painting made her deliriously happy.

'The brushstrokes are perfectly carried out, done in the old sfumato technique,' Marie murmured, as though she were back in the Louvre explaining it to an audience. 'A smoked sense is felt when gazing at the renaissance painting. The flesh tones are rich and vibrant. The eyes are filled with a story. She is beautiful.'

'So ... what are you saying?'

'Joey ... I can't really believe I'm about to say this, but I don't think this is a fake.'

'You don't? But how can that be?'

'She's perfect. I can't see any flaws.'

'What the hell was my dad involved in?'

'I don't know, Joey ...'

Marie couldn't take her eyes away from the painting, studying it, trying to find a fault; anything. After a while, she turned and directed her gaze into Joey's stark blue eyes and said, 'Joey, I can't explain how, but I think you might have yourself a genuine Leonardo da Vinci painting of the *Mona Lisa*.'

Chapter 3

The *Mona Lisa*. The best known, most visited, most written and sung about, as well as the most parodied work of art in the world, was staring Joey right in the face. *La Joconde's* eyes seemed to follow him as he walked to the other side of the room, deep in thought. A cold shiver ran down Joey's spine as his brain struggled to assess what he possessed.

'Come on, this has got to be a fake,' he said. 'The real one hangs in the Louvre.'

'If it's a fake your father sure has gone to huge lengths to keep it preserved,' Marie countered.

'Is there a way to find out?'

'There is.' Marie carefully lifted open the lid to the glass hatch, which was surrounded by a thick rubber seal to stop the outside air from getting in.

'Wait … is it safe to expose it to the open air?' asked Joey, with a concerned look on his face.

'The air-controlled environment isn't working. It makes no difference either way.'

Though it was true, Marie would have said anything at that moment to have the opportunity to hold the precious painting in her hands. As she opened the lid, she could feel the cool air escaping from inside on her fingertips. She extracted the small painting gently, avoiding the glass chamber, as if she were deactivating a bomb. When it was free of the case, she held it in front of her, taking it in anew. 'I wonder how long it's been in here?' she said.

'God knows,' replied Joey, his eyes fixed on the painting.

It appeared even more amazing, more vibrant, out of the glass. Marie gazed down at the small artwork in awe and just knew then and there that this was no fake. Millions of people had gazed upon the famous masterpiece from afar, behind bulletproof glass, and now Marie was holding her in her own hands.

'I can't believe this,' she said.

The painting was a mere thirty-one inches by twenty-one inches – painted on a poplar wood panel, she knew, with no frame surrounding it, which made it more delicate and vulnerable. It could be easily damaged, if dropped.

'It sure is small,' said Joey.

Marie smiled and said, 'You know what they say, good things come in small packages.'

This was an ironic reference to Marie herself, as she stood a mere five foot three tall. She slowly turned the painting upside down and looked at the back, searching for something.

'Be careful,' Joey warned, thrusting his hands out as if to catch the painting, just in case she dropped it by accident.

'I'm being careful, babe, relax,' said Marie. She knew she would have protected this priceless artefact with her life if necessary.

'So, what are you looking for?'

'There … that's it.' Marie nodded toward the lower right-hand side of the frameless panel.

'What is it, what does it mean?'

A red inventory stamp mark was clearly visible. 'That's the Louvre Museum's seal, which proves this painting once resided in the Louvre in Paris.'

'Fuck me,' Joey said in disbelief. 'So what the hell is this painting doing in my father's secret room?'

'I have no idea,' replied Marie, shaking her head.

Worried that her oily hands might damage the masterpiece, she laid it down, face-up, on Alexander's desk, after Joey had nudged away some of the architectural plans. Marie noticed that one of those had the words *LAPD Headquarters* printed in the header.

Marie knew from previous discussions she'd had with Joey that he'd grown up in an environment dominated by criminals and dangerous men. She knew that the Los Angeles Police Department Headquarters was the location of the last heist Joey's father had planned, the one that had ended up killing most of his crew and had inevitably led to his own death.

With the painting safe, Marie took a step back to think.

After a moment Joey turned to his girlfriend and said, 'Can I trust you to keep this a secret?'

'Why do you ask that?'

'If this is the real *Mona Lisa*, I need to know I can trust you.'

'Of course you can trust me.'

'The last woman I completely trusted corrupted my brother and killed my father.'

'I'm not Monica.' Marie heard the hurt in her voice, but Joey didn't respond.

Even though they had dated for the past six months, she didn't really know much about Joey's family history, and she'd never had a reason to ask until now. The moment they had been introduced at his Beach Club, she'd known Joey was the one. She was immediately attracted to him. He was different from the other men she had dated. When he entered the room, it was as if all eyes were on him. It had seemed an odd match at first, even to her; he was ten years younger than her and wasn't the most educated person in the room, but he had an energy about him and a thirst for knowledge that greatly appealed to her, plus he could hold a conversation with the best of them. He also had a talent for making you feel like you were the only two people in the room when he spoke to you. In the end his persistence had paid off. He had flooded her gallery with fresh flowers and purchased a new painting from her every week, just so he could see her.

Marie shook her head to clear her mind and asked him, 'Okay … what I don't understand is why you? Why do you have the painting? What's your connection?'

The way Joey smiled, it was clear to Marie that the stories of his family's history had flooded back to him, as he darted his eyes down to the wrist that bore the tattoo of the Vitruvian Man: the picture by Leonardo da Vinci that depicted a man in two superimposed positions with his arms and legs apart and inscribed in a circle and square.

'Vincenzo Peruggia,' Joey said.

'Who?'

'Vincenzo Peruggia. He was my great-grandfather.'

Marie frowned and said, 'Wait, I know that name.'

Suddenly, it came to her, and her astonished eyes met Joey's. It was a name that had long been associated with the *Mona Lisa*, a name that had given the painting an unexpected sense of meaning and importance. Before Vincenzo Peruggia stole the *Mona Lisa* in 1911, the painting was considered an exceptional piece of art, nothing more. But after its return in 1913, it became a legend. From that point on, the *Mona Lisa* was considered irreplaceable, a masterpiece. The robbery had catapulted her to stardom, and she was now the most recognizable painting on the planet. Joey's great-grandfather was the reason behind her celebrity status. He himself had become a hero in Italy, for trying to return *La Joconde* to his home country; the country of the artist.

'You've got to be kidding me! The man who stole the *Mona Lisa* was your great-grandfather?'

'Yep.'

'But he was caught and the Louvre took back the painting in 1913.'

Joey nodded thoughtfully. 'But what if that's not what really happened? How do we explain the presence of a painting of the *Mona Lisa* in my father's secret room? A painting that has been sitting in some kind of air-controlled vial and has the Louvre's personal seal stamped on it? This painting and the one in the Louvre can't both be genuine.'

'But if we're right, your great-grandfather must have exchanged the real painting for an exceptional fake, a fake that could escape detection. Can it be possible he succeeded?' Marie had a thought. 'Hang on, the letters in the safe, maybe they can help explain —'

Marie scooped up the two letters from where she'd dropped them and passed them over to their rightful owner, reading out the names as she did so. 'One is addressed to your father and the other is addressed to a Celestina; who's that?'

'Wow,' said Joey, sounding surprised. 'That's my grandmother, Vincenzo's daughter. Because of her, I have the Peruggia surname. Her son, my father, should have taken his father's name, but due to her falling pregnant out of wedlock she kept the family name. It would have been extremely hard to have raised an illegitimate child all on her own.'

Marie nodded. 'Can you read the letters? They're not in English.'

'Didn't I ever tell you I'm fluent in Italian?'

'Go on, then, read the oldest one first and translate it for me,' said Marie, leaning in to see the written handwriting.

Joey took the oldest letter, which was dated August 20, 1917. He took a breath, glanced over to Marie hovering over his shoulder and began to read it out loud in Italian, then translated it for her:

To my dearest daughter Celestina,

I am a free man. I have served my seven-month jail sentence and have also served my country in the world war. I am living in France, in a small town called Saint-Maur-des-Fossés. I like it here and think I will live out my days here. It reminds me of home. Celestina, I haven't seen you for four years now and often wonder what you are doing with your life, if you got married or had any children of your own. I know I have not been the greatest father, but I need to see you before I die. The war has made me ill and I don't know how long I will last. I must hand over something I hold dear to me, that I want to give you. Something that needs to be protected. Something I have guarded for many years. Something that cannot be named in this letter. If you can find the Forest Hill village, I live in a small house on the hill. There are olive trees on either side as you drive up to the house, you can't miss it. I will be awaiting your arrival and look forward to seeing your beautiful brown eyes.

Love always, your father,
Vincenzo Peruggia

Joey put down the letter on the table beside the painting, and felt an unexpected lump in his throat. He was wondering how his grandmother would have felt reading it. From what Alexander had told him, Celestina had lost all communication with her father the day he was sentenced to jail, and then he'd gone to war. Reading her father's letter, and knowing that her father had survived the war and was eager to see her again, would have brought tears to her eyes, thought Joey.

'Okay, so that letter explains the link from your great-grandfather to your grandmother,' said Marie. 'Let's see if the other letter explains the rest of it.'

Joey stared Marie dead in the eyes and said, 'What I just don't get is why he would go to all this trouble?'

'If what I've heard of the story is right, your great-grandfather felt the painting belonged to Italy. He felt it

24

was stolen by Napoleon. He must not have known that da Vinci took this painting as a gift for Francis I, when he moved to France to become a painter during the sixteenth century, two hundred and fifty years before Napoleon's birth.'

'Thanks for the history lesson,' said Joey with an impish smile.

Marie laughed condescendingly. 'Well, you asked me! Listen, Joey, I'm being serious now. I don't think you realize the importance of what you possess.'

Joey threw up his hands. 'I don't believe how this is even possible. You're telling me the painting now in the Louvre, the one that has been there for what, a hundred years, is a fake? How many experts, historians, yourself included, have seen the painting and not known it was a fake? And the big question: if the one we have here is genuine, then who painted the one in the Louvre? Could da Vinci have painted more than one?'

'Actually, yes,' said Marie frankly. 'There is a more recent version of the *Mona Lisa*, called the Isleworth *Mona Lisa*. It resides in England. Many believe it too was painted by da Vinci.' Then she stopped. 'Look … let's just read the other letter. It might explain more.'

Joey opened the letter dated 1964, which was also in Italian, and began to read it out loud, before translating it back to Marie:

Dear Alexander,

I am blessed to have you as my son. Words cannot describe how I feel about you and how proud I am of you. If you're reading this, I have gone to heaven. In my last will and testament I have left everything to you. The lawyers have a list of all my worldly goods, but one. I have in my possession something of grave importance to your grandfather and me. I have kept it safe and preserved for over fifty years and now entrust it to you. She is hidden away behind a false wall within my bedroom: the wall to the south that backs onto my walk-in closet. When you see her you will be shocked, you will doubt she is real, but let me assure you, son, she is the real thing. She is the original Mona Lisa that your grandfather stole in 1911, painted by the one and only Leonardo da Vinci. The one in the Louvre is a replica, a fake. Your grandfather commissioned a master painter by the name of Raphael Chaudron, who wanted to take on this task for personal reasons. It took him nearly two years to complete. He wanted to prove to himself that his talents were on a par with the master himself using the same natural pigment of oils and poplar wood panel your grandfather had found in the Louvre. He has had the last laugh all these years as millions of people line up to see not da Vinci's Lisa, but Raphael's. Not long after Raphael finished the painting, he passed away, and that's when your grandfather decided to allow himself to be caught, but to give them Raphael's version instead. The rest is history. Your grandfather and I never returned the genuine painting for reasons I don't want to explain. All I ask of you, son, is to do the same and keep her safe and out of sight. With my last words to you, I want you to know, I love you and Mamma will always be with you.

God bless. Love always,
Mamma

Chapter 4

Joey and Marie sat back on their heels, gobsmacked. It was a lot to take in, and neither spoke for a moment. The true *Mona Lisa* had been passed down from generation to generation and now was in the hands of the last living Peruggia descendant. Joey handed the second letter over to Marie, who examined it and mouthed quietly, 'I love her handwriting, such a lost art.'

Joey's thoughts were elsewhere. 'So I guess that explains how my dad ended up with the painting. Now I know why he spent millions renovating the club, and his rooms here, to conceal and preserve it. We all thought he was losing it at the time, with the amount of money he was splurging. But no one was game enough to ask why.' Joey smiled. 'Do you know, one night Dad and I got drunk together. We had just finished a bottle of Sullivans Cove Whisky. He told me he had treasures in this place that I would not have dreamed of. He said that one day I would see her face. I thought it was the booze talking; now I know what he was mumbling about. He had hidden the painting just like his mother had advised him to do.'

Joey cupped his chin in his hand, deep in thought, his mind traveling a million miles an hour. He glanced over to Marie, then back down to the painting and said, 'This has been in my family for decades, and they've kept it a secret all that time.'

'So what are you planning to do with it?' asked Marie, biting her lip.

'I don't know, display it on the wall in my penthouse suite?' he said lightly.

'Over my dead body! Don't be stupid.' Marie stepped in front of the painting, like a knight protecting her king. 'Sorry, Joey, but I can't let you do that. This is a priceless piece of artwork, which the world needs to know about. It belongs in the Louvre where it can receive the proper care.'

Joey raised his eyebrows at the heatedness of her response, but coming from Marie, it was completely understandable. Marie has spent most of her adult career studying, restoring and preserving paintings, and painstakingly caring for every single one. It didn't matter how old or damaged an artwork was. Everything was repairable.

'What do we do then, Marie?'

'We need to return it to the Louvre; that's where it belongs. And think about it: if we perform an act of altruism, they'll throw us the keys to the city. We'll be recognized all over the world. My own art studio will flourish, as will your Beach Club. We'll be the heroes who brought the *Mona Lisa* back to her rightful home.'

'It sure would help my public image,' said Joey, only half joking. 'It's taken some hard work to remove my father's tainted image from the club.'

'It's a win-win, for the painting and for the both of us.'

'I agree it would help our profiles,' said Joey, tapping

one finger against his leg. 'But I can't help wondering why my family didn't return it years ago. Why would they have kept it hidden all this time?'

Marie thought about it. 'Perhaps they feared retribution for Vincenzo Peruggia's theft of the original, or that their own reputations would be tarnished for having kept the secret? It's impossible to know, really. But I can't see any reason why we shouldn't do the right thing now. What's your decision?'

Joey studied her for a moment, weighing it up. 'Okay,' he said finally, 'let's do it. How do we get in contact with the Louvre?'

'I have Pierre Savard's number. He's the curator.'

'Can he be trusted?'

Marie grinned. 'Pierre's like an uncle to me. You can trust him. He's a good friend of the family. He gave me my first job when I was fresh out of university working inside the Louvre. He was the man who started my career and helped me develop my passion for art.'

'Did he?'

'Yes … And another thing you might not know, you owe him, too.'

'What are you talking about?'

'If it hadn't been for Pierre funding the charity event to promote my new art studio six months ago, we would never have met.'

'Are you talking about the function we hosted in the Beach Club, because you couldn't fit four hundred people in your art studio?'

'Yes, who do you think paid for it all?'

Joey chuckled. 'I guess I do owe him, then.'

Marie switched on her cell, dug into her contacts and

found the curator's number. As it dialed, she put the phone on speaker. After three rings a man with a strong British accent and a refined voice answered in English.

'Hello, you have reached Monsieur Pierre Savard's number. I'm his personal assistant. How can I help you?'

'Bradley, it's Marie, remember me? I'm the girl you used to tease for wearing the pink headbands.'

'Ah yes, Marie, it's been years, where have you been?'

'It has been years, Bradley. I'm in Santa Monica now. Why do you have Pierre's phone?'

'Sorry, Marie, he's in an important meeting and I have diverted all his calls to this number.'

'Okay. Listen, Bradley, I need you to do me a favor and interrupt Pierre's meeting. Tell him it's a matter of vital importance, and he needs to call me back immediately.' Marie's voice was straightforward and businesslike.

'Are you trying to get me fired?' said Bradley. 'I can't do that.'

'Bradley, I wouldn't ask if it wasn't absolutely essential. You won't get fired, you have my word.'

'Okay, Marie,' said Bradley reluctantly, 'I will do it for you. Whatever the problem, it sounds urgent.'

'It is. Thank you, Bradley. I'll be waiting.'

Marie ended the call.

Chapter 5

Bradley walked the long corridors of the Louvre's Sully Wing to the Pharaonic Egyptian exhibition. He disappeared into a secret entrance only known to a few people and hurried down the curved stone steps that led to a narrow hallway. The smell of musty dampness was in the air. He made his way through a system of underground tunnels that were home to a plethora of masterpieces, which were kept in cells to his right. Only a few people had ever had the pleasure of seeing them, guarded as they were 24/7 by the Louvre's personal guards, most of whom were ex-military personnel ending their service protecting France's greatest treasures.

Bradley carried his cell phone in his right hand as he approached two grand wooden doors, the kind you might see in an old Victorian church. Darting his eyes up at the doors that dwarfed him, Bradley felt like he was about to enter the giant's room from *Jack and the Beanstalk*. The doors, colossal in size, were themselves a masterpiece. They were covered in intricate carvings and painted a dark rich brown, and gold circular latches hung down from the handles. Bradley pushed inward on one of the doors with his left hand. The doors squealed a little as the hinges took on the enormous weight.

Inside, at the end of a long, dark wooden table carved in the same style as the doors, sat Monsieur Pierre Savard. He was the king in his throne room, and he looked the part. Tanned and tall with a Middle Eastern appearance, Savard was in his mid-seventies. Though bald, he had a slight beard with shades of gray in it. He was a man who carried himself well, who was always seen wearing a suit. His life revolved around his job and the men and women in it.

To both Savard's right and left were businessmen dressed in dark suits. They were of a similar age to Savard and just as distinguished, the kind of men who had abundant salaries and owned jets and Ferraris. Three of Pierre's personal guards stood unobtrusively around the room, watching. As Bradley let the door close behind him, he felt as though their eyes were burning a hole right through him. They were dressed in navy blue with all the weaponry needed to invade England. Their biceps pressed tight against their short-sleeved shirts. The room was dimly lit, with many masterpieces on all four walls. The painting that hung up high directly behind Pierre was a replica of da Vinci's well-known *Virgin and Child with St. Anne*. It was exquisite.

Frederic, the guard in charge, recognized Bradley as he stepped inside and let him proceed.

'Can I help you, Bradley? I'm in the middle of a meeting,' said Pierre irritably, his distinctive deep voice announcing him as a man of authority, wealth and power.

'Excuse me, sir,' said Bradley. 'Sorry to interrupt your meeting. There is an emergency.'

Bradley moved to where his boss was seated and whispered in his ear.

Pierre froze as he continued to listen. 'I'm sorry, my friends, we'll need to postpone this meeting, something extremely important has come up that needs my immediate attention.'

The men at the table stood up and were escorted out by two of the guards, who closed the doors behind them.

'She seemed stressed on the phone,' said Bradley.

After Bradley spoke, a silence fell over the room. Pierre looked Bradley in the eyes. There were noticeable frown marks on his forehead. Even at seventy-five years old, Savard's stare was intimidating.

Pierre broke the silence.

'Get her on the phone, Bradley, this day has become infinitely more interesting.'

Chapter 6

Joey and Marie stepped out from the secret room with their newfound treasure. Joey carried it over to the sunken lounge area and leaned the painting upright against one of the couches, as he and Marie sat on opposite ends admiring it.

The famed *Mona Lisa's* eyes seemed to follow them regardless of where they sat.

'She's freaking me out,' said Joey. 'The way she watches you even when you move.'

Marie's lips curled upward at the corners, and with a bubbly voice she replied, 'That's why Leonardo is the greatest painter of all time. It takes unbelievable skill to achieve this effect.'

'Yes, I understand he was a master craftsman. Believe me, my father never shut up about da Vinci when he was alive.'

Joey's eyes fell on his Vitruvian Man tattoo. Marie had never heard of the Peruggia blood family until she'd met Joey. She didn't know that the tattoo on his wrist had been worn by all the members of his father's gang. Now Joey was the last to wear it. Leonardo da Vinci was an important household name to Joey, even if he wasn't as big a fan as Marie certainly was.

'So, why do you think she's so important?' asked Joey.

Marie moved forward and sank down on her knees on the mosaic tiles, three feet away from the painting. 'This is a question asked by most people,' she said. 'It's a question with so many different answers. She's important because there are so many mysteries that surround her. Some believe she was a portrait of Lisa Gherardini, the wife of Francesco del Giocondo. Some believe Leonardo painted the *Mona Lisa* in his own likeness, as a female form, and some believe there are hidden secrets and symbols within the painting still yet to be uncovered. But forget about her mysterious smile and the eyes that seem to follow you. For a moment, look at the technique he used. Da Vinci used techniques unheard of in his time. He invented the sfumato technique. See how there are no firm lines in the painting? They're all soft and smoke-like, blending on top of each other and giving the painting a smooth, three-dimensional impression.'

'What are you talking about?' said Joey. 'There are lines all over the painting. So much for the sfumato technique,' he joked.

Marie looked annoyed. 'No ... they are crack marks from age.'

'I know,' he teased with a mischievous grin.

'Look at that smile.'

'She looks sad to me,' quipped Joey, playing with her emotions.

'Okay, at least that's an observation,' said Marie, exasperated. 'The way he painted her expression gives the painting an enigmatic aura, leaving the viewer to wonder what the model was actually thinking at the time. Who was she really, and why does she seem happy to some and so sad to others? This, for me, is what makes this painting so special.'

'So how much do you think she's worth?'

Marie stood up and sat back down on the couch. 'Well, the *Mona Lisa* was valued in 1962 at one hundred million, so you're looking at around seven hundred million today.'

'That's insane!'

'I'm sure the curator of the Louvre will give you a small fee when you return it.'

'I'm not after the money, Marie. I've got more than enough already,' said Joey. 'I just think it would be nice to bring some closure to these events for my family. There's been such a dark cloud over us for so long, and returning this painting could be the silver lining I've been waiting for.'

Joey scooted off the couch and walked out of the sunken lounge area toward the balcony doors, deep in thought. He then walked back to the couch and stared at the artwork from above. The *Mona Lisa* contrasted sharply with his white leather lounge. She had a yellow glow in her skin tone and the browns were rich and vibrant. The green background blended into the mountains. A hint of a smile appeared at the edges of Joey's mouth, mimicking *Lisa's* own.

Twenty minutes after the conversation she'd had with Bradley, Marie's cell phone rang. Pierre Savard's name was clearly displayed on the screen. Joey extended his right arm to Marie, indicating that he would take the call. Marie stopped, nodded and wished him good luck.

Joey answered, and put the phone on speaker. 'Hello, Mr. Savard.'

'Marie?' said a deep voice.

'I'm Joey, Marie's boyfriend. I have some news for you, and it seemed fitting that I be the one to deliver it.'

There was silence for a moment at the other end of the line. 'Do you indeed?' said Savard, his voice full of caution. 'Can you do me the honor of telling me your last name, Joey?'

'Peruggia.'

The silence seemed suddenly heavier.

'Are you there?' Joey asked, waiting for the old man's voice on the other end to reply.

'Peruggia … I thought I'd never hear that name again,' Savard said at last.

'Did you know my great-grandfather, Vincenzo?' asked Joey.

'I didn't, but my father certainly did. I have to say, he hated your great-grandfather. I've heard the story so many times. Peruggia took away the *Mona Lisa*. Then it was returned. Then, to my father's disgust, he found out the returned painting was a forgery. This is something I've never told anyone, but I have a feeling you already know about it. Am I correct?'

Joey's brows creased and his face tensed. There was no need to explain to Pierre how he had obtained the painting, it seemed he already knew. Ignoring Savard's question, he asked, 'So why didn't your father come out and tell everyone it was a fake? Why the cover-up?'

'Because, Joey, soon after its return, World War I began and everyone was on edge. People wanted hope; the *Mona Lisa* gave them hope. Coming out to the press would not have done anyone any good, especially my father, who was having health issues at the time. So he kept it a secret and passed on the secret to me before he died.'

'I just don't understand how in all these years no one worked it out,' said Joey.

'That's not entirely true, Joey. A close friend of mine, who I employed to restore the painting, did know the truth. But of course, you know who Bernard is. He was the only one allowed to work on the *Mona Lisa*. Then one day he turned on me and wanted to reveal it to the world. He planned to throw acid on the painting. We were lucky to have stopped him in time. If the acid had hit, it would have revealed the painting's true identity when it showed the reused painting from underneath.'

Joey's mind was scrabbling to keep up, but he kept his voice even when he asked, 'And what happened to Bernard?'

'He was shot dead at the scene. Hasn't Marie told you about Bernard? I'm sure she would be glad to tell you his story,' said Pierre.

Glancing at Marie, who flapped her hands at him as if to say *I'll tell you later*, Joey said, 'Pierre, I think you know why I'm calling. It seems my family has had the real *Mona Lisa* in our possession all these years. I would like to make things right again and bring it back to the Louvre.'

There was a sound at the other end of the line, as if Pierre had let out a long-held breath. 'It puts a smile on my face to hear you say that, Joey.'

'All Marie and I ask in return is to receive the credit

for doing the right thing. Maybe you can arrange a press conference or something?'

'Yes, of course,' replied Pierre smoothly. 'I will organize my personal jet to pick you both up.'

'I can't believe my first flight anywhere is going to be on a private jet,' said Joey with a laugh.

'You have never visited Paris?' asked Pierre, sounding slightly surprised.

'My father invited me many times to join him when he visited, but I was on another planet growing up. I now find it sad that I have a passport that has never been stamped. That's all about to change, though.'

'Well then, since it's your first visit to Paris, I will make it worth your while and organize a suite at the Hotel du Louvre. I have a private plane on standby already based in America, when it arrives in LAX, I will have someone call you.'

'Thank you, sir. I'm looking forward to meeting you.'

'No, thank you, Joey,' said Pierre. 'May I ask one thing of you both?'

'Yes, of course.'

'Please tell no one what you possess, for safety reasons.'

'No problem, that won't be too hard,' Joey replied.

'Excellent, I will instruct the pilot to call you before he lands. See you in Paris.'

Chapter 7

'Pack your bags, babe, we're going to Paris,' said Joey with a grin that could not be contained. He flung his hands in the air as if he had scored a goal in a World Cup soccer match.

With an untamed expression on her face, Marie bounced on the balls of her feet and rubbed her hands together, then hurried into Joey's embrace.

In the arms of his girl, Joey said, 'I'm so looking forward to seeing Paris for the first time.'

'I'm so excited,' said Marie, taking a step back to look into Joey's stark blue eyes. 'I can't believe I'm going back home.'

'Hang on, how are we going to carry the painting? I presume we can't just shove it into our luggage.'

'No, my dear,' joked Marie. 'I have a carry case in my studio, we can use that.'

'What about customs?'

'I'm sure Pierre would have thought of all this if he's sending us his private plane. Besides, we're just taking a painting on a plane, nothing wrong with that.'

'We'll soon find out,' said Joey a little nervously. He wanted to make sure there were no obstacles in his path before he left the United States for the very first time.

MONA LISA'S SECRET

★ ★ ★

At 3:00 pm on Monday, Joey received the call he had been waiting for. The pilot instructed him that the plane would be refueled for a quick turnaround and would be ready to fly out within the hour. He also provided the landing bay and gate number, so they could start to head over.

Carrying one piece of luggage each, Joey and Marie strolled casually into the airport terminal.

'Gate seven is this way,' said Marie with a hand gesture, and Joey had to restrain himself from actually breaking into a run.

Joey held the shoulder strap of the case carrying the *Mona Lisa* tightly, making sure no one bumped it as they walked through the crowds. Marie had picked up the carry case from her art studio in Santa Monica. It had brass-plated hinges along one side and a leather handle and linen shoulder strap for easy carrying. Made out of lightweight basswood, it could carry as many as three canvases in a range of sizes. It was perfectly able to fit the *Mona Lisa* without causing it any damage. Around the airport and up on the walls were plasma screens displaying arrival and departure times. In the background soft classical music played, giving the airport a relaxing ambience. Long rows of people lined up at the check-in desks to weigh and check in their luggage. Joey observed a bag being thrown onto the conveyer belt and wondered how they were going to treat his own bag.

At that moment, a tall man with a chiseled jawline and a strong French accent interrupted them.

Joey was quick to strengthen his hold on the strap on his carry case.

'You are Joey and you are Marie, right?' the man said in English.

'Yes, we are,' said Marie with a smile. 'How did you know?'

'Nice to meet you both, my name is Frederic, your pilot. I could tell it was you from the carry case you're holding.' Frederic's voice was low and raspy. 'I also work in the Louvre as Pierre's personal guard, and have seen many of them in my time.'

With his fading hairline, Frederic looked to be in his sixties, though he was still built like a soldier, albeit one who gave the orders. He was dressed completely in navy and on his shirt was an embroidered logo reading *Police Française Louvre*.

Frederic shook Joey's and Marie's hands. His grip was strong and he looked Joey in the eyes. For all his civility, Joey got the feeling there was more to this man than met the eye. He made a mental note to treat him with caution. Joey had been around enough criminals in his time to know that this man probably wasn't as affable as he seemed, and that underneath that unassuming smile loomed a dangerous man. If he was the pilot as well as Pierre's personal guard, he must have once been some kind of special-ops military man.

'I like your necklace,' said Frederic to Marie, leaning in to touch it.

'Thank you,' said Marie with a smile, though Joey noticed that she looked slightly uncomfortable as Frederic entered her personal space. 'It's been in my father's family a long time.'

'The green in it compliments your eyes,' said Frederic. Marie blushed and flashed another smile.

The necklace Frederic was referring to had a silver heart-shaped pendant with a green flower kaleidoscope image inside it, covered in a durable epoxy. Marie had told Joey she always wore it because it made her feel closer to her father, who had died before she was born, something she never wanted to discuss.

'Is the plane waiting for us?' asked Joey pointedly. He felt decidedly uncomfortable with Frederic's overfamiliar manner.

'Yes ... yes ... of course,' said Frederic. 'Come this way, please.'

Frederic led them through customs, flashing his identification card for the American woman standing at the metal detector. They already seemed to know each other, as she gave Frederic a friendly nod and a smile and let Joey and Marie walk through the detectors without feeding the carry case through the x-ray machine.

'The plane is this way,' said Frederic, guiding them through an unassuming door that led outside to the tarmac. Instantly, their nostrils were filled with the acrid smell of aviation fuel, and standing before them was the jetliner owned by the curator himself.

'That's for us?' said Joey, surprised by its size.

'Knowing the curator is one hell of a thing,' said Marie, squeezing Joey's left arm in elation. 'It's first class all the way, baby.'

They followed Frederic up the airstair and into the Airbus 319, where the pilot took his leave of them and headed toward the cockpit. A friendly female flight attendant was waiting to greet them and show them to their seats. Joey looked around the plane with interest. It appeared to seat around thirty passengers and was no doubt designed with the model of a filthy-rich businessperson in mind, someone who traveled the world on a regular basis. Complete with executive lounge and divan, lavatory, shower and with all the technological devices you could ever need, Joey knew the flight would be no ordinary experience. Taking a seat next to Marie in the spacious cabin, he placed the carry case on the shiny wooden table in front of him.

Marie began pressing buttons like a curious schoolkid. 'I've been in business class a couple of times, but this takes the cake,' she said. 'Look, Joey, this chair turns into a bed.' She laughed in delight.

Joey shook his head, loving the fact that even though she was a sophisticated woman who had seen far more of the world than he had, she was a child at heart. He also felt that the difference in their ages meant that Marie felt comfortable letting her guard down and being her true self around him.

The plane's intercom chimed.

'Hello, my American friends, this is Frederic, your captain, speaking. You have the entire plane to yourselves. We'll be arriving in Paris in just under eleven hours. Feel free to roam around the plane when the seatbelt sign is off and enjoy a bottle of Cristal champagne compliments of Monsieur Pierre Savard. Thank you and have a pleasant flight.'

After traveling 5,642 miles across the Atlantic Ocean, the Airbus landed safely in Paris. It was three o'clock on Tuesday morning in LA, but in Paris it was midday Wednesday. Joey felt completely disoriented. After all, the City of Love was situated to the east of the United

States and Joey and Marie had just lost nine hours. It was as if they had stepped into the future, a first for Joey.

'We made it,' said Marie, nudging Joey playfully. Marie seemed fresh and rejuvenated, having slept most of the flight.

Joey, on the other hand, hadn't slept a wink, and now he was paying the price. He sat, tired-eyed and slumped over his table. The flight attendant opened the exit door and Frederic stood beside her as Marie and Joey disembarked the aircraft.

'We have a car waiting for you outside,' said Frederic. 'It will take you to your hotel. I hope your flight was comfortable.'

'It was, thank you, Frederic,' said Marie.

Holding the carry case firmly, Joey shook Frederic's waiting hand and asked, 'Do you know where Monsieur Savard is meeting us?'

'Yes ... sorry about that, I forgot. He's instructed me to tell you to meet him at seven tonight in your hotel's restaurant, Brasserie du Louvre. You can conduct your business then.'

Joey thanked Frederic again and followed Marie down the steep steps to a shiny black Bentley that had pulled up right beside the Airbus. He suddenly felt the cold air and glanced up in search of the sun, but saw nothing other than a mass of gray cloud. It was the complete opposite of the warm Californian climate he was used to.

'Welcome to Paris,' said the driver of the Bentley, who was dressed smartly in a three-piece suit. 'I will be escorting you to your hotel.'

Joey climbed into the vehicle behind his girlfriend,

and in spite of his exhaustion enjoyed the short drive through the streets of Paris. When they reached their destination, he stepped out of the car and felt a jolt of excitement return when he caught sight of the beautiful old building in front of them. A substantial white sign four stories up announced that they were at the HOTEL DU LOUVRE.

The hotel was five stars and was surrounded by the best of Paris, with four façades facing the most famous cultural sights. Marie had explained on the plane that the Hotel du Louvre was a two-minute walk from the Louvre Museum and ten minutes away from the Opéra Garnier. It was situated right in the heart of the fashion district, just steps away from the boutiques on the Rue Saint-Honoré, and had direct access to the Champs-Élysées and to the business district of La Défense.

Joey and Marie entered the rotating glass doors that led to the hotel's patterned marble foyer. Standing inside, they both drank it all in, impressed by its grandeur. Joey felt like he was in a museum. The color scheme on the walls was of warm yellows and greens. The furniture was antique with contrasting orange fabrics. An enormous antique chandelier hung overhead and two black marbled pillars framed the center of the room. The balcony could be seen from ground level, tapering down to a staircase on the right-hand side.

After a quick check-in, the concierge escorted them to the most luxurious suite in the building called the Pissarro Penthouse Suite. If one were inclined to pay for the room, Joey thought, it would undoubtedly cost thousands of dollars per night. Joey saw Marie's jaw drop as she stepped inside the open-plan room. Not only was the room opulently appointed, the view from the floor-to-ceiling windows and balcony doors, which opened up onto their own private balcony, was to die for.

Once the concierge had left, Joey took a glance outside, smiled, then placed the carry case beside the king-sized bed and lay down with a sigh, allowing his eyes to close.

'No! Wake up, don't sleep,' said Marie, jumping onto the bed and straddling him. 'You need to adjust to French time.'

'But I'm so tired.'

'I'm not taking no for an answer, I'm afraid. It's lunchtime,' said Marie in a way that was far too chirpy for Joey's liking. 'Look, babe,' she said in a more conciliatory tone, 'I'll buy you a strong cup of coffee. Come on … let's go, we have places to see. Sleeping is overrated anyway.'

Joey couldn't help grinning. 'Yeah, coming from someone who was snoring the entire way over here.'

Joey climbed wearily out of bed and ran a hand through his hair.

'Hang on, what about the painting?' he said, pausing.

'It'll be safe here. Just leave it.'

'Are you for real? It's a seven-hundred-million-dollar painting.'

'That nobody would look twice at. Everybody thinks the real one is in the Louvre. But if you're worried, hide it. We can come back for it tonight when we meet Peter.'

'Who's Peter?'

'Peter is Pierre,' said Marie with a smile. 'I'm the only one who calls him that, though.'

Joey walked into one of the two grand bathrooms in

search of a hiding place. The room was designed like a hammam, a Turkish bath or steam room. That would never work, he thought.

The other bathroom was capacious and ultra-modern. Nothing but the best for a presidential suite like this, he thought. It sported gleaming granite countertops, walnut-framed mirrors and fluffy towels neatly arranged. Joey could feel the under-floor heating through his shoes and admired a spacious Jacuzzi that sat alongside the window. He found himself looking forward to relaxing into the tub and enjoying the same breathtaking view over Paris that they had from the main living area.

What caught Joey's attention, though, was a white storage pantry filled with Egyptian-cotton towels, robes, blankets, and toiletries.

He quickly removed the painting from its wooden case and gently placed it inside the bathroom pantry, moving the folded towels over it to conceal it. Exiting the bathroom, he then slipped the carry box under the bed.

'Okay, happy now?' said Marie teasingly.

'Yes, I am,' said Joey, picking himself up from the floor. 'I have a feeling today's going to be a very long day.'

He was not wrong.

Chapter 8

As promised, Marie bought Joey a coffee to go from a local coffee shop, situated to the right of the hotel entrance. The white awning and yellow sign reading *Café de la Comédie* made it hard to miss. The air inside the café was thick with the scent of coffee and pastries. It was a traditional-looking French café, the kind you see throughout Paris. Red-and-yellow-striped cane chairs and circular wooden tables sat outside on the pavement, inviting customers to come in and dine.

With a regular-sized latte in hand and a smile finally on his face, Joey followed Marie onto the old cobblestone street.

'Can you believe we're in Paris?' said Marie delightedly. 'There's so much I want to show you. Come on, this way.'

'Why is it so cold here?' asked Joey, sipping his warm latte.

'This is how the weather is in the fall. Don't worry, you'll get used to it.'

Taking his free hand in one of hers, Marie ushered Joey toward the main road, Rue de Rivoli. He quickly drank his coffee, hoping that the caffeine would kick in fast, then threw the empty paper cup into a bin as they strolled through the old Pavilion, the palace walls and into Napoleon's Courtyard, where the Louvre was located.

Joey looked around in awe when he saw the sights before him. To his left was the architect-designed glass pyramid, and ahead on the Place du Carrousel was the museum's inverted pyramid skylight. A giant roundabout with a hedge of green plants decorated its rim. Made famous by the movie the *The Da Vinci Code*, Joey knew the greenery had been designed to stop people from stepping onto the square of glass within.

'Do you know where we are now?' asked Marie, smiling.

'Oh yeah, that's where Mary Magdalene was supposedly buried,' said Joey, taking in the glass floor covering the two pyramid shapes that pointed toward each other as if one was a reflection of the other. 'That's impressive.'

'If you look to your right, Joey, you'll see the Arc de Triomphe du Carrousel, and past that is the famous Tuileries Gardens.'

Joey peered at the giant stone archway in the distance. He was impressed, but knew nothing about its history. Lucky for him he had an art and history major by his side, he thought.

'Who built that?' he asked.

'The structure was built to commemorate Napoleon's military victories and the arch is derivative of the triumphal arches of the Roman Empire; in particular that of Septimius Severus in Rome. Around its exterior are eight Corinthian columns of marble. And the quadriga on top is a copy of the so-called Horses of St

Mark that adorn the top of the main door of St Mark's Basilica in Venice.'

Joey chuckled. 'You're a walking textbook,' he teased.

Marie grinned. 'I just love this stuff.'

Joey turned back to the arch. 'So that's the famous Arc de Triomphe,' he said. 'I thought it would be bigger.'

Marie burst out laughing. 'No, Dumb-dumb, the one you're talking about is the Arc de Triomphe de l'Étoile, across from the Champs Élysées, and on the largest roundabout in the world. That's twice the size and one hundred and sixty feet high.'

Joey gave an upward look as if to say, *Whatever*. It was all French to him anyway.

Marie continued, 'This one was built first by Napoleon in 1808 and is only sixty feet high.'

'You sure know your history. How do you remember all those dates?'

'Sorry, do you want me to stop? This is just my thing, that's all.'

'No, it's actually nice having my own free tour guide.'

Marie entwined her arm in Joey's and gave him a peck on the cheek before continuing with her commentary. 'Okay, so if you continue looking westward you'll see that the arch is perfectly aligned with the Obelisk of Ramses in the Place de la Concorde. Its twin obelisk is still resting outside the Luxor Temple in Egypt.'

'Cool,' said Joey appreciatively. Marie's passion and love for her European roots were clearly apparent.

She now turned to face the square that was surrounded by the Louvre's walls. 'Hey, since we're here, let's go inside,' she suggested.

'But we're supposed to meet Pierre tonight at seven.'

'We have heaps of time before then. Don't you want to see the fake *Mona Lisa*?' She pulled on Joey's arm. 'I've seen it so many times. I want to see it again now that I've seen the real one.'

Joey wasn't sure he had the energy, but Marie's enthusiasm persuaded him and he nodded and followed her lead.

As they walked, Joey examined the Renaissance palace that had become the most famous art museum in the world. The main entrance was encircled by seven triangular pools, which Joey knew spouted illuminated fountains at nighttime. Joey looked upward, trying to absorb the entire mass of the edifice. It was larger than he had imagined from the pictures and movies he had seen. From its roots in the expansive plaza, the imposing façade of the Louvre rose like a mountain into the Paris sky.

A line of tourists stretched a mile back, waiting to enter. It would be at least an hour's wait, thought Joey. Marie was no tourist, though. She strode purposefully to the front of the queue and pulled a white card out of her jeans pocket. On the shiny surface of one side was a simple illustrated drawing of the Louvre, and on the other was a QR code. Marie explained quietly to Joey that it was a special VIP card given to her by the curator himself. The pass gave her priority and unlimited access to the Louvre at any time.

'*Je suis un VIP*,' said Marie to one of the two Louvre guards manning the door. Her card was scanned on a hand-held device, and she was identified from a picture that flashed up on their screen. It all happened extremely fast and before Joey knew it, they had been moved to the front of the queue, entering through the enormous revolving doors.

'Did I ever tell you you're amazing?' Joey said, stopping to gaze at the view inside the glass structure.

Marie flashed him a smile and held his hand as they descended the famous curved marbled staircase into the sunken atrium beneath the glass pyramid. Joey could hear his own footsteps reverberating from the glass above. He gazed up at the overcast sky, then returned his attention to the foyer below, which was flooded with tourists of all nationalities.

The newly constructed seventy-thousand-square-foot lobby was an incredible sight. Joey had read about it on the plane. It was built fifty-seven feet beneath ground level, and was constructed from a warm ochre marble in order to be compatible with the honey-colored texture of the stone façade.

'So how big is it down here?' asked Joey, taking in its grandeur.

'To give you an idea, the Louvre is said to be three times the length of the Eiffel Tower, or a bit over ten times the size of the Statue of Liberty, or three times the size of the Chrysler Building in New York.'

'Far out, that is big,' said Joey, trying to get his head around it. From above ground, you could never truly appreciate the museum's size.

'The *Mona Lisa* is this way,' said Marie, pulling on Joey's arm as they headed down an arched hallway covered in wall-to-wall masterpieces. 'This is the Denon Wing on the first floor; we are heading for the *Salle des Etats* room that is between the Denon Pavillon and the Grande Galerie. It was designed by architect Hector

Lefuel between 1855 and 1857. It cost 4.8 million euros to refurbish and is the place where Leonardo da Vinci's *Mona Lisa* hangs behind an unbreakable, non-reflective glass covering to protect it from climate changes and camera flashes.'

Joey continued to listen and take in the artworks he glimpsed as they walked. Eventually, they arrived at the large wooden doors of the *Salle des Etats*. The room was a dead end; it was the only room off the middle of the grand gallery. One entry faced a fifteen-foot Botticelli that hung on the far wall. Inside the room, everyone was facing the northwestern wall, where the *Mona Lisa* was displayed. A rope barrier was in place, and beyond that a curved wooden barrier, and then the unbreakable two-inch-thick pane of protective Plexiglas.

Joey laughed, catching Marie's hazel eyes as he whispered, 'That's a lot of protection for a painting that's not even the real thing.'

'Yep,' said Marie, but she was clearly a little more conflicted about it than Joey was. She had loved this painting for years. The news that it wasn't the original *Mona Lisa* had been a blow, he knew.

Taking her hand, Joey led Marie over to join the line of people waiting to see the painting. When they reached the front, the *Mona Lisa* was merely feet away. Drinking it in, Joey found himself grinning.

'What is it?' asked Marie.

'What I find funny is the *Mona Lisa's* smile.'

'What about it?'

'She's smiling like she knows a secret that we'll never be privileged to know.'

'And?'

'So that's why I'm doing the same thing back at her. I know *her* little secret.'

Marie grinned back at him. 'And to think we're among only a handful of people in the entire world who know it,' she said. After fifteen seconds or so of closely examining the painting, a standard viewing time for the Louvre, they were pushed along by tourists jostling to get to the front.

Joey turned and said jokingly to a Chinese man in his sixties standing beside him, 'Do you know she's not real? She's a fake. I have the real *Mona Lisa* back in my hotel.'

The non-English-speaking tourist smiled right back and said, 'Ah yes ... yes ... a *Mona Lisa* ... a good.'

Marie rolled her eyes at Joey and he chortled to himself while they gazed at the painting from afar over the heads of the crowd of tourists. The imposter up on the wall was impressive to say the least. Even Joey could tell that she was an exceptional copy of the authentic painting. The painter, Raphael Chaudron, who had stayed anonymous all those years, must have been a genius. Joey turned to Marie to gauge her opinion and was surprised by the almost angry look on her face.

'I feel cheated,' said Marie, her eyes glued to the painting.

'It's impossible to tell them apart,' said Joey. 'This version does look a little newer, though.'

'That's because it has been restored and looked after all these years, and placed behind safety glass. The one you have has probably been kept in drawers, cupboards and hidden behind walls for the past hundred years. What did you expect? That's why it needs to be returned, so it can receive proper care.'

'Well, tonight they can have it back,' said Joey evenly. 'How about we head back to the hotel? I've seen enough for today.'

Just as Joey turned around, a strong man's hand weighed down on his shoulder. 'Excuse me, Monsieur Peruggia, Mademoiselle Martino? Come with me, please,' the man asked in clipped English. Joey glanced at the man, who was about six foot three with a very muscular build and dressed in a navy uniform. He had been perfectly polite, but something about his shaved head and his square-jawed, unshaven face made the hairs on the back of Joey's neck stand up.

Marie asked the stranger, 'What's this all about? Who are you?'

The man peered down at Marie's petite frame. He towered over her. 'Mr. Savard knows you're here and has instructed me to invite you to his secret room.'

Marie blinked. 'What secret room? I used to work here and never knew about a secret room.'

'That's because he only recently began conducting his work there. It is below ground level. Not many people know of it.'

'How does Pierre know we are here?' asked Joey.

'As soon as you entered the Louvre and used Marie's VIP card we were instantly notified. I have clear instructions to bring you both to him. Please come with me, Pierre doesn't like to be kept waiting.'

Joey glanced at Marie but she only smiled and nodded, and began to follow the man into a lift that descended to the lower level of the ground floor. There were signs here for eight sections: Arts of Islam, Sculptures, Egyptian Antiquities, Greek, Etruscan and Roman Antiquities, History of the Louvre, The Medieval Louvre and temporary exhibition halls.

Turning into the area reserved for Egyptian antiquities, Joey and Marie trailed behind the guard, who didn't say much. All of a sudden, a second male guard appeared out of nowhere and fell into step not far behind them. Both men wore earpieces and strangely resembled each other. Same height, same shaved head and appearance.

Joey felt a stab of fear. Something didn't feel right and the presence of these two guards seemed a bit strange. He tried to catch Marie's eye to see if she felt the same way, but she seemed relaxed and unconcerned.

They reached a dead end, or what seemed to be a dead end. Now Marie moved closer to Joey, who knew she didn't like confined spaces. Rows of spotlights were strategically placed to face upward onto the sandstone walls, giving the feeling and essence of an Egyptian tomb. The carpenters had carved the plaster to give the impression that they were inside a pyramid. An Egyptian cartouche was on one of the walls, and it was to this that the man leading the way went. Glancing around to check that the area was clear of tourists, the guard pressed his finger up against the cartouche where a picture of an eye resided, and instantly the wall slid open, revealing a dimly lit winding staircase. 'Monsieur Savard is this way,' he said, pointing the way with an open hand.

They all began their descent down the secret passageway, and the wall slid smoothly closed behind them. Joey could see Marie's facial expressions; she was in awe, and she had clearly never known this place existed. Joey recalled the article he'd read about the Louvre on the plane. The rumors of underground tunnel systems and secret rooms within the Louvre were true. The article had said that there were thousands of paintings down here, some of which might be masterpieces, that would never see the light of day.

Joey and Marie reached the bottom of the damp stone steps. The guard held out a flashlight that cut through the darkness. They were in a narrow, stone-walled tunnel that stretched away from them into the gloom. Three unlit fire torches hung on the left-hand wall, spaced evenly apart from one another. On the opposite wall were rows of what looked like jail cells, now clearly used as storage rooms. Through the bars Joey could see hundreds of paintings piled on top of each other in countless stacks.

'What an amazing place,' breathed Marie.

In the distance Joey could make out a set of enormous double doors. In the light shining under the doors, he could see the silhouettes of moving feet in the room beyond.

Marie continued to look around, her eyes wide, her grin wider.

Following the lead guard, Joey approached the wooden doors, his heart thumping. He couldn't put his finger on why he felt so apprehensive, but he couldn't shake the thought that once he entered the room behind those doors, there would be no turning back.

Chapter 9

The doors opened wide, and a familiar face appeared in the doorway. It was Frederic, the pilot who had flown them over. He wore the same attire as the two guards, who walked into the room behind Joey and Marie. Joey saw that all three men were tall and wore blue cargo pants, blue short-sleeved shirts and thick black boots, the kind used for combat in the military. Tucked into their holsters were Glock 19, third-generation semi-automatic pistols.

The two men acknowledged Frederic with a nod as they entered the room. It was clear he was their commanding officer. Joey hadn't noticed it before, but he could now see a tattoo on the back of Frederic's neck. It comprised three sharp-looking arrows that pointed upward above a five-pointed star, below which three curved arrows were arranged. Joey felt a jolt of recognition; he remembered once seeing a similar tattoo on one of the men in his father's crew. The man had served in the United States army and the tattoo had depicted his military ranking.

'Hello, Frederic,' said Marie as she stepped inside with a grin.

Frederic smiled right back at her, but when Marie

averted her gaze his smile fell lifelessly from his face. Joey witnessed this and again felt a frisson of fear trickle down his spine. Suddenly Frederic seemed a stranger. He stood still and silent, his feet apart and with a look of cold detachment on his face.

'Welcome … welcome, my American friends,' said a voice from across the room, and Joey turned to look at the man who was surely Pierre Savard, sitting at the end of a long table, half his face still in shadow in the softly lit room. His English was flawless. He was obviously a man who dealt with many people from all over the world and was comfortable speaking in English.

'Peter … it's been such a long time,' said Marie, who hurried over to greet the old man.

'My dear Marie, how lovely to see you again,' replied Pierre, rising from his chair and holding his arms wide open. Laughing, Marie rushed into his embrace. When they pulled apart, Savard turned to Joey. 'And you must be Joey.'

Joey strolled over and introduced himself, shaking Savard's outstretched hand as he did so. 'Sorry to say this, sir, but this place gives me the creeps.'

The thin-faced man gave a wry laugh.

'Joey,' said Marie in an admonishing tone, as if she was embarrassed and afraid to disrespect the curator.

'Sorry, I didn't mean to offend you,' said Joey contritely. He knew from what Marie had told him that Pierre had saved and ordered the restoration of thousands of paintings. It was because of him that the Louvre had become and remained the number-one art museum in the world.

'That's okay, my dear, he's right,' replied Pierre. 'It

does have a creepy feel to it, but that's why I like it. There's a lot of history in this room. It once belonged to Napoleon. It was his secret room. The things he did down here during his heyday would turn people's heads if they knew. I have journals that were found in this room that I have read, and believe me, he was no saint, that's for sure.'

Joey glanced upward to the carved ceiling cornice and the detailed moldings on the walls, which supported a row of old French rifles.

'You like those?' asked Pierre, following Joey's gaze.

'Nice collection,' said Joey.

'All these guns are from the late 1800s,' said Pierre. 'This one is an 1890 Meunier and this is an 1886 Lebel.'

It was clear by the way he spoke about his guns that they were important to him.

'Do any of them work?'

'They all work,' said Pierre dryly.

Joey spotted many classical oil paintings around the room and a large ten-foot-by-six-foot carpet that hung up on the southern wall. It depicted a man Joey guessed was Napoleon, on a horse with his army marching through what was undoubtedly the Arc de Triomphe.

'Please take a seat,' said Pierre.

Joey and Marie sat together on the same side of the wooden table and gazed up at a towering, gold-framed painting. Marie could not take her eyes off it.

'Ah, Marie, I see you've spotted *The Virgin and Child with St. Anne*,' said Pierre with a hint of a smile.

'It's amazing,' said Marie. 'It's an exact replica of the original that hangs in the Denon Wing, is it not? It's *magnifique*.'

'Yes it is, my dear, painted by an unknown artist who was never truly recognized for his incredible work. He was obsessed with Leonardo da Vinci, and the people who witnessed his work believed he was just as talented. His name was Raphael Chaudron. Have you heard of him?'

Joey stiffened and Marie's eyes darted over to meet his.

Pierre grinned as though he knew more than he was letting on and, without waiting for an answer, asked out of the blue, 'So where's my painting?'

'It's in a safe place back at the hotel,' replied Joey. 'We thought we were going to discuss this tonight, over dinner. Have you organized the press so we can tell the world what we've found?'

Savard paused and steepled his fingers on the table in front of him. 'Sorry, Joey, I'm afraid I have reconsidered the situation. There will be no such thing. The world cannot know about the cover-up. It needs to be kept a secret.'

'You're being unreasonable, Peter,' Marie's voice trembled with outrage.

Joey sat back in his chair, stunned. 'But I thought we had a deal?' he said, trying to hold his voice steady.

'You're mistaken. There will be no deal,' said Pierre blandly, his eyes boring into Joey's. 'Why should I give you credit for returning a painting that was taken away from the Louvre by your family in the first place?'

'Don't you think people need to know the truth?'

'Sorry, I cannot allow that to happen.'

'But I came to Paris to clear my family name,' said Joey, frustrated. He scrabbled to order his thoughts, wondering how things had deteriorated so rapidly.

'I cannot allow it to happen,' repeated Pierre in a cold voice.

'I don't care what you say,' said Joey angrily. 'If you're not going to arrange a press conference, I certainly will.'

Pierre closed his eyes, shook his head and said to the guards, '*Fermer la porte.*'

'What are you doing, Peter?' said Marie, understanding the tongue.

Joey observed Marie's alarmed reaction as the guards approached the large wooden doors. He turned to Pierre and said, 'Now just a minute. Seven tonight at our hotel's restaurant, wasn't that the plan?'

'Well, things change, you're here now.' Pierre's tone was hard.

Joey shook his head slowly. 'I can't believe this.'

All of a sudden, the enormously heavy doors slammed shut with a loud thump. Joey startled in his seat and so did Marie. Getting to his feet, Joey berated himself for not trusting his instinct that something wasn't right when they'd first been led to the secret room. You didn't need to be a genius to know this was going to end badly.

'Why are the doors closed?' asked Marie, her voice high and frightened. 'Peter, you're scaring me, what's going on?'

Without replying, Pierre eyeballed Frederic, who seemed to know his role in this, as though they had planned it ahead of time. He stepped toward Joey, looming over the American's smaller frame. Joey tried to calm himself, but he felt panic rising in him. Frederic seemed like a man who had fought a fight or two in his time.

'Open the effin' door!' said Joey bluntly.

Pierre's smile left his face.

Frederic turned his body side-on, facing Joey, and unleashed a powerful knee into his stomach that made him drop to the cold floor, gasping for air.

'Stop! What are you doing?' shouted Marie, leaping to her feet. 'We are practically family, Peter! We'll give you the painting and not tell anyone, there's no need for this.'

Joey watched from the floor as Pierre stood up and walked toward Marie. He was an old man, but he clearly commanded an unquestioned authority among the guards and that made him unpredictable – and very dangerous. Marie took a little step backwards as he approached her. 'I want my painting back. My father and I have gone through hell to keep the fate of the *Mona Lisa* a secret, and now you two idiots could jeopardize it all.'

'We wouldn't do that, Peter, we promise,' said Marie.

'That's what your father told me. We were friends, and then he tried to betray me.'

'What's he talking about?' said Joey, still holding his stomach as he tried to get to his feet.

Marie went quiet and lowered her head.

Pierre laughed snidely. 'You haven't told your boyfriend, have you?'

'Told me what?' asked Joey.

'Bernard Martino, the man who was shot dead in the Louvre thirty-five years ago, was Marie's father,' said Pierre smugly. 'Can you believe it, he tried to throw acid at the *Mona Lisa*.'

'Because he knew the truth?' asked Joey.

'Yes, he did,' said Pierre. 'But he betrayed me.'

'You were like an uncle to me,' Marie interrupted. 'Why are you doing this?'

'And I've been a great uncle. After your father died, I felt responsible for his death and promised your mother I would help you with your career. I did a good job, don't you think? And here we are.'

Tears started running down Marie's cheeks, ruining her otherwise perfect makeup.

'This is what needs to happen,' Pierre continued smoothly. 'Joey is going to retrieve the painting and then I will put you both on a flight back to America.'

'I ain't getting shit,' said Joey, keeping a safe distance away from Frederic's long legs.

'Oh, I think you will. Maybe you just need a little incentive. Have you met the twins, Lamond and Thierry?'

Joey felt his gorge rise as one of the shaved-headed guards sauntered in Marie's direction. Unlike his brother, this one had a scar on his lip, most probably caused by an army knife, Joey guessed. Marie stepped behind Pierre as if for protection, but was grabbed by her long hair and forced to the ground. She screamed as her hair was pulled back from the roots.

'Stop!' shouted Joey.

The guard holding Marie slid out his Glock 19 from his back belt, switched the safety off and pushed it up against her temple. Marie squeezed her eyes shut. She was shaking like a leaf. *This was it, this was how she was going to die*, thought Joey as she cried uncontrollably. In a dark underground chamber by the hands of the same man who had ordered her father's death. He had no choice.

'Stop! Okay ... I'll get it ... please,' pleaded Joey.

Pierre approached Joey and stood toe-to-toe with him. 'Peruggia,' he said in a low, pitiless voice. 'If you only knew how much my father hated that name.'

Joey exhaled and didn't answer back.

'Go back to your hotel, get my painting, and I'll release you both.'

Joey nodded. He needed to obey. It wasn't worth dying for.

'Thierry, you go with him,' ordered Frederic, nodding toward the guard without the scar. 'If he tries anything, kill him.'

Frederic looked down at Joey in a menacing way. 'A warning to you: the man who is escorting you can sprint a mile without stopping. His aim with a firearm is unmatched, even by his brother. If I were you I would think twice about trying to grow a brain and escape.'

Joey nodded his agreement and tried to send a reassuring look to Marie, who looked absolutely petrified. He was ushered out into the hallway by Thierry, and as he left the room he overheard Pierre say something in French. Joey didn't know any French, but he thought he recognized one of the words. On the plane on the way over, he had watched a French movie with subtitles. The movie had been a thriller featuring an assassin, and the word Joey recognized had been often on the assassin's tongue: *Tuer*. Kill.

Chapter 10

Holding his panic firmly in check, Joey proceeded to walk through the dimly lit tunnel and up the steps. Even though the man who accompanied him was of above-average height, it was his muscular, bulky physique that made him look like a giant. One thought crossed Joey's mind as he entered the lift and exited the Louvre via the escalators in the lobby: once Pierre had possession of the *Mona Lisa*, he and Marie were expendable. Why would Pierre keep them alive? It was too risky. Joey and Marie knew a secret that had been kept quiet for over one hundred years, a secret that could undermine the very foundation of the Louvre Museum's authority and respectability. All pieces of artwork in the Louvre would be scrutinized. The curator would be disbarred and ridiculed and his father's legacy would be destroyed. There was too much at stake for Pierre. Joey was just another obstacle that needed to be dealt with. Joey felt a flush of anger at himself for not considering the consequences of the return of the true *Mona Lisa* from Pierre's point of view. He and Marie had been naïve.

As they left the Louvre, Joey peered back at the glass pyramid in wonder. Its architectural design and beauty were superb, and he felt a sudden despair that he would never see it again.

'Let's go, Hotel de Louvre,' ordered Thierry in broken English. 'Walk!' Thierry held his right hand under the hem of his untucked shirt. Joey could make out the shape of a gun's barrel aimed at him from behind the fabric. Joey walked out of Napoleon's Courtyard, passing through the palace walls.

The weather had not improved. The sky was the same dull gray and seemed to be closing in even more. A strong wind was brewing and the hairs on Joey's arms began to stand on end as he made his way along the cobblestone street to the front entrance of the hotel.

'Move! No funny business,' said Thierry as they entered the foyer of the Hotel de Louvre.

Inside the elevator, Joey gave Thierry a cold stare and pressed the button to the penthouse. The elevator ride seemed to take an eternity. Joey tried to decide what to do. He knew he was at a disadvantage here, but he would not go down without a fight.

A year ago when Joey's older brother, Phil, was killed, Joey had hired a professional UFC fighter to teach him how to fight. The only unusual thing about that was that he hadn't done it sooner, given that his father was the so-called godfather in the criminal world. His father, Alexander, had once sparred with him, and he'd proved to be an animal in the ring. In fact, Alexander had knocked him out, a feeling Joey never wanted to relive again. Alexander had been a hard man, but he had explained that he wanted Joey to be strong and to be prepared for any situation that might arise in the future. That situation had come sooner than either of them had expected.

Standing in a confined space only feet away from a trained ex-military soldier made Joey re-evaluate his chances. Attacking Thierry in the elevator was not his best option. He needed to be smart and choose his moment carefully.

Joey was the first to step out into the blue-carpeted corridor. He went straight to the penthouse door and opened it with his key card before turning to the guard. 'Look, Thierry, I need to go to the toilet,' he said. 'The bathroom is just here.'

'Shut up and move,' said Thierry, pushing him forward with his free hand.

'No, I'm serious. I really need to go,' begged Joey.

Thierry took out his Glock as he locked the door behind him. No one was getting out. 'Get the painting,' he ordered.

'I will get it, relax, but first I need to go to the toilet. I'm not going anywhere, you've locked us in. You don't want me to leave a puddle on the penthouse floor that your boss has paid for, do you?'

Thierry paused, looking annoyed. 'Okay, but make it quick,' he said.

Joey hobbled over to the bathroom.

Thierry cast a trained eye around the suite and spotted Joey and Marie's luggage, still packed and sitting near the king-sized bed. Then he noticed a strap that was sticking out from underneath the bed. Intrigued, he kneeled down, pulled the strap, and found a wooden box attached to it. His eyes lit up. This was what he had come for: The *Mona Lisa*.

He gently removed the carry case and placed it on

the expensive hand-stitched duvet. He was careful with how he handled the box. Inside was the priceless masterpiece his boss would do anything to have back. He unclipped the two brass-plated latches and the lid swung smoothly open.

'*Baise*,' he cursed in French. Nothing but an empty box. He frowned. *Where was it?*

Just as the guard turned back toward the bathroom, he caught a movement in his peripheral vision. It was outside on the balcony, moving quickly. Thierry felt a momentary flare of anger as he saw something red, followed by blue eyes that stared right back at him for an instant.

It was Joey, he was outside, and he was carrying the painting.

'Stop!' Thierry shouted, '*im vais vous tuer.*'

Chapter 11

Joey's plan had been simple, mainly because his options had been so limited. He had secretly retrieved the painting from where he'd hidden it in the bathroom's pantry and climbed out of the window onto the penthouse balcony. It was not really ideal, since he was five stories above the ground, but he was desperate and he'd really had no other choice.

Thierry slid open the balcony door in a hurry.

Joey climbed over the metal railing and free-climbed down to the next level using his right hand, the *Mona Lisa* safely in his left. He used the grooves in the old rendered wall to continue his descent.

'What are you doing, you idiot?' shouted Thierry through gritted teeth as he pulled out his firearm and took aim. It would be an extremely easy shot.

'Wait,' Joey shouted back quickly. 'If you shoot me and I slip, da Vinci's masterpiece will be destroyed in the fall.' He had to trust that Thierry wouldn't risk damaging the painting.

One onlooker from below began to point and cause a commotion.

Thierry's eyes were full of frustration as he watched Joey use the coping around the rendered window frame to climb down another level. Placing all his weight on his outstretched feet and right arm, Joey prepared to jump down onto a third-floor balcony.

Sounds of distress emanated from the crowd that was building watching this unfold.

'No, don't,' warned Thierry. 'The landing is too small.'

Joey jumped.

The drop was larger than he had anticipated, and the momentum of his jump tilted him forward. The painting, held in his weaker hand, was going to break his fall. With razor-sharp speed, Joey thrust out his right hand, which took the brunt of the fall onto the balcony's tiled surface. He held the position for a moment, as if he were about to do a one-handed push-up, then got up to his feet in a hurry, testing his hand for injury. Nothing broken; he'd been lucky. Joey peered upward at Thierry, who now began to climb down after him. The guard moved fast and with precision as though he were back in military training camp.

With sweat running down his face, Joey looked around wildly for a way down. His gaze fell on a thick cylindrical pipe tinted the same color as the building that ran all the way down to the second level. He could use it to spider-walk down, he thought. But it was several yards away along a small ledge that wrapped around the entire building. With a growing sense of urgency, Joey sidestepped along the ledge, moving from window to window and carefully avoiding the protruding walls that separated each room. Glancing back, he saw that Thierry was gaining on him with every step.

Below, the city flowed in its tense way, bustling and honking, while Joey clung to the 160-year-old structure.

With relief Joey reached the pipe, and began climbing down it, placing his feet on each small bracket that held it to the wall. One foot after the other he continued his one-armed monkey climb, gathering speed as he went. Sweat dripped off him and his leg muscles burned. The fact that he was so sleep-deprived didn't help one bit. To make matters worse, he could see that Thierry was gaining on him.

If Joey lost his balance …

Then out of nowhere a flock of pigeons startled and took flight below him, brushing past his face and causing him to lose his grip on the pole. His fingers fought to grab onto the flat rendered wall.

A loud sound of fear rose from the street.

'Oh shit …!' Joey screamed with terror as he began to fall.

'No!' said Thierry above him.

Joey flailed as he fell away from the building. If he hit the ground at this speed, his legs would snap like toothpicks and the seven-hundred-million-dollar painting would be destroyed. He free-fell six feet, but it seemed like thirty.

The gods must have been watching.

It was only a small groove in the wall, but Joey's right hand managed to find it and cling on to it, causing his feet to swing inward, hitting a window. He had found the rendered coping of a window frame, and it was from this that his entire weight now hung from his four fingers. His legs scrabbled in search of a footing. He found one on the window ledge and climbed shakily down to the second level from there.

Trembling, Joey sighed with relief and quickly

checked that the painting had made it through the ordeal unscathed.

'Stop,' Thierry's voice boomed from above.

On this level, there was no way of climbing down. Long Greek-style columns ran the rest of the way to the ground, and they were too wide to slide down. Joey searched for any open windows, but they were all shut.

'Fuck,' mouthed Joey. He was trapped.

'Stay there,' shouted Thierry, kicking in a window with his combat boots, breaking the glass and hurrying into the building.

Joey knew he had only seconds to decide what to do. Thierry was on his way, and this time he would show no mercy. Joey moved to the edge of the balcony and peered down over the long second-story drop to a throng of people that had been watching him this whole time. The glimmer of an idea presented itself to him.

Joey exhaled and said to himself, 'It could work.' He looked down at the white awning of the coffee shop he had visited only a couple of hours ago. It was risky, he could break bones, but he thought a few broken bones would be infinitely better than his inevitable death at Thierry's hands.

'God help me,' he said, and with one last breath, he jumped.

It was like nothing he had ever experienced. Everything was a blur. The wind hammered into his face and his hair lifted upward as he clutched the painting to his chest with his left hand.

The white awning of the Café de la Comédie took the hit, and Joey bounced off it as though it were a trampoline. His feet hit the pavement and he crash-rolled onto the ground on his right-hand side to avoid damaging the painting. Pain shot through his elbows and forearms, which took most of the hit, and his skin was badly grazed, but the painting was unharmed.

Rolling onto his back, Joey saw that the men and women sitting beneath the awning had jumped up and were shouting in fear, caught off guard by the lunatic who had landed in front of them. The owner of the establishment, a short slender male wearing a suit, came out cursing. Simply happy to be alive, Joey picked himself up and took off down the uneven paved street. He had survived the jump, but it wasn't over yet.

Thierry exited the hotel and ran into the café, panting and wild, hoping to find Joey. He scanned the terrified faces staring right back at him and realized he was still holding his Glock. With a yell of frustration he stomped his foot and kicked a chair in front of him, which hit the next table and spilled freshly brewed coffee on the patron sitting at it. With a frightened scream the woman rose from her chair. The owner ran back into the café behind Thierry but shut his mouth and took a step back when he spotted the semi-automatic weapon in Thierry's hand. This was not a man to mess with.

Joey sprinted north up Avenue de l'Opéra in the direction of the famous Opéra Garnier. With one arm held protectively across the painting, he did not stop and he did not look back. The street was colorless under the dark gray blanket of cloud above. A few drops of rain began to fall. Joey knew he needed to find shelter before the rain started or the priceless painting would get wet.

An aqua-painted bus with the number sixty-eight had pulled over ahead, and Joey made the snap decision to hop on. He knocked on the closed door of the bus and the driver ignored him. 'Open the door,' he shouted, hoping the driver would understand.

'*Non*,' said the driver.

Joey thumped the door again. 'Please, let me in.'

'*Non*.'

Joey glanced back down the street in dismay, his heart pounding wildly in his chest. He knocked again, this time hard enough to leave a small crack in the glass. The driver threw his hands in the air and opened the door, shaking his head as he muttered something in French to himself. He seemed stressed as he ran his hand through his gray hair.

Joey stepped inside with haste and took a seat among the first ten empty rows. It was only then that he understood why the bus driver was so frustrated. The bus had been taken over by a gang of thugs.

Chapter 12

'I don't believe this,' said Joey under his breath.

The gang was bothering a group of girls, playing with their ponytails and touching them inappropriately. Three of them stood covering the back exit, while the other five sat and watched on, laughing. They were behaving as if they were above the law and could do as they pleased.

Joey turned back to the front of the bus, holding on to the painting and avoiding all eye contact with the gang members. He wanted nothing to do with this. He wiped the sweat off his forehead and gazed out the window as the bus continued on its route.

A few minutes into the trip Joey heard a man's voice say, '*Enlever ses pantalons.*' He sensed by the tone in the thug's voice that this person was the leader, and it certainly wasn't hard to guess the meaning of *pantalons*.

'No! Please don't do that.' This came from one of the girls, whose accent was distinctly Australian. Joey squeezed his hands into fists and punched the seat in front of him.

'*Arrêtez ça,*' yelled the bus driver, who pulled over now to the side of the road. Joey observed the driver exit his bus in a hurry, running to a police vehicle parked a hundred yards down the street.

Joey turned in his seat to see the fear in the girls' eyes. One of them was trying to fight the youths away. The girls seemed to be in their early twenties, maybe younger. Tears were pouring down their faces.

'No, stop! No, please! No!'

Joey stood up. This was wrong. The last thing he wanted to do was get involved, but he knew he had to do something. He remembered that not so long ago his father had strangled a boy to death for doing the same thing to a girl in his own club. These thugs needed to be taught a lesson; his father wouldn't want it any other way. Leaving the priceless work of art to rest on his seat, he swung around and approached the back of the bus.

'Let the girls go,' said Joey, his hands clenched in fists by his sides.

'Mind your own business, American,' said the leader in heavily accented English, leaning against a pole with a look of utter nonchalance. Joey took in the youth's muscular form, denim attire and spiky hairstyle. He wore studs in his ears and nose and had a hint of a mustache that didn't quite belong with the rest of his image.

'Let them go or there'll be consequences,' said Joey evenly, his hands now gripping the seat handles in front of him in the narrow carriage.

The attention instantly turned to Joey, and the girls clung to each other and moved as far away from the gang as they could on their seat. Eight youths faced Joey now, the confident leader in front.

'Why are you not in school?' said Joey sarcastically.

'Why are you in France?' said the leader, poking his

finger into Joey's chest. This was not going to end well, Joey thought.

'Touch me again and —'

The French kid shoved him harder this time. 'Or what?' he said with attitude.

'What's your name?' asked Joey.

'Rocky Balboa,' said the leader with a smirk that was mirrored by his posse.

Joey smiled right back, but under his grin his rage was building. This was a rage that had begun smoldering the moment a gun was pointed at his girlfriend's head. He'd had a hell of a day. 'You like raping girls, do you?' he sneered.

'Screw you,' said the teen, spitting in Joey's face.

Joey wiped away the saliva from his nose and growled through gritted teeth, 'Today you messed with the wrong guy.' That was the moment Joey exploded in a frenzy of anger, delivering a knockout punch to Rocky, who landed in his friends' arms before hitting the floor. The fury consumed Joey as he unleashed left and right punches. He plowed through the gang as they stepped up to defend their leader. He felt their bones cracking but he wasn't about to hold back. He rammed one teen's head into a pole and elbowed another who tried to grab his shoulder. He kicked them when they were on the ground and kneed a fat kid in the head when he tried to grab hold of his legs.

It became a bus filled with cries of pain. Several of the gang members had bleeding noses or were spitting out loosened teeth as they lay curled up on the floor.

Joey approached the girls and helped guide them to the front of the vehicle, where they exited the bus and ran out to safety.

It was at that moment that Joey felt arms grip him around his lower torso. A quick glance over his shoulder told him that Rocky hadn't given up yet. The muscular youth wrapped himself around Joey's legs, trying to sandbag him. He then screamed out to his cohort, '*L'emmener.*'

The dead weight of Rocky's body prevented Joey from moving. He watched as the fat kid in the back of the bus plowed toward them, and the momentum of his run saw him fall on two of his friends before all three fell to the ground on top of Joey. Joey tried to crawl free but he was pinned face-down to the floor of the bus.

Joey used his hands to protect his face from punches and kicks coming in from all directions. He managed to block the first two but the third connected, giving Joey a ringing headache.

Having untangled himself from Joey's legs, Rocky stepped up and stomped at his body, one hit in the groin region that made Joey wither and gasp for air. Somewhere at the back of his mind he looked on incredulously. Lying on the bus's hard, gray floor, delirious from lack of sleep and with grazed arms and a bruised face was not what he had envisioned this trip would be like.

But there was worse to come. A teen barely five feet tall spotted the painting Joey had left on his seat and picked it up. He stared at it for a moment, seeming to appreciate its beauty. '*La Joconde*,' he said to himself.

Feeling fear like a trickle of ice down his spine, Joey suddenly found the strength to heave the thugs off him and leap to his feet. He took in the food stains and dirt on the youngster's shirt, hands and fingers. He cringed as he watched the kid hold the *Mona Lisa*, without having the faintest idea of its value. Rocky said something to the boy in French, and the youth tossed the painting over to Rocky, who extracted a razor-sharp, flip pocketknife in a single move.

Joey was rooted to the spot. 'The painting is a gift for my wife,' he babbled, his hands up.

The knife was a hair's breadth away from touching the artwork's surface, in the place where the *Lisa's* eyes resided.

'*Police*,' one of the gang members hissed.

Joey followed Rocky's eyes down the busy street. A policeman was being escorted by the bus driver. Rocky gestured to the rest of his beaten crew, who hobbled out of the bus and made a run for it, leaving their hapless leader alone with Joey.

'Go … I will not come after you. Just leave my wife's birthday present behind.'

'Fuck your present,' said Rocky, his knife now touching the poplar board.

'No!' breathed Joey. 'I paid a hundred American dollars for it. I will give you half now to walk away.'

'No.'

'Okay, here.' Joey extracted a hundred-dollar Benjamin Franklin note from his wallet and offered it to the youngster with the knife.

With a faint smile, the spiky-haired teen snatched the money off Joey and, tucking the painting under his arm, he bolted out of the bus. He began sprinting in the opposite direction from the policeman headed his way.

'Shit!' Joey castigated himself. He leapt off the bus

and took off after the youth. Weaving dangerously in and out of the traffic, his injuries throbbing with pain, Joey remained focused on the figure ahead of him. The boy was younger and fitter, but Joey was determined. Marie's survival depended on that painting. He needed to stop the teen at any cost.

Glancing over his shoulder, the youngster crossed a busy intersection and stumbled on a pothole in the road. He tripped, twisted his ankle and fell to the ground, grazing his face. Joey's heart leapt into his throat when he saw the painting fly up in the air in front of oncoming traffic. The next couple of seconds seemed like an eternity for Joey, as if someone had pressed the slow motion button on a DVD remote. The *Mona Lisa* flew, spinning like a frisbee in midair. It ended up in the middle of the street. Luckily, it had skidded to a halt with its good side facing up.

Joey nearly gagged with relief as he scrambled toward the artwork. The scratched backside was one thing, but he quickly realized that was the least of his worries. An enormous semi-trailer with deep thirty-two-inch treads was heading its way.

Chapter 13

Joey could only stand there and watch in horror. There was nothing he could do. It was too late. He covered his eyes with his hands, too scared to even imagine the outcome. The truck was heading directly toward the painting. The ground shook and a candy wrapper on the street scattered in the wind as the enormous load rushed by.

It was over in seconds. But, to Joey's astonishment, the *Mona Lisa* was still in one piece, lying in the same vulnerable position. The semi-trailer had passed over it, its huge tires treading a path on either side of the painting but missing it completely as it lay centered on the road.

Joey let go of the breath he was holding. That had been a fraction of an inch away from being the catastrophe of the century: at least for the small group of people who knew the secret of its existence.

His heartbeat racing, Joey bolted to the rescue of the undamaged *Mona Lisa*. He knew his luck couldn't hold; the next vehicle heading its way would not be as forgiving. He scooped up the board with his right hand, avoided the oncoming traffic, and darted to the other side of the road. Finally on safe ground, he turned the oil painting around to assess the damage. The backside was covered with dents and scratches and remnants of gravel from the road. However, the front was still intact and untouched, and that was a relief.

Joey peered down the street to see Rocky being pressed up against a parked car by a police officer, his hands forced behind his back. The officer handcuffed him and began to read him his rights, while the bus driver stood by and gave him a noisy talking to.

A few feet away from the man being arrested were the two traumatized girls who had just dodged a bullet thanks to Joey. A female police officer had brought them some water to drink and was comforting them as they sat on the curb. Joey thought as he watched the tears flow down their faces: it would be an experience in Paris neither of them would ever forget.

Hearing the sound of police sirens fast approaching, Joey left the scene. The last thing he wanted was to be involved in this any further when he had bigger problems to deal with. Hurrying up a side street, he dug his free hand into his pants pocket and pulled out his leather wallet, which was filled to the brim with Benjamin Franklins. He had money, that was something. What he needed right now was to find a hotel. Some place to rest. He was tired, beat up, his clothes were filthy and smelled of sweat and he needed to work out his next move.

After a short stroll, he spotted a black car with a white Parisian TAXI roof sign, illuminated with a green LED light; an indication that it was vacant. He flagged it down, climbed in and said slowly to the driver, in case he didn't speak much English, 'Please take me to a hotel. Not too far from the Louvre, though.'

'Yes, sir,' said the taxi driver. 'Is this your first time in Paris?'

'Yes it is,' said Joey, surprised at the man's fluency. 'Are you American?'

'I'm actually Canadian,' said the driver, smiling at Joey in the rear-vision mirror. 'I've lived in Paris for twenty years. I love it here, man.'

'It's nice to hear a familiar accent,' said Joey.

'Have you been to the Arc de Triomphe yet?'

'No, why?'

'Because, my friend, that's where we're headed.'

Finally allowing himself to relax back into his seat, Joey gazed out his window at the black-and-white city beyond. It had been cold and gray from the moment the plane had landed, but apart from the few drops of rain he'd felt earlier, it had yet to rain properly. Now, however, as the daylight faded, a dense fog had begun to descend. His eyes fought the urge to sleep as the taxi drove on the western end of the Champs-Élysées, to where the largest roundabout in the world resided. As they approached the 160-foot high monument, Joey recalled what Marie had told him about it, and looked appreciatively at its simple design and immense size. 'She's right, it is big,' said Joey in a whisper.

'See the enormous single arch in the center?' said the driver. 'It's inspired by the Roman Arch of Titus and was designed to honor those who fought for France and in particular, those who fought during the Napoleonic Wars. The inside walls of the monument list the names of six hundred and sixty people, including five hundred and fifty-eight French Generals of the first French

Empire. And the cost to build it? Over nine million French francs, a gigantic amount of money for the time.'

'Wow,' said Joey in admiration as the taxi quickly took the fourth exit onto Avenue de Neuilly. He heard honking horns as people changed lanes desperately, ducking and weaving and occasionally missing their exit. Looking back over his shoulder through the cab's rear window, he could see how the roundabout branched out in every different direction, like a spider web with the monument in its center.

The next site in view was the foggy Seine River, where another bridge could just be seen in the far distance. Exiting the bridge, the car turned right and followed the road that ran parallel to the river. They drove past a quiet residential area with cafés and restaurants that gave the area a metropolitan vibe.

The driver pulled over and said, 'Hear you go. Hotel de la Jatte, it's a good family hotel. I've stayed here many times myself.'

Joey thanked the man and left him a generous hundred-dollar bill, more than enough to cover the twenty-minute fare. He grabbed his painting and approached the hotel's white-painted façade.

As he entered through the hotel's front doors, he felt a warmth that rejuvenated him a bit from his exhausting escapades in the cold streets of Paris. The hotel was much smaller and less grand than the Hotel de Louvre, but with its color scheme of warm browns, reds and whites, accompanied by fabric couches, it had a comfortable, homely feel about it. Moreover, the staff seemed to resemble each other in some way, as though they were all members of one large Greek family.

Joey headed to the front counter and checked in. He pretended he'd been mugged, since he looked the part. He used an alias and left a bond deposit in cash so that he could not be traced. In his room he opened the oversized white French-style windows to see the river view he had requested. The long Seine River stretched to his left and right, disappearing into the dense fog. It was the place where cruise ships and houseboats all shared the same green waterway. The smell of seafood was in the air as fishing boats drifted by the hotel, stopping to offload their catch to the locals.

Just outside the hotel on the bank of the river an art class was taking place. Funnily enough, they were replicating the *Mona Lisa*. The instructor was a middle-aged woman with gray hair, who was standing beside an easel with brush in hand. Her students, most of whom seemed to be elderly, were looking at her with admiration and amazement as she showed them the wet-on-wet technique. Joey recognized it immediately from what Marie had told him about the *Mona Lisa* and watched, curious. Though he couldn't hear what the woman was saying, he could tell from her hand gestures that she was explaining that the darks were painted on first, followed by the lighter highlights on top to build depth and give the painting its realistic appearance. Leonardo da Vinci was known for his layering, which gave his works of art a smooth, blended effect.

Joey ran his hands through his hair. He wished he had never laid eyes on the painting. It had caused him nothing but pain and sorrow. To make matters worse, the *Mona Lisa's* face was everywhere. As soon as they'd arrived in Paris he had seen her on billboards, on street posters, on freaking coffee cups, you name it.

He closed his window and laid the painting on a lime-green antique chair. He heard the seniors outside applaud as their lesson drew to a close. Going into the bathroom, he stepped into the shower and allowed the hot water to ease some of the pains of the day.

What was he going to do now? he wondered. And how the hell was Pierre going to react when he found out Joey had run away with his precious *La Joconde*?

Chapter 14

Thierry barged into Napoleon's secret room. The large wooden doors opened wide then came crashing back to a close behind him, catching Frederic and Lamond off guard. Fires of fury and hatred smoldered in Thierry's narrowed eyes. He ran his hand over his shaved head three times and fixed his brother with a stare that could have frozen the halls of Hades.

'What happened, brother?' asked Lamond in his native French.

'Where's Joey?' asked Frederic. 'And most importantly, where's the painting?'

Thierry peered over at Pierre, who was sitting at the long wooden table that was made out of solid timber, writing in a notebook. As silence fell in the room, Pierre's only reaction was to continue to write in his precious notebook. Thierry knew Pierre had assembled decades of research and information relating to the *Mona Lisa* in that book. All the conspiracy theories and stories concerning her were contained in this considerably thick but small A5-sized tome. After a full minute, Pierre gently put it aside and got to his feet, coming over to face his towering soldier. 'Tell me, son, what happened?' he asked in a calm voice.

Thierry brought a shaky hand to his forehead, mortified that he had failed in his mission. 'I'm sorry, boss, but Joey got away.'

'What ... come on, bro,' said Lamond, shock and disappointment clear in his voice. 'How did you let that happen?'

'I let him go to the bathroom,' said Thierry.

'*Stupide*,' replied Frederic in his usual deep, unassuming voice.

'Let him finish,' said Pierre.

'How was I to know he had the painting in there? He snuck out of the window and free-climbed down the hotel. What was I supposed to do?'

'Shoot him,' said Lamond.

'I couldn't shoot him while he was carrying the painting,' replied Thierry. 'He would've dropped and destroyed it.'

'You were right in not doing so,' said Pierre, tapping Thierry on the shoulder, then sauntering back to his chair.

'He'd better not contact the authorities,' said Frederic. 'You know we need to keep a low profile. We're meant to be dead, remember.'

'Fuck!' barked Thierry, biting his lip and punching his right arm in the air. He hadn't thought of that possibility. The three soldiers had a secret of their own they needed kept quiet, and this stupid American posed a real threat to them.

'Don't worry, no one is going to find out about you three,' said Pierre, still the calmest person in the room. 'If he wants his girlfriend back, he will call. Believe me, he will call, unless he wants her back in tiny little pieces. In due time, my friends, we'll find him and take back what is ours.'

Chapter 15

Deep in thought and running on adrenaline, Joey picked up the cordless phone in his room and asked the operator to direct him to the office of the Louvre curator Pierre Savard.

'One moment, please,' the woman replied, and seconds later he heard the phone ring through. A man answered and said something in French, but Joey could make out the name of Pierre's assistant, Bradley.

'Hello, Bradley, it's Joey, Marie's boyfriend. Can you get your boss on the phone for me, please?'

'Certainly,' said Bradley, switching to English. 'Mr. Savard has been expecting your call.' There was a click on the line as the call was put through.

'Joey, Joey, Joey, what have you done?' Pierre's distinct rasping voice was unmistakable.

'Is Marie okay?' Joey asked. 'I want to hear her voice.'

'She's fine, relax. If you had just done as I asked, both of you would've been free by now. I don't understand why you decided you needed to run.'

'That's a load of crap and you know it. There's way too much at stake, and now too many people know the truth. You weren't just going to let us walk.'

'What do you want me to say, Joey? Let's cut to the chase: what do we do now?'

Pausing to think, Joey peered out the window. What was he to do? The rain was holding off, though the sky was the same intense gray and the daylight was almost gone. In front of him was the green river filled with boats cruising south, while a line of houseboats was parked up against the sidewall. Opening the window, Joey stuck his head out and glanced to the left and right. Bridges could just be seen in the distance in both directions. Down below, the art school had packed up for the day.

'Are you there?' said Pierre.

'Listen, let Marie go and I'll give you the *Mona Lisa* back,' said Joey. 'I don't care about this stupid painting. I don't even like it, to tell you the truth. All I care about is Marie's safety.'

'Sorry, I can't do that, Joey,' said Pierre smoothly, as if he were negotiating with a terrorist.

'If you can't do that, then I will burn it.'

'No! Don't be so melodramatic. You Americans; you're all the same. Okay ... let's do an exchange. Name the place and I'll be there. The painting for Marie, and no one gets hurt.'

Joey doubted very much that any transfer would be as straightforward as Pierre made it sound. He knew Pierre's guards would treat it like a military operation, and he still expected Pierre to try to kill him and Marie if he could. Joey needed to be clever and try to outsmart them at their own game.

'Joey, are you there?'

'Hang on.'

Joey dove back into the room. The table near the flat-screen TV was piled up with handfuls of pamphlets. He flicked through them and found the one he was searching for. It was a map of Paris. He unfolded the map and laid it on the bed's white duvet. *Hotel de la Jatte* was circled in red ink.

'One minute,' he muttered under his breath.

'What?' Pierre replied testily.

Joey started at the hotel and moved his finger northeast to a walking bridge half a mile away. Leaning in to read the small print on the map, he said to Pierre, 'Okay, here's the plan. Drop Marie off at Quai Michelet, at the bank of the Seine River, at 10 am tomorrow morning. Walk with her across the Place de la Jatte Bridge. When I see she's safe, I'll return your painting. You have my word.'

'No funny business,' said Pierre.

'The same goes for you.'

Pierre laughed.

'What's so funny?' asked Joey.

'Nothing … I'm just not used to taking orders,' said Pierre. 'I guess you're calling all the shots.'

'You get what you want and I get what I want and we never see each other again,' said Joey. 'And by the way, if there's any attempt to shoot me or Marie by one of your puppets, your precious painting will be destroyed. Do we understand each other?'

'Of course.'

Joey hung up the phone, not wanting to engage in further conversation. Now he needed to plan for every possibility.

★ ★ ★

Pierre faced his towering, gold-framed painting of *The Virgin and Child with St. Anne*. He thought about Raphael Chaudron and his *Mona Lisa* hanging in the *Salle des Etats*. There was no higher accolade. His achievement was unheard of. Many artists had tried to put their painting beside the great Leonardo da Vinci's and failed. But Raphael's version was uncannily good, aided, Pierre had to admit, by the expertise of the renowned restorer Bernard Martino, who had spent years fixing any idiosyncrasies. Together they had transformed Chaudron's *Mona Lisa* into the painting that millions of people saw each day. The museum had kept this secret for over one hundred years, and now an ordinary American and his girlfriend could destroy that painstaking work with a single word in the right ears.

Pierre turned to Thierry, who was standing three feet away waiting to receive instructions. His eyes were filled with hatred and bitterness. He knew he could not afford to fail a second time.

'Tomorrow morning a swap is in play,' said Pierre in French, with a relaxed demeanor. He outlined the directions Joey had given him. 'I want you three to formulate a plan, get back my painting and then and only then, kill them both.'

Thierry flashed a cold smile. 'This time, sir, he's not getting away. I promise you that.'

Chapter 16

Wednesday, 10 pm

From the moment Joey and Thierry had disappeared together to pick up the *Mona Lisa*, Marie had been left locked away in a dingy, damp cell. It had given her plenty of time to think about the events that had just transpired. She felt utterly betrayed. Pierre had been like a father to her in the absence of her own father, who had died before she was born. She had never thought in a million years that he of all people would put her in a situation like the one she was in.

As a child, Marie had grown up in a very cultured environment and could speak three languages by the time she was a teenager. She learned English from her mother, who was born in the United Kingdom and had studied Theology at the University of Cambridge. She was raised in Switzerland, her father's native land, and shared his love and passion for the arts even though she'd never known him. As a young adult she'd lived in Paris, where Pierre had taken her under his wing and put her on a path that began the career she had always wanted. All those years with Pierre, she thought: the friendship, the trust, it had all slipped away as if it had never existed the moment the barrel of a gun was pressed up against her head. She could hardly take it all in.

The air underground was dank and humid. Rust consumed the bars of her cell and the walls were in a terrible state, crumbling and mold-spotted all over, with small broken holes in the old brickwork. Nonetheless, they were solid enough to keep Marie captive until Joey returned – she'd tried to force the door open the minute the guards had left, but to no avail.

Mountains of decaying Renaissance canvases that would never see the light of day were piled in the cell behind her. Her curiosity piqued, she scrounged through the heap, hoping to find a jewel that had been lost or forgotten. The only problem she faced was the dim light, which was only just enough to see the aqua-blue of her shirt. Her fingers scoured the canvases for undamaged flat surfaces with their frames still intact. She found one and lifted it up. It could have been a masterpiece, but it reeked of mold. She squinted, trying to help her eyes adjust to the darkness, but all she could see of the painting was the composition of a face, without the detail.

She gave up, realizing it was pointless. Anything down here would have sustained too much water damage, not only from the humid air but also from the water that was dripping down from the rusted pipes above. Not wanting to dirty her clothes on the filthy floor, Marie used the canvas as a base to sit on, and the frame broke at the seams.

Feeling the snapped frame, a thought crossed her mind. She sprang to her feet and twisted the timber free with her hands. She wrapped some of the torn canvas around the base of the wood to protect her hands from splinters, then looked for a crumbling section of wall. Her goal was to dig a hole in the wall big enough to squeeze through, or at least big enough to allow her to loosen a bar or two and climb through the gap. She knew it wasn't the best of plans, but it was better than doing nothing.

As she prepared to swing her makeshift implement at the wall, she heard the sound of the doors to Napoleon's room creakily moaning as they opened. The light from inside the room found its way into the darkness of the corridor that ran past her cell. Marie dropped the timber and kicked it over to the pile of paintings just before Pierre emerged, looking relaxed and overdressed in his pristine suit. Behind him were Frederic, Lamond and Thierry, who continued up the curved stairway and out of the darkness, leaving Pierre alone to chat with Marie.

Pierre peered inside her cell and gave her a crooked smile. 'You know, during war times, Napoleon filled these cells up with naked women and used them for his own pleasures.' He spoke in English, the language they had always spoken together.

'What do you want?' asked Marie bluntly, cringing away from the bars.

'I just want to thank you for bringing me back the *Mona Lisa*.'

Marie glared up at his smug face, half in shadow. He moved in closer and grabbed hold of the rusted bars.

'You've used me all this time, haven't you?' said Marie. 'You knew Joey had the painting and that's why you insisted I have my launch event at his venue. Tell me I'm not wrong.'

'You're not wrong,' smirked Pierre. 'However, I never had any proof that the Peruggia family still had the painting, although everything pointed to it. It was worth the gamble, though, wasn't it? I knew once Joey saw you he wouldn't be able to resist your beauty. And I knew once you had found the *Mona Lisa* you would be a good girl and call me.'

'You're a real piece of work,' she said, averting her gaze. 'How did you know?'

'I have known for quite a while now, my dear. My suspicion started when Joey's father, Alexander, visited our museum with an engineer friend of his. He claimed he had purchased a rare Picasso painting and wanted to preserve it. He said he was constructing an air-controlled environment and wanted to know the optimal temperature needed for its longevity. At first, I thought nothing of it, until I realized he was the grandson of Vincenzo Peruggia, the man my father despised. The man who stole the *Mona Lisa* and returned a fake.'

'So that's when you knew?' asked Marie.

'No. To be sure, I sent one of my men undercover. He stayed a couple of nights at Joey's Beach Club and I had him ask about the Picasso painting Alexander said he owned. And to my joy, there was no such painting. It never existed. That's when I knew.'

'So why didn't you go after it?' Marie asked, curious in spite of herself.

'You obviously never met Joey's gangster father and his crazy son Phil, did you?'

'No, I never had the pleasure,' said Marie.

'They were unpredictable, dangerous. Believe me, you didn't want to cross them, if you valued your life.'

'So you waited for your opportunity?'

'Yes ... Well, after Alexander and his son miraculously both died, I knew it would only be a matter of time before Joey would find out about the painting. I set in motion the events that now have led us here, and waited for them to play out. Apart from this latest hiccup, everything has worked out spectacularly successfully. My dear, you have returned to France her *La Joconde*.'

'Yes,' said Marie heavily. 'And when you get her back you'll kill me and Joey. Great reward to look forward to.'

'Yes, well, this secret needs to be kept a secret.' Pierre shrugged theatrically.

'You would kill for it?'

'Yes, I would. There's more to this painting than you'll ever know.'

'What do you mean?'

Pierre chuckled. 'Not today, my dear. Not today.'

'I thought you were my friend. I looked up to you like an uncle. If my mother finds out about this she will kill you.'

'No, I think your mamma would agree with me on this one. She's one of the few people in this world who knows how important that painting is.'

Marie didn't reply, instead giving him an intense, fevered stare.

'Okay, my dear, it was nice chatting with you. I'll see you in the morning. Sleep tight and don't let the rats bother you.' Pierre laughed and ascended the stairs, extinguishing the lights as he went and leaving Marie alone to spend the night among the critters in complete darkness.

Chapter 17

Thursday, 9 am

This was it, the big exchange: the painting for the girl. Joey stayed up most of the night planning, knowing the men he was up against would be ready to take him down. He needed to be smarter and he needed key pieces of his plan to be carried out with absolute precision. There was no room for error. His life – and Marie's – depended on it.

Joey stuck his head out his bedroom window to see a deep-sea fishing boat with a dredge positioned at the stern. Its heavy steel frame, in the form of a scoop, towed along the bottom of the sea, collecting edible bottom-dwelling species such as scallops and oysters. The fishmongers waited with anticipation on the riverbank to receive their fresh produce, and going by the smiles on their faces, they were not disappointed. Large polystyrene boxes were all piled up on top of each other, filled with fresh oysters and fish, ready to be purchased and picked up.

But what brought a smile to Joey's face was the sight of a boy and his boat.

★ ★ ★

The previous day, after Joey had spoken to Pierre, he'd decided to take a walk around the block to familiarize himself with his surroundings. On the bank of the Seine, he had bumped into a teenage boy who was working on the deck of a twenty-four-foot timber boat. It was an old classic 1956 Fisher boat in need of a paint job, but it looked to be in good working order.

'Would you like a trip down river?' the boy called over to Joey. He spoke rather good English, but with a strong accent. 'I'm much cheaper than the taxi boats and can offer you a history lesson on the way, too,' he added.

Joey smiled at the young teen. He needed a haircut; his hair was long and curly, covering his forehead and overlapping his ears. He wore an old checked shirt with two buttons missing and baggy jeans that had seen better days. 'Is your father or the captain of the boat here?' he asked.

'No, sir,' the kid said boldly. 'This is my father's boat, but I'm looking after it for him this week.'

Joey raised an eyebrow. 'What's your name?'

'My name is Boyce. Are you interested in taking a ride on my boat? Or perhaps tomorrow?'

'How old are you?'

'I'm fifteen.'

'Won't you be in school tomorrow?' asked Joey curiously.

The boy flicked his hair out of his eyes. 'I'm on school holidays.'

Joey thought fast. 'Listen, Boy, I have a proposition for you. You can make some money and I could use your help.'

'It's Boyce. What help?' asked the teen, crossing his arms warily.

'Is there any way I could borrow your father's boat tomorrow?'

'Sorry, sir,' replied Boyce, shaking his head. 'My father would kill me.'

'I'll only need it for a few hours, tops,' said Joey, watching the boy's eyes drift away, unconvinced. 'I will give you five hundred American dollars and another five hundred when I'm done.'

Joey watched Boyce's eyes dart back toward him at the mention of the money. Joey guessed from the clothes Boyce wore that one thousand dollars would have been worth a lot to him.

'What do you need the boat for?' Boyce asked.

'I can't tell you specifics, but I will need it for three hours, then I will return it to you.'

'Three hours?' repeated Boyce. 'Is that it?'

'No ... I also need you to do something for me,' said Joey.

'What do you want me to do?'

Joey gave the young man a list of instructions Boyce would need to follow for the deal to go ahead, the first of which was to have the boat ready to go at 9 am sharp the next morning.

Boyce considered this for a moment and then hesitantly agreed.

Joey sealed the deal with a friendly handshake.

Now, as Joey prepared to leave, he took one last look around the hotel room, running through a mental checklist of all his preparations. He opened the door to his bathroom and a strong smell of the ocean rushed out of it, caused by the hundred or so oysters bunched up together in the bathtub. Wiping his hands down the same sweaty red shirt and blue jeans that he'd been wearing yesterday, he picked up a large rectangular polystyrene box, carefully cleaned and dried.

It was time. He locked the door to his hotel room and walked through the lobby, glancing over at the nine easels that were stacked neatly in the corner of the hotel's sitting room area.

Exiting the hotel, he flashed a friendly smile at the two young girls standing at the front counter and strolled as casually as he could around to the promenade, where he felt the wind rush through his hair, nearly lifting the lid of the polystyrene box he was carrying. A strong southerly had picked up and the gray sky now had hints of green in it: ominous signs of a brewing storm.

As promised, at 9 am sharp Boyce was waiting alongside his moored boat, holding the handlebars of an old bicycle.

Joey approached his new partner and watched as Boyce rubbed the back of his neck with trepidation. It was clear he was on edge.

'Good morning, Boy. Relax, she's in good hands,' Joey reassured him. What he didn't say for fear of making the kid's nerves even worse was that if anything did happen to the boat, Joey would have no problem replacing it.

'One thing I must tell you,' said Boyce. 'If you decide to run away with my boat, Marcel Couraud will come looking for you. He's the gangster my father won this boat from.'

Joey cracked a smile, stepped on board the boat and pulled out a set of red-and-blue walkie-talkies that had been inside the white box he was carrying. He handed one to Boyce. 'This is yours. Don't forget to do as we discussed.'

'I won't forget,' said Boyce, peering down incredulously at the childish set of Spider-Man walkie-talkies.

It was one of the many items Joey had purchased the previous night. He had found them in an all-purpose store that sold everything from toys to toilet paper. The walkie-talkies were elementary, but they were good enough to do the job that was required today.

'Here are the keys to the boat,' said Boyce with a shaky hand. 'Please, sir, be careful with my boat.'

'Don't worry, I will treat her like she was my own,' said Joey, digging into his pocket and extracting five hundred dollars in cash. 'Here you go. The rest I promise to give you when I return.'

Joey gave the boy a wink and started the sixteen-horsepower Nanni diesel engine. Up at the wheel, under the oak coach-house canopy, he steered the boat away from the riverbank and through a group of other boats. 'Can you hear me, Boy?' said Joey, testing the walkie-talkies.

Glancing over his shoulder, he saw Boyce climb onto his bicycle and follow the boat along the bank of the river. 'Yes, I can hear you,' the teen replied. 'But can you do me a favor and stop calling me Boy? It's Boyce.'

Joey laughed, amused that he had managed to rile the teen. He chuckled to himself and said back, 'Roger that, Boy, over and out.'

Chapter 18

Thursday 10 am

Thierry dropped Marie and Pierre off at Quai Michelet, a beautiful tree-lined street facing the white pedestrian bridge Joey had instructed them to cross. He then drove the white van further down the street.

Thierry drove a quarter mile northeast to the first bridge crossing, which was the Pont de Levallois. He pulled the van over to the side of the road, turned on his hazard lights and placed three traffic cones around the vehicle. He then lifted the van's engine hood and slid open the door facing the river. To the cars passing by, it would have looked like the van had broken down. But on the inside Thierry moved a Heckler & Koch HK417 sniper rifle into position and aimed it at the bridge where Marie and Pierre were about to cross. He focused in on his riflescope, making the bridge seem only feet away. The river was busy that morning; while he adjusted the rifle, twenty or so small boats cruised past.

Thierry observed Frederic position himself on the left side of the bridge behind a wide tree trunk. His brother was on the opposite right-hand side crouched down in the bushes. They were all armed and communicating through their earpiece plugs. For them this was a military operation, a snatch-and-grab job.

'I'm in position, locked and loaded,' said Thierry, waiting for the opportune moment to place a bullet through Joey's head.

'Roger that,' said Frederic. 'No sign of him yet. Lamond, you see anything?'

'No, not yet,' said Lamond.

Marie was the first up the concrete steps that led to the designated meeting point. Pierre followed right behind her, listening intently to what was going on through the communication earpiece in his right ear. They walked slowly across the narrow bridge, which was laid with wooden boards. Pierre glanced down through the white metal fence to see the Seine River and the many boats coming and going beneath them. 'Thierry, can you see me?' he murmured, with his finger on his earpiece.

'Yes, sir, don't worry, I have you covered,' Thierry answered.

'Take your finger off your ear, sir,' said Frederic. 'You don't want him to know we are here. Hang on ... I have movement ... Thierry, are you seeing this?'

Thierry's voice came through the earpiece. 'Yes ... it's a boy on a bike; he has stopped at the end of your bridge, sir. He's holding something in his right hand. He's staring right at you.'

'Is it a gun?' asked Pierre quickly.

'No ... I can't make it out, but it's not a gun, sir,' replied Thierry.

Pierre turned to face the end of the bridge and saw

the boy staring at him. He squeezed Marie's arm tight as they approached the boy, who seemed to be waiting for them. *Who is this*? thought Pierre, looking around in wonder. And what did he want?

Pierre met the boy's brown eyes. They did not betray any fear.

'*Bonjour*,' said the boy, and continued in French, 'I was told to give you this.' He handed over a toy walkie-talkie to Marie.

She accepted the unusual gift and thanked the youngster, who turned around and jogged away, leaving the bicycle he'd ridden on next to the bridge.

'Hey, you forgot your bike,' Marie called after him, but he didn't respond and disappeared out of sight. All of a sudden, the sound of static was heard coming from the walkie-talkie in her hand. She pressed the button. 'Hello ... Joey ...?'

'Hello, beautiful, nice day for a bridge walk, ain't it?' replied Joey, sounding as calm as a frog in the sun.

Pierre pursed his lips in displeasure. The fact that Joey had three trained mercenaries on his tail didn't seem to bother him one bit.

Marie pressed the receiver button again to answer, 'Joey, I hope you know what you're doing.' She didn't seem to share his confidence.

'It will all ...' Then the crackling noise started up again. '... be okay ...' *Shhh* ... 'Trust me.' If he said anything else, the static overpowered it.

'Where is he?' asked Pierre in annoyance.

Marie pressed the button again and paused for a couple of seconds, looking over at Pierre, who was watching her every movement. Then quick as a whip, she said into the toy's microphone, 'Joey, they're going to kill you after you return the …'

Pierre felt a flash of rage and immediately slapped Marie across the face, his handprint leaving a red mark on her left cheek. Marie's head snapped back, but she raised her arm to try to reciprocate with a slap of her own. Pierre grabbed her and pulled her close to him, holding her tightly with one arm. Aging he might have been, but he was strong enough to hold Marie at bay.

He snatched the walkie-talkie out of her hand with his free arm and pushed the button to talk to Joey. 'Where are you, Joey? I brought you what you wanted, where is my part of the bargain?'

Shhh … Then over the static came Joey's angry voice. 'You touch her again and I'll —'

'You'll what?' said Pierre, directing Marie away from the bridge, over to the right. He realized Joey could see them, so he was somewhere nearby. 'Now, where's my painting?'

Shhh '… I …' *Shhh* '… when …' *Shhh* '… hold.'

Pierre stopped. The static from the walkie-talkie was worsening the further he moved. It meant he was moving away from Joey, so Joey was somewhere on or near the river. He turned around, hauling Marie along with him. As he walked back the way he'd come the sound slowly repaired itself and he heard, 'You touch one hair on her head …'

Pierre scanned the river in front of him. The water was green, darker in the shadows and paler in the light, but still green. He searched the many boats drifting down it and said in French, 'I think he's on a boat somewhere on the river.'

'I'm on it,' Thierry said quickly, then after a few seconds, '*Baise* ... I can't see inside the boats from this high position.'

Pierre saw Frederic come out from the cover of the tree he was positioned behind and start to scan the boats on the river.

Lifting the walkie-talkie to his mouth, Pierre pressed the button and said, 'Okay, Joey, are you going to show yourself or what?'

This time there was nothing but static at the other end.

Pierre cursed in French. Marie cringed away from him, but he gripped tightly.

'JOEY! Cat got your tongue?' Pierre shouted in his best American accent, his tone filled with frustration.

The only sound that could be heard was the soft rustling of the boats cruising gently on the waters of the Seine River.

Chapter 19

An old wooden boat drifted by Frederic's position. The stocky Frenchman squinted in search of the driver. Then he saw a head bobbing low in the coach-house, just high enough to drive the boat without being seen. His eyes went wide with excitement. 'It's him,' said Frederic.

'Which boat is it?' said Lamond from the bushes opposite, standing up to take a closer look.

'The one with the oak cabin,' said Frederic.

Thierry moved his scope to the boat in question. He could see the man driving the boat fiddling with something in his hands, but he was hunched low, so Thierry couldn't get a clear shot. 'I have the target in range, just waiting for him to stick his head up,' said Thierry.

'Can you take the shot, brother?' said Lamond.

'Wait … can you see the painting anywhere on that boat?' warned Pierre, moving to stand with Marie at the side of the river not far away from Frederic's position.

'Hang on,' said Thierry. 'I don't see the painting, but Joey is out in the open. I have a shot. Permission to shoot?' he asked, his finger tight on the trigger, his open eye concentrating on the target. It was a matter of pride; Joey wasn't getting away this time; he was as good as dead.

Joey was seen by all holding on to a large white box that was attached to a rope.

'I see him,' said Frederic.

'I see him, too,' said Lamond. 'What's he doing?'

'Give me the go and he's a goner, sir,' said Thierry.

'Something's not right,' said Pierre. 'It's too easy.'

'He's placed a white box in the water,' said Thierry.

'What's he doing?' repeated Pierre. 'What's in the box?'

The polystyrene box was now floating in the river behind the boat and continually moving further and further away in the current, though it was kept tethered to the boat by a single rope. Joey held the end of the rope in his hand as the box bobbed up and down in the water like a fishing float. Then a strong gust of wind buffeted the box and the lid on top flew off like a lone sheet of newspaper on a windy street.

Thierry aimed his scope at the lidless box to get a closer look and what he saw next made his jaw drop. 'Holy shit!' he said.

'What is it?' replied Pierre.

'The *Mona Lisa* is inside the box, floating on the river. Do I fire, sir, please confirm?'

'No! Don't fire,' screamed out Pierre.

'Hold your fire, Thierry, I repeat, hold your fire,' yelled Frederic. 'Joey has the upper hand.'

Chapter 20

Joey had placed the seven-hundred-million-dollar painting inside the rectangular polystyrene box that had been used to hold the oysters that were now in his bathtub. He had known he needed to do something drastic to get Pierre's attention, so that is what he had done.

'What are you doing, Joey?' shouted Pierre through the walkie-talkies. 'I brought you Marie, what's with these games? If any water touches the painting —'

'Good. I'm glad I have your attention now,' said Joey, knowing they wouldn't dare shoot him and risk relinquishing the *Mona Lisa* to the murky river. 'If your men try anything foolish, the *Mona Lisa* will go into the river.'

'All right, Joey, what do you propose?' said Pierre in a flat, defeated tone.

'This is what's going to happen. First, give the walkie-talkie to Marie.'

There were a few moments of silence, and then Marie's voice came through the walkie-talkie.

'Joey, it's me, what's the plan?' said Marie.

'Hey, gorgeous, listen to me carefully. Grab the bike left by the boy, turn to your right and ride it all the way down river. I have a taxi boat waiting to pick you up and take you someplace safe.'

'Okay,' she said, sounding nervous.

'Listen, Marie, this is important. I will not be able to communicate with you once you reach a certain distance. But when you board the boat, to let me know you made it there safely, I need you to press the button on the walkie-talkie five times. I'll be able to hear the tones, I tried it yesterday.'

'What about you?' said Marie. 'I can't just leave you here.'

'Don't worry about me, I'm fine,' said Joey, and a memory came flooding back to his mind. The last time he'd said he was fine was to his brother's girlfriend, who had turned out to be an evil, vindictive bitch. She had told him the word *fine* stood for: Freaked out, Insecure, Neurotic and Eccentric.

Joey continued, 'Is Pierre listening?'

'Yes, he is,' replied Marie.

'Pierre, when I get the sign that she is safe, I'll continue to release the rope from my end, so that you can pick up the painting from the bridge you just walked over. There's a ladder in the middle of the bridge on one of the piers, you can use that to get down to the water. One more thing. If you or your men try anything funny, I promise you I will yank the rope and tip da Vinci's greatest masterpiece into this water. Do we understand each other?'

'You Americans, you think you're all fucking MacGyver,' said Pierre tonelessly, as if through clenched teeth.

Glancing up at the bridge, Joey saw Marie jogging over to the bicycle, clipping the walkie-talkie to her pants as she went. She flung her leg over the saddle.

Within seconds, she was pedaling fast along the riverbank, just like Joey planned.

'I can't believe we have given this American total control,' said Pierre in a jarring tone, kicking a small rock across the ground as he watched his hostage escape.

'I have an idea, Pierre,' said Frederic. 'I overheard everything through your earpiece. Now it's our turn to take control. Listen up, everyone, change of plans. Lamond, you go after the girl. I will give you further orders when you have her in your possession. Thierry, I'm going to enter the water. When I'm in position I will give you the order to shoot the rope that is tied to the box. Then you can take the American out. Are we clear?'

'Roger,' said Lamond, who kept low so as not to be seen by Joey, then took off like an Olympic sprinter once he crossed the bridge.

'Roger that,' said Thierry. 'It'll be my pleasure.'

Pierre sighed heavily and said to all listening, 'That painting must NOT hit the water.'

'Don't worry, I'll intercept it before it does,' said Frederic confidently, and then he ran to the edge of the bank, where two fishing kayaks were secured. He grabbed one, untethered it and rushed into the water, inserting his legs into it as he did so. The paddle in his hands balanced his weight as he dug into the water from both sides.

Joey spotted Frederic enter the water and attempt to paddle over to the priceless jewel in the box. He darted his eyes back down to the walkie-talkie left on the carpeted floor of the coach-house, but all he could hear was static. Marie had not reached the taxi boat yet, but now that Frederic had entered the river, it made him feel a little on edge. He decided to pull away from the bridge so as to keep a safe distance. As he did so, the rope tied to the polystyrene box trailing behind the boat tightened. At the same time, the wake waves of another vessel traveling in the opposite direction caused the box to wobble jerkily.

Chapter 21

As he watched the box pitch from side to side in the swell, Pierre grabbed his head and squeezed his eyes shut. He felt like he was going to have a panic attack. 'Don't get too close, Frederic,' he warned between anxious breaths.

In all his life, he had never had to endure such stress.

He watched as Frederic backed off and the boat once again came to a stop.

Two minutes had gone by before the static from the walkie-talkie changed.

Clank. Clank. Clank. Clank. Clank.

Joey released a tightly held breath. Five presses in total, Marie was safe. She had made it to the taxi boat. Joey flashed a smile. Now it was his turn to get as far away from Paris as he could.

He glanced at Frederic in the water. The Frenchman had stopped paddling, but he was close. Too close. The box now floated between them. Suddenly the wind changed, blowing up alarmingly fast, and out of nowhere a loud thunderclap erupted, making them all jump.

'Oh NO!' screamed out Pierre, who was now

standing on the bridge overlooking the boat, and close enough for Joey to hear him. 'The rain!'

Joey felt the first spatter of water from the thick clouds above.

'JOEY!' yelled Frederic from his kayak. 'Don't be stupid, man, the painting is now at risk from the weather.'

Joey didn't respond.

'I can't believe this,' Pierre cried as little pinpricks of water began to rain down over him. 'Whatever you have planned, Frederic, do it now. NOW!'

Joey tensed, even though he had expected the Frenchmen to attempt something. He tried to keep both Pierre and Frederic in his sight as he scanned the river for other threats.

The drops of rain pierced the river around Frederic, who turned now to look up river at the next bridge along and shouted into his earpiece, 'Take the shot!'

'Oh, God,' said Pierre with dread.

Then to make matters worse, there was lightning.

Thierry cracked his neck, revealing a dragon tattoo, and prepared himself for a shot he had to make in extremely windy conditions, a shot he could not afford to miss. He concentrated on his target; no thunder, lightning or strong winds were going to distract him as he breathed out and pulled the trigger three times. The gunshots cracked into the air as loud as thunder, then the silence returned.

As soon as the words Frederic had uttered sank in, Joey immediately dropped to the ground, his right hand still holding on to the rope. The shots rang out almost instantly, and that was when Joey realized the rope was now as light as a feather. The polystyrene box had been cut free and left to drift.

'Oh, shit,' muttered Joey to himself, knowing he had just lost his only bargaining chip. All bets were now off.

Chapter 22

Holding on to a useless piece of severed rope, Joey peered over the port side of Boyce's boat to see the white box drifting toward Frederic, who paddled over to collect it. He saw the Frenchman carefully lift the box from the water and sit it on the kayak, then quickly take off the waterproof jacket he was wearing and lay it over the painting to protect it from the incoming rain.

Immediately after the box was secured, Frederic pulled out a nine-millimeter semi-automatic pistol from under his clothes, took aim, and emptied a cartridge at the stern of the boat. Bullets entered the wooden frame just as Joey crawled inside the canopy to safety. An instant later there was an onslaught of bullets that came in from the opposite direction.

Thierry had been poised to shoot the American ever since he'd arrived, and was finally free to do so. He pointed his twenty-inch accurized barrel, which held twenty rounds in the magazine, and let loose on the bow of Joey's boat. The top half of the canopy was blasted within an inch of its life. The 1956 boat took a beating, as wood fragments chipped everywhere. The three large glass panels smashed into pieces and fell on top of Joey, who was curled up on the carpeted floor. Thierry grinned.

Joey lay on the floor, covering his head, waiting for the hail of bullets to stop.

He knew this old boat couldn't take much more gunfire and he spared a thought for the poor teen who would be gutted when he brought it back – if he brought it back – shot to pieces. He crawled over to the steering wheel and dropped the handle to the accelerator, which set the boat in motion. The only problem was that it was heading in the direction of the oncoming gunfire.

Waiting in the cold rain for Frederic to disembark from the kayak was Pierre, who took the polystyrene box out of the guard's hands at the first opportunity and ran for shelter under a vast network of large trees. Standing again on solid ground, Frederic reloaded a fresh clip extracted from his knee pocket into his Glock and took off on foot along the bank. He trained his eyes on the boat as he sprinted beside it. 'Thierry, don't you let him escape this time!' he shouted as the heavens opened and the rain began to bucket down.

Chapter 23

The old Fisher boat approached Thierry's bridge. Joey prepared himself for the next assault of bullets to come his way. He grabbed a stainless-steel frypan that Boyce must have used to cook his dinner and ducked under the steering wheel for cover.

A rain of bullets hit the starboard hard, much too close for comfort.

'HOLY SHIT!' screamed Joey, who let go of the steering wheel, protecting his face with the frypan. He tried to take stock of the situation. His plan had been simple: to set Marie free first; that was his top priority. That, at least, he seemed to have succeeded in doing. Then he was going to flee for the canals while the Frenchmen struggled to collect the *Mona Lisa* floating in the river. But he had underestimated the lengths to which Pierre and his group would go to retrieve the painting. They were behaving as though they were in a military training exercise and he was the target. His thoughts were broken when one bullet came down through the shattered window and ricocheted off the pan, saving his life.

The damaged boat, running on its sixteen-horsepower engine, must have looked like it had been in World War III, Joey thought ruefully. As they passed the bridge from which the rain of bullets had originated, the gunfire ceased and Joey breathed a sigh of relief. He had just lifted his head cautiously to steer the boat, when an unexpected bullet zinged passed his right ear, causing him to drop back down again. A dozen or so more bullets followed on the starboard quarter of the stern. Joey realized that these were coming from Frederic, who Joey could hear cursing in French as he fell further and further behind the boat. Glancing ahead through the heavy rain, Joey saw that the river broke off into two channels, so he had to make a quick decision. Wanting to get away from Frederic, he veered in haste to his port side.

BOOM! The sound of thunder roared from above and the rain dramatically increased, to the point where visibility was low. Joey had survived a plethora of bullets and now entered a fog that loomed as far as the eye could see. He wasn't sure whether this would be a hindrance or a help. The only things guiding him were the lights along the side of the river and an upcoming bridge, along which fog lights were strung. He kept calm as the deluge pounded the broken boat, and rain dripped down on him through the bullet holes in the roof.

He passed under the next bridge, which was much lower than the previous one, and the sound of the rain completely ceased for a moment before starting up again as the vessel exited the other side. The rain was a problem, but it would soon become the least of his worries.

Joey heard a loud thump, and turned his head in the direction of the sound. It was Thierry, who had leaped off the bridge and landed on the bow. Adrenaline coursing through him, Joey fixed his eyes on the trained killer in front of him. There was no place for him to hide this time.

Entering with his legs first, Thierry charged through the broken window and tackled Joey to the ground. Joey swung back at him, but only hit air. Thierry smiled and took advantage of his soaring height to throw two killer jabs at Joey's nose. Joey reeled backwards with the power of the hits, struggling to keep himself up on his feet. Blood rained down from his nostrils as he prepared to deal with another onslaught of punches coming his way.

At that moment the port side of the rogue boat hit and scraped against the stone walls bordering the river. Joey shook off Thierry's punch with gritted teeth and glimpsed another about to connect, and that's when the boat impacted against the wall a second time, throwing Thierry off balance. Joey saw his chance. He stepped back and came in with a powerful swing of his own.

Thierry fell to his knees in a daze.

Joey became aware of a loud noise like a washing machine behind him. He turned around to see a sizeable riverboat approaching, its dangerous revolving blades smashing into the water. Boyce's wooden boat was heading straight for the rotating paddles. Joey recognized the vessel. He remembered seeing a similar one in Disneyland. It was a large floating restaurant, which took tourists on a joy cruise up and down the Seine River. The riverboat blew its horn, warning the smaller vessel that was dangerously close. There was no way around it and, at this late stage, no way to avoid the collision.

Joey decided he was going to jump before the impact. But as soon as he ran out the door and approached the stern of the boat, he was tackled to the ground.

'Stop, you fool, we're going to get squashed,' roared Joey. The vessel's rotating blades were now only feet away.

Thierry seemed either not to have heard him or not to care. The big man straddled Joey and punched him in the stomach, and then elbowed him in his jaw. 'You're not getting away from me this time,' said Thierry, throwing another punch.

'We are going to die,' warned Joey, his mouth full of blood.

'No, you're going to die,' said Thierry.

Joey knew that the impact with the riverboat was imminent. Desperate, he pummeled Thierry's body with his hands, searching for something, anything, to use as a weapon. Then he felt something hard and boxlike in one of Thierry's pockets, and pulled it out. It was some sort of radio transceiver. He swung it at Thierry's face and heard a satisfying sound as it connected. Thierry's grip loosened momentarily, and Joey pulled the giant to the ground and brought a fist to his face, snapping his nose into a grotesquerie. Thierry retaliated, his broken face filled with hatred, slamming Joey to the edge of the boat, both men still holding on to each other.

'You wanna play,' screamed Joey, spitting out rain and blood from his mouth. 'Okay then, let's play.'

With all his might, he forced Thierry off the boat and into the churning river water, which looked white in the pounding rain.

They both hit the surface hard.

The world went eerily silent.

The two men fell into the cold, murky green darkness in a rolling struggle, their flailing feet and twisting arms hidden amid a cloud of bubbles.

The vibrating hum of the two boats' engines echoed under the water. Joey knew he could never defeat Thierry on solid ground, but in water, he had a chance. It was an environment he was familiar with, being an avid surfer. He had learned years ago how to hold his breath for long periods of time as heavy surf pounded from above.

They sank deeper and deeper in a vertical descent, bodies locked together, each trying to strangle the other. From above came the muffled sounds of wood being annihilated as Boyce's boat's timber frame was crushed by the turning propellers of the bigger vessel. The rotating blades destroyed the boat as if it were made of toothpicks.

At that moment, something unexpected happened.

Thierry was jerked upward and away from Joey's arms.

Joey felt a surge of adrenaline rush through him. *It worked*, he thought with some astonishment. In their last moments on the boat, while Joey was getting his head punched in, he had spotted the boat's mooring rope coiled neatly next to them on the deck. Using his foot, he had tugged the loop end of the rope free and secretly slipped it around Thierry's leg. Then, hoping the rope wouldn't come loose, Joey had pushed Thierry into the water.

Thierry was now pulled upward legs first. Bubbles exited his mouth as he was yanked toward the enormous spinning blades of the riverboat. The other end of the rope had been secured to Boyce's boat, and now it was hopelessly tangled in the bigger boat's paddles. Thierry's hands flailed uselessly in the water as he tried to stop himself from entering the mouth of death.

But he managed to catch Joey's feet on the way up. Joey agitated his hips and lost his shoes, leaving Thierry to try to find purchase on his jeans. Feeling his lungs start to burn, Joey kicked hard in the opposite direction as they were both pulled toward the churning blades. Joey knew he only had a few moments left before he would start to lose consciousness. He found his belt buckle and undid his belt, and, with Thierry still gripping his jeans, he shucked them off and kicked hard toward the surface.

In a final attempt to save himself, Thierry let go of Joey at last and his hands moved to the rope that was strangling his feet. The bubbles around him intensified, but there was no escape. Thierry's legs bent inward and snapped out of place as they made contact with the riverboat's blades.

As Joey hit the surface of the water and gulped deep breaths of air, all he could hear were screams of unimaginable pain. The enormous blades smashed and churned through the water around him, struggling against the heavy load. With a shiver of horror, Joey noticed the dragon tattoo on the back of Thierry's neck as the Frenchman's lifeless, mutilated body surfaced and floated away in the beating rain.

But the blades were still much too close. It was Joey's turn to swim for his life. As the water around him turned crimson, Joey lit out for the shore, carefully keeping his mouth above the red-stained surface.

Finally, exhausted and cold, soaked to the bone and with his heart beating painfully fast in his chest, Joey reached the stone wall at the river's edge. Shaking from the effort, he scaled the exposed stone, scraping his hands and knees, and collapsed on the ground on the other side, where he took a few moments to catch his breath. Then, with a glance in each direction to ensure Pierre and his gang hadn't spotted him, he got to his feet and jogged away into the rain and fog, having escaped by the skin of his teeth.

Chapter 24

A taxi boat pulled up to the wharf where Pierre and Frederic stood waiting. When he had lost sight of Joey's boat, Frederic had decided to cut his losses and return to Pierre to discuss their next move. Pierre now proceeded to the vessel, carrying Leonardo da Vinci's *Mona Lisa*, still covered by Frederic's jacket, up high in his arms. The rain showed no sign of abating. The taxi boat driver, his face hidden beneath a yellow baseball cap that matched the yellow boat, pulled back on the accelerator, causing the boat to reverse and dock up against the wharf.

The driver had a scar on his lip.

It was Lamond.

'I intercepted Marie just like you planned,' said Lamond to his new passengers, who jumped aboard and stared down at Marie, who sat alone, huddled away from the splattered blood on a long metal seat that could fit up to five people across. A dead man lay spread-eagled on the floor. You didn't need to be a genius to work out that his death had been caused by one of Lamond's bullets. His right eye oozed blood: the kill shot.

Lamond's eyes darted to the painting in Pierre's arms

and he continued, 'Once I had her hostage, I pressed the walkie-talkie's receiver five times, just like you told me to.'

'You did good, Lamond. It worked,' said Frederic, patting his friend on the shoulder.

Marie glanced up, her angry eyes filled with hatred.

With studied nonchalance, Pierre sat down across from her. Rain ran from his bald head into his eyebrows. He continued to look unblinkingly into Marie's eyes. Then he placed the *Mona Lisa* to one side, seemingly unconcerned that the rain was coming in at an angle. A puddle had pooled on the seat.

Frederic advanced toward Lamond at the steering wheel and asked, 'Have you heard from your brother?'

'The last thing I heard from my earpiece was him boarding Joey's boat. I heard them fighting. Then it went dead.'

'I got that, too,' said Frederic. 'They must have gone in the water. Don't worry, there's no way the American would have got the better of Thierry.'

'I hope you're right,' said Lamond, who pushed the accelerator's lever down and headed back out into the river in the heavy rain.

Pierre continued to stare, deep in thought. He ignored the painting, exposed and at the mercy of the rain. But he chose not to say a word.

A tear fell down Marie's face. The thought of seeing her boyfriend floating in the Seine River somewhere was unimaginable. She hated the man in front of her, a man she had once thought of as family. Her eyes fell on the masterpiece by Pierre's side. Raindrops were hitting the surface of the painting and sliding down to the seat beneath it. Marie's rage grew with each droplet. 'Peter, what are you doing? The painting.'

'What about it?' said Pierre, calm as ever.

'It's in the rain. The board will warp. The damage will be irreparable.'

Pierre sighed. 'The only thing that will be irreparable, Marie, will be Joey when I get my hands on him.'

'What are you talking about?'

Pierre picked up the *Mona Lisa* and turned it around so that the back was facing Marie.

Once Marie saw it, she understood. The Louvre's seal stamp was not present, and the back of the board was not old. In fact, it was brand new. There was also a Mont Marte sticker and the words *Renée's Art Academy* were printed at the top. A name, presumably that of the student who had painted it, was written in black texta: *Margret Francsois*.

'Now you know,' said Pierre, tossing the painting onto the dead body on the ground.

'What's going on? Where is the real *Mona Lisa*?' asked Marie.

'It looks like your boyfriend has been playing games with us this whole time.'

Marie tried to hide her delight but couldn't. She smiled.

'I don't like playing games,' Pierre said, in a slow, menacing way. 'Someone needs to pay for his little stunt today.'

Marie's smile left her face just as Pierre's began.

They drifted toward the place where the river forked, and took the left-hand exit. The taxi's mounted floodlights shone downward into the dark water, which was a rich greeny-gray, reflecting the dark clouds above. The storm had caused a swell that didn't look like it would let up anytime soon. Even though it was daytime, the dark, gray shadowy world made it feel much later.

After they passed under the second bridge, Marie could make out some sort of commotion in the distance. A large riverboat was banked up against the wharf, surrounded by the flashing lights of police and fire vehicles. A boat accident had clearly taken place. This couldn't be a coincidence. Marie's heart leaped into her mouth and she craned her neck for a better look. The enormous steel framework of the riverboat's paddle blades was being examined for damage. It looked like a rope had somehow become tangled within them. Dozens of police officers with flashlights were searching the river. Using the power of a four-wheel drive's pulley system, they extracted out of the water a remnant of a wooden boat. It looked like the damaged boat had been split in two. All around them, hundreds of pieces of broken timber floated in the river, as though a deadly plague had hit the water.

Lamond steered the taxi boat around the scene, keeping a safe distance as the floating timber pieces hit up against the bow. Marie noticed Frederic turn his eyes to a torn piece of rope, one end of which was pulled tight into the abyss. It was far enough away from the wreckage that the police hadn't noticed yet. 'Hang on, Lamond, stop the engine for a second,' he said.

Lamond killed the engine and maneuvered the boat closer so that Frederic could reach the rope.

Marie bit her lip, dreading the possibility that they would find Joey at the end of it.

'I got it,' said Frederic, tugging on the rope as if he were a fisherman waiting to see what he had caught. There was a considerable weight on the rope, and the weather conditions were not helping.

Lamond angled one of the boat's floodlights in Frederic's direction, and they all saw a strange shape appear at the end of the rope as it neared the surface. 'It's a body,' said Frederic.

Marie closed her eyes, her hands shaking with dismay.

'Ah, shit,' said Frederic, lifting up the body part.

Those two words said it all. Marie opened her eyes and her gorge rose in her throat when she saw half of a man's body sliced in two. The sight was disgusting. The half-body in view were the legs and part of the torso. There were boots on the corpse's feet.

'Is it Joey?' asked Lamond, still behind the wheel.

'Stay there, Lamond,' ordered Frederic.

'Why ... What the hell's going on?' said Lamond, his tone rising. 'Something's wrong, isn't it?'

Lamond approached the edge of the boat and his face collapsed. His legs buckled and he fell to his knees as Marie watched his salty tears flow unchecked from his eyes. Then his features changed, and a look of pure rage overcame him.

'I'm going to kill him,' he said. 'He's mine ... he's fucking mine.'

'Don't worry, you will get your chance,' Frederic replied.

Chapter 25

Pierre sat across from Marie and tried not to see the smug look in her eyes. Though he was doing a good job of hiding it, he was furious and felt sick to the stomach. How could it be that they were all back to square one, with Joey still in possession of the *Mona Lisa* and more dangerous than ever? If he wanted, he could reveal the truth to the world. The truth Pierre had tried so hard to keep hidden. Joey was in control yet again, and this feeling was making Pierre's blood boil.

Marie glanced over at the police in the distance.

'Scream all you want, they won't be able to hear you over this rain,' said Pierre, his face reddening with anger. He had had enough of her. All those years spent helping Marie, even though she was the daughter of a friend who had betrayed him, had allowed the hate and resentment Pierre felt for them both to build up. Now he was at breaking point. He had never loved Marie; he had felt responsible for what had happened to her father, and later when he realized who she'd met, she had become a pawn he could use to get his *Mona Lisa* back. A way she could repay him for all the years he'd invested in her. It was high time she was sacrificed for the cause.

He stood up and charged at her like a raging bull, grabbing her by her long brown hair and forcing her entire body off the side of the boat.

Marie couldn't believe what was happening. She tried to loosen his grip on her hair, but couldn't stop the momentum of her body as it entered the cold, murky water of the Seine. Pierre had gone mad; she could see the whites of his eyes as he screamed down at her, taking out all his frustration on her, she guessed.

'Help!' she screamed, trying to stay afloat as she gulped for air.

'I told you they can't help you.' Pierre laughed hysterically as he pushed her head under the water. She struggled to break the surface, her hands flailing everywhere.

'Help!' she screamed again.

Under the water all she could hear was the sound of her own panicked bubbles and muffled cries. Then, when she managed to break the surface, she could hear the sound of the crashing rain all around her.

'No one messes with me,' said Pierre. 'Nobody!'

With superhuman effort she broke the surface again, gulping in air and rain, then she was shoved right back down again.

This time panic had her heart hammering against her ribs, and every cell in her body was screaming for oxygen. Trying not to breathe, she swallowed some of the dirty water and started choking. It would only be a few more seconds and she would drown in the city she loved so much. She felt herself weakening, losing the will to struggle anymore.

★ ★ ★

'Boss, we'll need her,' said Frederic. 'She's our bargaining chip. Now's not the time.'

Through the red mist of his rage, Pierre had no desire to let Marie live. But he thought of the *Mona Lisa*, and his years of effort spent trying to get it back. 'Yes,' he finally said reluctantly. 'Yes, you're right.' He let go of Marie's hair and turned away, moving back to his seat and rolling up his wet sleeves.

Marie surfaced, gagging and spluttering. She could barely keep herself afloat.

'Get yourself in the boat, Marie,' ordered Frederic.

Marie weakly grabbed the edge of the boat, continuing to gasp for air.

Ignoring her, Frederic took control of the wheel, leaving Lamond hunched in a corner with his grief. Starting the taxi's engine, he began to steer the boat past the damaged vessel.

Pierre watched as Marie hauled herself back into the boat, her limbs shaking with the effort. She curled herself into a ball, shivering uncontrollably and her teeth chattering. As she looked up Pierre met her gaze. Her eyes were filled with utter hatred.

Chapter 26

Thursday, 12 pm

Joey had survived certain death. In the end, it had been a matter of pure luck and a bit of smart thinking on his part that had saved him. Any day you were up against a trained soldier whose only purpose was to take you out, and you came out on top, was a good day. Joey had pre-organized the taxi boat to take Marie to a waiting cab, which would bring her to his hotel. His only objective now was to get to the hotel, retrieve his girlfriend and get out of this country.

Shoeless, and wearing only his sodden underwear and red shirt, he jogged back to his hotel in the cold rain. He entered the foyer in a hurry and approached the girls at the front desk, who gaped at the bloodied, beaten and unsightly image in front of them. Other tourists, kids and staff members in the lobby stared curiously and pointed when they saw the man in his underwear.

'Can I please get another room key,' asked Joey with an embarrassed grin. 'As you can see, I've had a rough morning, and I seem to have lost my pants.'

'Of course,' said the brunette with a smile, while the blonde asked, 'How did you lose your pants, *monsieur*?'

'Believe me, you don't want to know,' replied Joey, who accepted the new card, turned and headed for the elevator doors, knowing that all eyes were on him.

He pressed the elevator button and waited. Behind him he heard an elderly woman talking as she headed his way. She was complaining about something. The tone of her voice was one of frustration, one Joey knew all too well. He turned to look.

'My name is Margret!' the woman said to a hotel staff member, who appeared to have taken down all her information on a piece of paper. 'If you find it, please let me know.'

'*Certainement, madame,*' replied the staff member politely, though Joey saw him roll his eyes as the woman hurried away.

Margret stood next to Joey. She seemed flushed in the face, her cheeks pinched red. She would have been in her late seventies. She had freckles across her nose and her hair was as white as snow and tied back in a ponytail. As they both entered the elevator, Joey saw the woman glance at his state of undress and take a step away from him. It wasn't an everyday occurrence to see a grown man in his underwear, waiting to catch a lift, he supposed.

'Are you from the Netherlands?' asked Joey.

The old woman glanced across at Joey nervously. 'Yes. I am.'

'I recognized your Dutch accent. I have many friends with the same accent.'

'Do you,' she replied with cold detachment.

'If you don't mind me asking,' said Joey, 'why are you so upset?'

'My oil painting was stolen,' she answered abruptly. 'Were your pants stolen, too?'

Joey flashed a smile. 'Ah, I'm really sorry about that.'

'It's not your fault,' she said.

If she only knew the truth, thought Joey, and he felt a stab of guilt.

'What upsets me about the robbery was the fact that my painting was the only one taken in the entire class. Everyone else's was left behind.'

Margret was genuinely upset, and Joey felt awful for what he had done. He needed to say something, at least to make her feel better. He said, 'Maybe the thief chose your painting because it was the best one among the lot? It's kind of a backhanded compliment.'

Margret gave him a crooked smile and said, 'You're a sweet boy, but please do me a favor and put some pants on.'

'Will do,' said Joey, stepping out of the elevator. 'See you around.'

Joey hurried down the carpeted hallway, longing for the warmth and comfort of his room, only to see a figure sitting in front of his hotel door. For a second a feeling of fear pierced his brain, but it disappeared just as quickly when he saw the curls. It was his partner in crime, Boyce, and judging by the expression on his face, he wasn't happy at all.

'How did you find me?' asked Joey.

'I followed you the entire time,' replied Boyce, his voice choked with emotion. 'I can't believe you destroyed my boat. I trusted you. Now I have nothing. No home ... no job ... nothing.'

Joey opened his door with his new card key. He was

cold, wet and tired. 'If you know what happened, why are you here?' said Joey. 'I could be dangerous. Why take the risk?'

'I know a dangerous man when I see one,' said Boyce, following him into the room. 'Dangerous people don't walk the streets in their underwear. Plus you owe me money. And a new boat. Don't think I'll let you get away that easily. By the way, why aren't you wearing any pants? What's going on? And who the hell are you?'

'Okay ... Okay ... Give me a minute.' Joey closed the door, then snatched a green towel from the bathroom towel rack and dried his hair with it. He then took off his shirt and wrapped the towel around his waist. Next he opened the minibar fridge and took out two Cokes, threw one over to Boyce and retired to a comfy chair that was facing the bed.

'I'm waiting,' said Boyce with folded arms.

'Yes ... your boat was destroyed.'

'It's all I had,' said Boyce raising his voice.

'Relax, Boy. I have lots of money. I'll buy you and your father a new and better boat, don't worry.'

'Firstly, my name is Boyce. Stop calling me Boy. And why should I trust you? You lied to me once; you'll most likely lie to me again!'

'Look, Boy.'

Boyce shook his head, but didn't bother correcting Joey again.

'Can you just give me a break, kid? I'm tired, my nose is bleeding and I was nearly killed not so long ago. What do you want me to say? You just have to trust me.'

'*Salaud*,' said Boyce angrily. 'I have no choice but to

trust you, but I'm not leaving your side until I get my money back.'

'That's not a good idea,' said Joey. 'Go home, kid.'

'You don't seem to get it, do you? I have no home to go to.'

'What do you mean?' said Joey, watching the youngster's brown eyes fill with tears.

'I lied before, this wasn't my father's boat. I live alone and have lived alone for the past three years. My mother was a junkie and died when I was eight years old and my father is a criminal doing time in jail.'

'Ah,' said Joey delicately. 'You know, we aren't so different after all,' he added. 'I never met my mother, and my father was a criminal, too.' He watched Boyce for a moment, thinking. 'But how have you escaped social services all these years? I can't believe they haven't picked you up already.'

Boyce's eyes darted away shiftily. 'Even though he's in jail, my father is still well connected, and I've had help from his friends on the outside. My father told me never to get involved with the authorities. He taught me how to avoid them, and I have.'

'So you are now practically homeless.'

'Yes, that boat was my everything.'

Joey sighed. 'Boy, look at me. You can trust me, okay? I promise you I'll buy you a better boat. We can go to a bank and I'll transfer you over some money.'

'Okay, but until then, I'm with you,' said Boyce. 'I have no place else to go.'

There was no point debating the point with the teen. He was here to stay. Joey sank back in his chair and sipped on his Coke. He thought about the decision he had made not to make the exchange with the real painting, putting Marie in danger. She still had not arrived at the hotel and the possibility that she could have been recaptured toyed in his mind. He knew the type of people he was dealing with, and he just couldn't bring himself to hand the masterpiece over to them. But more importantly, he couldn't help wondering why his forebears had kept the painting hidden for so long. They, too, might have done the philanthropic thing and returned it, but they hadn't, and Joey wanted to know why not. If they had had a good reason for holding on to the painting, then Joey needed to know what it was. In that moment, Joey decided that he was going to make it his mission to discover the reason.

Boyce sat down on the bed. 'So tell me, Joey. Why are these people after you? What did you do?'

Joey pointed to the wall, to a painting of the *Mona Lisa* that hung above the bedhead. Before he had left the room that morning, he had hung his precious masterpiece up on the wall. He thought hiding it in plain sight would be a much safer option than trying to hide it under the bed or in the closet. If room service had entered they would have thought it was part of the décor and ignored it – if they'd even noticed it in the first place.

'*La Joconde*, what about it?' asked Boyce.

'That's why they are after me.'

'I know I'm only a kid, but you're not making sense. Are you planning to steal it from the Louvre? Are you a professional thief?'

'Professional thief,' Joey laughed. 'No. But I come from a line of professional thieves. You might have heard of my great-grandfather, Vincenzo Peruggia?'

It only took a second or two for the new information to sink in. There was no need to continue; Boyce was French, after all. What French person didn't know about the greatest art theft of all time?

'Peruggia was your great-grandfather?' he asked with widening eyes.

'I guess, after destroying your home, I at least owe you the truth,' said Joey, sighing. 'The painting up there is the original *Mona Lisa* that my great-grandfather stole in 1911. The Louvre knows of its existence and wants it back at any cost. That's why I'm in danger and that's why they tried to kill me. To make matters worse they've taken my girlfriend hostage – she's the one you gave the walkie-talkie to on the bridge – and the curator has three – actually two – military officers trying to track me down, so being around me isn't safe.'

Boyce's mouth dropped open in astonishment and he stared back into Joey's eyes as if he was trying to register what he had just heard. Finally he managed, 'If what you're telling me is true, yes, that would explain why they want you dead.'

Boyce stepped up to the painting, his young untrained eyes appreciating the artwork of the master and said, 'So what do we do now?'

'What do you mean what do *we* do? You're not going to do anything,' said Joey. 'Didn't you hear what I just said? It's too dangerous.'

'How about we make an arrangement? I can help you, for a fee. You destroyed my boat and I need to continue to make money.'

Joey was about to refuse when something stopped

him. He was undeniably in need of assistance. It was his first time in Paris and a guide around the city would be useful, and the fact that this teen spoke excellent English was also a plus.

'Okay, Boy,' said Joey.

'My name is Boyce!'

Joey flashed a smile. He was never going to call him Boyce. He enjoyed riling the kid way too much. 'Hey, by the way, how did you get your boat in the first place, and how come you speak such fluent English?' asked Joey, stretching his arms behind his head.

'I won my boat in a poker game. I had an unbeatable hand.' Boyce smiled as if remembering the day. 'My English is good because my father is British. He moved to Paris when he fell in love with my mother.'

Joey couldn't help liking the kid. He was young, but he was resourceful and brave, and frankly, Joey knew he needed all the help he could get to stay alive in this situation. 'Okay, Boy, a brand-new boat, fully equipped, plus five thousand dollars cash if you help me around town while I'm here. But for us to work together you need to listen to what I say. Is that a deal?'

'Deal,' said Boyce with a wide grin. He looked as though he had won the lottery. 'So what's the plan, boss?'

'First, I need some fresh clothes. I can't roam around the city without pants and smelling like shit, can I? Nothing fancy, just a pair of jeans, thirty-two-inch waist, a plain shirt and sweater in size medium. Also if you can find me some US-size-nine sneakers, I'd really appreciate it.'

'No problem. Money?' said Boyce, holding out his hand.

Joey got up from the chair and stepped into the closet,

where the hotel-room safe was situated. He entered the four-digit combination and extracted his wallet, which he had left behind that morning. 'Here's my credit card. Use it only to purchase the clothes. My PIN is 2604, I assume you know how to use it. If you decide to run away with it, I'll cancel it immediately, and you'll get no new boat, no money. Do you understand?'

'I do,' said Boyce, who plucked the card out of Joey's fingers and headed for the door.

'While you're there, Boy, buy yourself some new clothes, too. We're partners now. I need you looking the part,' Joey added, eying Boyce's old torn shirt, dirty jeans and worn-out shoes.

At the door Boyce turned, gave him a smiling salute, and left the room.

Chapter 27

The stress spread through Joey's mind like ink on paper. An hour had gone by and Marie had yet to arrive at the hotel. He needed to know if his plan had worked or if she had been captured by Pierre's men. While Joey waited for the teen to arrive back with new clothes, he stepped outside in his hotel robe and paid a stranger fifty US dollars to use his cell phone. The male who looked like a businessman wearing an expensive dark suit, agreed and handed it over to Joey. Making sure the private setting on the phone was activated, he googled the Louvre curator's number and dialed it.

After being greeted by Bradley, he was transferred immediately to Pierre's office.

Pierre's voice was present, but he spoke in French.

'Hello, Pierre, it's Joey.'

'Joey, my favorite American,' said Pierre. 'When are you going to learn? I have someone here who would like to talk to you.'

Screams erupted from a female. Joey cringed at the thought that it was Marie, but he knew it to be true.

'Joey!' Marie cried out.

'Marie, are you okay?'

'Marie will be sleeping with the rats tonight because of you,' said Pierre.

With a burst of rage Joey kicked the bin in front of him, which scared the businessman, who gave him space to discuss his issues. 'If you harm her I will come for you, Pierre!'

'I want my painting back, Joey.'

Joey didn't reply and hung up the phone.

Chapter 28

Thursday, 2 pm

It seemed like forever, but Boyce finally returned from his shopping spree. He was dressed in dark-blue jeans and a white shirt underneath a navy-blue sweater. His shoes were Italian leather, brown and pointy. He had had his long curly hair cut short and styled. His appearance was totally transformed.

'Look at you, what did you get me?' asked Joey, digging into the bags to find a pair of dark-blue jeans, a white shirt and navy-blue sweater. It was exactly the same outfit Boyce was wearing. The only difference was the pair of size-nine sneakers he had requested. Joey had to laugh.

Showered and dressed, and finally free of the rotten smell of the river, Joey looked his younger twin up and down. 'You know, you could've bought us different-colored sweaters. We look like half of a boy band.'

'I think I did okay,' said Boyce, smiling from ear to ear. 'So tell me, what's the plan, JP?'

'JP … Are you trying to be funny?' replied Joey.

'From now on, I'm going to call you JP, until you start calling me Boyce.'

Joey smiled at the young punk giving him lip and asked, 'Do you know where I can use the internet?'

'The hotel lobby should have free internet; I think I saw a Mac on the way in. What are you looking for?'

'The Louvre curator mentioned something about a restorer named Bernard Martino,' said Joey as he tied his shoelaces. 'This Martino knew the truth about the painting's fake status and was shot dead inside the Louvre. Coincidentally, I recently discovered he was also my girlfriend's father.'

Boyce raised his eyebrows in surprise. 'Yes, I know about him,' he said. 'He was killed because he was about to throw acid at the *Mona Lisa* in 1981.'

'But I thought the *Mona Lisa* was protected behind bulletproof glass, so how could he?'

'Bernard Martino was the *Mona Lisa's* main restorer. He knew how to disarm the glass. He even had his own personal key. That's why they had no choice but to shoot him down.'

'Somehow, I believe there's more to that story. If Bernard had known all that time the painting was a fake, why did he decide to destroy it in 1981? Why not earlier? What tipped him over the edge?'

'I have no idea,' Boyce replied.

'I think there's something else going on here. My family went to great lengths to keep the real painting hidden, and I need to find out why. Plus there's something that doesn't add up about what happened to Martino, and I can't help feeling it has something to do with all this. We need to find out. Only then will I consider returning the painting to the Louvre.'

★ ★ ★

Joey and Boyce left the room and Boyce led the way to a computer terminal in the hotel's designated computer room. The girls at the front desk giggled behind their hands when they saw the man and boy wearing the same outfit. The 'stupid American' had become a talking point in the hotel due to his famous underwear incident a couple of hours ago.

'You had to get us the same clothes,' whispered Joey in dismay, shaking his head as he turned his attention back to the screen.

'Next time you do the shopping, then,' replied Boyce as he pulled up a chair.

Opening up a search engine, Joey typed in the name *Bernard Martino*. Many sites appeared to mention him. Joey clicked on one and Bernard's story unfolded in front of their eyes. The article was in English with a large header that read, *Vandal Is Shot* at the top of the page.

The media had branded Martino as the ultimate vandal, who had been stopped in the nick of time. The story went into detail, explaining how close the art restorer had come to damaging the painting. How he had concealed acid in a Pellegrino water bottle. How his sick plan was to destroy the greatest artwork of all time, but that he was stopped by the Louvre guards, who disrupted the crime and shot him dead.

Joey scrolled down the page and saw a picture of Bernard's family taken a couple of years after his death. His young wife was holding her two-year-old daughter in her lap. The picture had been taken in an interview for a TV special about her husband. It was an old photo. The lady's hair was blonde and cut in a bob. She sat in an old cane chair in front of her house, reported to be an old abandoned church that had been converted into a home. Being an artist, Bernard had transformed the inside but had retained the exterior façade, a cross still prominent at the highest point.

'Do you know where this place is?' asked Joey, pointing to the name of the village, which was listed underneath the photo.

'Why, do you want to go there?' asked Boyce curiously.

'We need to find out more about Bernard. Maybe his wife can help us. I know I'm clutching at straws, but she might know something about Pierre that could help us. Plus she's Marie's mother. I have to find a way to rescue Marie.'

Boyce took control of the computer mouse and entered the address into the search engine. 'It's in Switzerland,' he mumbled. 'It's a five-hour drive from here. The house shouldn't be too hard to find, being an old church in a small town.'

Taking the mouse, Joey switched the page back to the previous one and continued to study the photo. The old lady's sad eyes looked back at him. But what caught his eye this time was the green heart-shaped necklace that hung around her neck. The exact same heart-shaped necklace that Marie wore all the time. As he gazed at the little girl he knew to be Marie, he wondered how he was going to save her and what he could possibly discover in Switzerland. He knew he was taking a risk leaving Marie in Pierre's custody while he went searching for answers, but he had to trust that just as the painting was Joey's bargaining chip, Marie was Pierre's, and he'd keep her alive until he had his painting back.

'I have a feeling, Boy,' Joey said, 'that we're about to find out more than we bargained for.'

Chapter 29

Joey tucked the *Mona Lisa* inside a pillowcase after removing the pillow. He took a clean white towel from the bathroom and picked up a flat-head screwdriver that had been left in a toolkit just under the bathroom sink.

They left the hotel on foot and wandered south down the narrow street. It was still raining, though the intensity of the storm had passed, so they jogged to a nearby undercover parking lot belonging to some luxury apartments. They waited for a car to exit, and then slid discreetly underneath the roller door before it shut behind them. The vast parking lot was full of expensive BMWs, Mercedes and Porsches.

'What are we looking for?' asked Boyce quietly, following Joey.

'There … the visitors' spots,' replied Joey. He had spotted an old mid-nineties Renault. 'We're going to steal this car.'

For all his worldliness, Boyce looked taken aback. 'Why? Why don't we just rent a car?'

'If we rent a car we'd have to fill in paperwork and give our names, which would be stored on a database somewhere. We don't have time to organize a fake ID and rent a car that way. I'm not taking any chances with Pierre. This way there's far less chance we could be traced.'

Joey rolled up the towel around his right arm as a guard and elbowed the driver's side window. The glass shattered.

'So that's why you brought the towel. You're crazy,' said Boyce, his eyes flashing. 'But why are you stealing this car, when there's a Porsche over there?' he added.

'Watch.' Joey snaked his hand through the broken window and opened the door. He entered first and hit the flat-head screwdriver as hard as he could into the ignition, then turned it like a key. He had seen his older brother do this before, when they were just kids. The car buzzed to life with a coughing chortle.

'On new cars the screwdriver-in-the-ignition trick doesn't work, which is why I chose this shitbox,' Joey explained. 'Quick, get in before someone comes.' Joey unlocked the passenger-side door.

Boyce climbed in, carefully swiping away the shattered glass from his seat. Before he had time to put on his seatbelt, Joey had planted his foot on the gas, leaving the underground parking lot in a hurry.

Chapter 30

Pierre's black Rolls-Royce pulled up in front of the Hotel de la Jatte. Frederic exited the car first and stood on guard. Lamond opened Pierre's door with an umbrella at the ready and Pierre emerged, wearing an overpriced gray suit and matching hat. All three men entered the hotel and Lamond approached the front desk.

After flashing a badge that read *Louvre Police* on it, Lamond asked a predetermined question Pierre had given him on the drive over. He then re-joined Frederic and Pierre in the hotel's sitting room, where they were waiting to hear the answer.

'You were right about this hotel,' said Lamond, facing his much shorter boss. 'The artist Margret Francsois is a guest here. And yes, her painting was stolen overnight.'

'You've got to give the kid credit,' said Pierre, but in a tone that lacked enthusiasm. 'He sure did outsmart us.'

Pierre left the two soldiers and advanced over to the counter. Frederic and Lamond followed, standing discreetly behind and on either side of him.

'Good evening, ladies,' said Pierre smoothly to the two girls at the reception desk. 'I'm looking for a friend of mine, and I believe he checked into this hotel. He's in his mid-twenties with long blondish hair and blue eyes.

Can you help me?' Pierre smiled charmingly at them.

'You must be talking about the underwear man,' laughed the blonde-haired sister, trying to keep a straight face.

'I'm Pierre Savard, the curator of the Louvre, and I have important business with this man. His name is Mr. Joey Peruggia. Can you please tell me what room he's in?'

The girls' smiles disappeared when they realized who the powerful man in front of them was. Pierre understood what this was about; it wasn't an uncommon occurrence. He knew how well-known he was, how highly regarded in the art and religious sectors. The brunette spoke first. 'Ah, Mr. Savard, I'm sorry we didn't recognize you. The name you have mentioned is not what we have on file.'

'Did he pay in cash?'

'Yes, sir, he did.'

'He is covering his tracks. The man staying here is Joey Peruggia.'

'Well, you just missed him. He went out about an hour ago. We don't know where he was going, but he's staying in room twenty. If you'd been here a few hours ago you would have run into him right here – he was using our free internet service.' She pointed a finger toward the computer room off the foyer.

Pierre smiled, doffed his hat and thanked the girls before turning his back on them. 'Follow me,' he said to his men, and headed for the computer room.

'We know his room number,' said Frederic. 'How about we set up a trap?'

'Before we do that, I want to see what he was looking

for,' said Pierre, pulling up a seat. 'Let's see your history,' he said to himself, controlling the mouse.

After a few clicks, information on Bernard Martino flashed up on the screen. Pierre tapped the desk distractedly, thinking.

'Why was he researching Bernard?' asked Frederic, leaning over. 'Wasn't he killed in the Louvre?'

Pierre sighed. 'I know where he's going.'

'Where?' asked Frederic.

'He is heading for a church in Switzerland.'

'Why?'

'He is going to meet an old friend who lives there. The small town is called Romainmôtier-Envy. You two need to find the church that is situated high up on the hill. Take the Chevy pickup.'

'What about you?' asked Frederic.

'I have a business meeting I can't postpone or reschedule, but when I am done, I will take the helicopter.'

'Yes, sir.'

'Like I said before, make sure the painting is safe before you kill them.'

Frederic acknowledged this instruction with a nod and left with Lamond.

Pierre turned back to the screen and scrolled down to see pictures of Bernard's wife and child. A hint of a smirk shone on his face. Then as quickly as the smile had appeared, it fell away. It had been over thirty-something years since the last time they had spoken, and it had all ended in tears.

Now an unwelcome reunion was about to take place.

Chapter 31

Three hours on the road and the city was only a distant memory. The landscape around them was green as far as the eye could see. The setting sun illuminated the hills and the purple mountains, which were gradually rising into view in the distance. On either side of the highway cows, sheep and horses grazed contentedly in their pastures.

The drive took a little over five hours and they stopped only for food and petrol. Crossing the stunning France–Switzerland border, they took in the breathtaking view of the majestic Jura Mountains, whose peaks projected up into the clouds on the north of the Western Alps.

What remained of Joey's driver-side window was all the way down. He took in the panoramic views and breathed in the clean but extremely cold fresh mountain air. A wide river separated a golden wave of sugar cane farm territory, which stretched for miles in every direction.

While he drove, Joey turned over in his mind the contents of the letters his grandmother and great-grandfather had written, and the effort his father had made to preserve and hide the *Mona Lisa* in his secret room. There had to be a reason why his family hadn't returned the painting to the Louvre when they had the chance. Joey knew he couldn't hand the painting over until he knew what that reason was, but unearthing that secret was not going to be easy. Not able to come to any conclusions, he turned his mind to the matter at hand. He hoped he was doing the right thing following up on the unusual circumstances of Martino's death. He sensed there was a clue to be found there, and it was as good a place to start as any, but he felt he was risking Marie's life in the process. If this trip turned out to be a waste of time, she might well be the one who paid the price.

The time was 7:30 pm, and they entered the small village of Romainmôtier-Envy just as night was falling. A sign informed them that the town was a heritage site and of national significance, with a total population of five hundred and four people. The homes all resembled each other. Built from medieval-era brick, they were joined together like a row of townhouses. Joey continued along the old bumpy road out of the main town, and he and Boyce looked around for signs of the converted church.

'There,' said Boyce, pointing up at the mountainside. Above a row of trees they could see the top of a church spire. A little further along the road they came across a dirt access road, which they followed up the mountain. After a short drive they turned into a clearing and before them sat an old Romanesque-style church with a crucifix atop its spire.

'That's got to be it,' said Boyce with excitement in his voice as the car fought its way through grass that had grown knee-high. 'It sure looked nicer in the photo.'

'That's because inside this church is an old lady,' replied Joey. 'Probably too much for her to keep it maintained on her own.'

Joey drove the Renault up to where the land leveled itself into what must once have been the church's parking area. The entire site was filled with pebbles and wet rocks that crunched as they drove over them.

After parking the car and removing his screwdriver key, Joey opened his door and stood up, stretching his aching muscles. His breath was visible in the crisp, chill air. He had never experienced forty-five degrees Fahrenheit before and he was amazed at how cold it was. He took a moment to enjoy the beautiful view around him and the smell of rosemary before turning to peer at the structure they'd come to find.

'Well, it's now or never,' he said, and he reached into the car and pulled out the pillowcase holding the painting. He flung it across his back as though he were Santa Claus, and he and Boyce strolled to the front entrance. The grass and weeds around the premises were out of control. The front fence was broken and leaning over to one side, and the floor of the porch was strewn with silt.

Raising a clenched fist, Joey knocked on the old wooden church doors. He waited a couple of seconds then knocked again, and this time he called out, 'Mrs. Martino, I'm a friend, are you here?'

'I'll go around the back to see if there's another entrance,' said Boyce, hopping off the porch and hurrying around the side of the building. It was clear from the way he moved that he was trying to keep himself warm.

Still no answer.

It seemed like the house was empty.

If you lived out here on your own you could die and no one would know, thought Joey uneasily. He walked back to the broken fence.

Boyce reappeared around the other side of the property. 'There are no other access points,' he said, rubbing his hands together. 'The church was built like a hall, one way in and one way out. She's not here.'

Gazing back at the church, Joey suddenly smiled and replied, 'Someone's here. Look.' He pointed up at the smoke curling out of the chimney.

He walked purposefully back to the church's front doors. 'Mrs. Martino, I need your help. I'm desperate. My girlfriend's in trouble. Yesterday, I saw a picture taken of you in 1983. You were wearing a green heart-shaped necklace and you had a little girl in your lap, a girl who is thirty-five years old now. That girl is my girlfriend. She wears that exact same necklace. Can you please open the door? Your daughter needs your help.'

There was nothing but silence.

'She's not here, JP.'

Joey sighed. He had no idea what to do next.

Just then came the sound of a key turning in a lock, then a scraping noise that Joey realized was a large wooden beam being lifted from across the inside of the door. Then the door opened to reveal a little old lady with a walking stick who hobbled to a stop in the entrance.

'Come in,' she said softly in accented English. Her eyes darted toward the unusual pillowcase that rested on Joey's back as she ushered them inside.

The interior of the old church had been entirely gutted out and redesigned. The only church-like features remaining were the high ceilings, pitched roof and stained-glass windows, high up on the walls. The layout was open plan, warm and comfortable with different living areas. A larger-than-usual feature fireplace found in contemporary homes was lit, surrounded by comfortable gray fabric lounges.

'Nice place you have here,' said Boyce.

Even though the ceiling must have been thirty feet high, it was still warm inside.

'Take a seat,' the old woman said, gesturing them toward the couches.

Joey and Boyce sat together like schoolkids about to be told a story by their teacher. The light from the fireplace bounced off their faces. Like a knight protecting an important religious relic, Joey held the *Mona Lisa* by his side under his arm.

'So you're dating my daughter,' the old woman said with a hint of a smile as she eyed Joey up and down.

'Yes, Mrs. Martino,' Joey replied formally.

'Please, call me Edna,' she said. 'And what's your name, son?'

'My name is Joey Peruggia.'

'Peruggia ...' she repeated, and her smile widened. 'Your being here is fate,' she said, as she observed Joey with something like adoration. 'So I assume your great-grandfather left you something special? A painting, perhaps?'

'How did you know about that?' asked Joey.

'You have no idea what I know, son,' she murmured.

Joey reached into his pillowcase and extracted the

Mona Lisa. He watched Edna's eyes glisten in the light of the fire. Her mouth fell open.

'Your daughter's in trouble,' said Joey, holding the painting. 'Pierre, the Louvre curator, has taken Marie hostage and will kill her if I don't give him back the *Mona Lisa*.'

'You can't give it back to him,' Edna said quickly, her voice choked with tears.

'But if I don't, they'll kill her,' said Joey.

'You still don't get it, do you, son?'

'What I don't get is why so many people have died because of this painting,' said Joey. 'Why it has caused so much pain and suffering. That's what I don't get!'

Boyce didn't say a word. He just slumped against the cushions on the couch, watching the two adults go back and forth like he would a tennis match. It was obvious he didn't want to get involved in this family squabble.

'Pain … believe me, I know of pain,' said Edna, her voice raised. 'My husband died because of it.'

'Why did he?' said Joey. 'Why would he want to destroy the painting he'd worked so hard to restore? I just don't understand.'

'Do you want to know the truth?'

'Please. That's why I've come.'

'Okay, great-grandson to Vincenzo Peruggia,' said Edna with a sigh. She paused for a moment, as if unsure whether or not to continue. 'Here it goes … It's because of a secret that lies within the painting you hold in your hands, a secret that has been kept hidden for centuries.'

'What are you talking about?' asked Joey. 'What secret?'

'It's a secret your great-grandfather had found out while working inside the Louvre. It's the reason why he stole the painting in the first place. It's a secret that Pierre Savard is now obsessed with, and has spent all his life in search of.'

'What is it?' asked Boyce, sitting forward. 'Do you know the secret?'

Edna nodded her head slowly. 'I do,' she said. 'I was going to take it to my grave, but now that Vincenzo's great-grandson is in my home ...'

She took a breath, paused and refocused.

'Does Marie know the secret?' asked Joey.

'No, she does not,' said Edna. 'I didn't want to put her in harm's way. I feared that if I did, she would end up dead like her father.'

'Well, she's in deep trouble now,' said Joey. 'If you want to help her, you need to tell me everything you know.'

Joey stared at the old lady and could see his girlfriend's hazel eyes peering back at him. For the first time he saw fear in them, and then she dropped her gaze and he noticed that her hands, which she was twisting in her lap, were trembling. What the hell had his great-grandfather been involved in? What secret could be so important?

Chapter 32

'Okay, start with my great-grandfather,' said Joey as patiently as he could. 'Why is he so significant?'

'Vincenzo Peruggia ... your great-grandfather was branded a thief.'

'Yes, we know that,' said Joey.

'But did you know what he did before that? He was working in the Louvre in the early 1900s, and he was one of five men enlisted to work in the underground chambers.'

'I know of the place; so what?'

Edna continued. 'His job was to scour through thousands of paintings that were piled up on top of each other, in search of a hidden gem among them.'

'Did they find anything?' Boyce asked curiously.

Edna smiled. 'After months of searching and cataloguing through works of art that were too damaged to be repaired, but too old and valuable to be thrown away, Vincenzo came across a document that was stuck to the back of an old canvas.'

'Whose canvas was it?' asked Boyce. 'Do you know who painted it?'

'No one knows,' said Edna. 'The painting was too far gone to be recognized. It didn't matter anyway as a large slash ran right through the center of it and mold had built up all over it.'

'So what was on the document?' persisted Joey.

'At first your great-grandfather thought it was nothing, so he folded it and put it in his pocket. Later that evening he examined the half-ripped document, which was made out of stone paper, but it was in terrible condition and he couldn't even read one word. However, he did recognize the signature at the bottom. It was that of Leonardo da Vinci.'

Joey whistled slowly and sat back, taking in this news. Edna nodded. She was a genuine storyteller and the passion in her voice was undeniable.

'Once he knew the paper had been handwritten by da Vinci himself, Peruggia guessed he had written it in his favorite left-handed mirror-writing: a style that was read from right to left. It was something Leonardo did to prevent his ideas from being leaked.'

'Did Vincenzo decipher it?' asked Boyce eagerly.

'Yes,' she said. 'He did. He could read it with a hand-held mirror.'

'What was written on it?' asked Joey.

'Written in black ink was a short paragraph that spoke of a long-lost treasure and how it could be found,' said Edna.

Joey and Boyce froze.

'Like a treasure map?' said Boyce.

Joey's mind suddenly churned with visions of a lost city of gold.

'Not just any treasure map,' said Edna, sitting up a little straighter. 'The greatest treasure of all mankind.'

'Come on, Mrs. Martino,' laughed Joey incredulously,

'that's a big claim. Whose treasure is it? And how come no one has found it yet?'

'Da Vinci's document alleged that the location was secretly concealed in his most loved painting.'

'The *Mona Lisa*?' said Boyce, gazing upon the renaissance painting to his side.

'That's correct,' said Edna with a twinkle in her eye. 'I memorized the contents of that document long ago. Would you like to hear the translation?'

Joey and Boyce nodded, aware they were about to hear a secret that only a handful of people had even known existed.

'*Look underneath the Mona Lisa's hands to be guided on your quest, but only once placed under a red light. The man known as the great one will be revealed, and the location of his tomb and all his prized possessions. But be prepared for what you might find, as many have killed to keep this a secret.*'

'Under a red light,' repeated Joey out loud. 'Da Vinci must have created an ink that was visible only under some kind of infrared light.'

'Leonardo was a man ahead of his time,' said Edna. 'The American military invented infrared light in nineteen sixty-four, but it seems that Leonardo was already toying with the idea four hundred and forty-five years earlier.'

'So that explains why your great-grandfather stole the *Mona Lisa*,' said Boyce, facing Joey. 'He was trying to keep the secret safe.'

'So, he wasn't a thief after all,' said Joey. 'Or only in the literal sense.'

'I'm afraid your young friend is right,' said Edna.

'After Vincenzo read the letter he felt he had to protect Leonardo da Vinci's secret.'

Joey frowned. 'But why did he feel he needed to do that?'

'No one really knows. Your great-grandfather was an uneducated man. He was a hard worker, but he was on the bottom of the food chain. Maybe this made him feel important? Maybe it became his obsession.'

'So let me recap. After discovering this long-lost secret, my great-grandfather organized Raphael Chaudron to duplicate the painting so as to be able to keep the secret hidden in the real one. I wonder if he ever went to find the treasure? Hang on, whose treasure is it? You still haven't told us.'

'It's the treasure of all treasures,' said Edna, smiling. 'The tomb of all tombs. The resting place of the greatest general who ever lived: Alexander the Great.'

Joey and Boyce gawked at her, trying to process what she had just said.

Edna continued, 'Alexander the Great wanted an Egyptian-style burial in a tomb mounted with gold, and he requested that the most secret doctrine from the Library of Alexandria be buried with him. Over the years and even after his death, his cult of followers collected scriptures that dated back to the fourth century and to the days of Christ and the beginning of Christianity, and they placed them in his tomb. Some believe Jesus himself had even written his own bible, which had been rejected by the church, and that this was also placed within Alexander the Great's hidden tomb. Can you imagine what the Vatican would do if such documents came to light? What if they portrayed

Jesus in a bad light, or showed him to be something different from what they claim he was? Now do you understand why your great-grandfather's actions were so important? Now do you understand why my poor husband was part of a plan to maintain the Chaudron *Mona Lisa* in the Louvre until the real one was returned, and why he was murdered? That's why I took a vow to never speak of it again.'

'Until now,' said Joey.

'Until now,' repeated Edna in a whisper.

'And how did you find out about all this?'

'The da Vinci document Vincenzo had in his possession was recovered at his home by Pierre's father when Vincenzo was arrested. It was hidden behind a picture frame. But the information it contained was useless without the real painting. Although Pierre's father did everything he could, he was unable to track down the genuine *Mona Lisa*, though he always suspected that Peruggia's family was harboring it.

'When Pierre's father handed the curatorship of the Louvre to his son, he entrusted him with the secret, and with da Vinci's document. Pierre kept it in a notebook in his personal safe. He knew he needed to restore the fake *Mona Lisa* to the highest of standards, to protect both the secret and his father's reputation. He hired his trusted and good friend Bernard to do it, and that's how I found out about everything.'

Joey let out a long breath. He could hardly believe it. 'So how do you think Leonardo da Vinci knew about Alexander the Great's tomb?' he asked, his index finger hovering over the painting where the clue was said to be hidden.

'I believe the location was passed down through Alexander's cult to many important pagan leaders of the time who were stonemasons. After a period of time the secret finally penetrated the secret society, the Priory of Sion. Leonardo da Vinci was known to have been the head of the group, which had long harbored exceptional knowledge. Sir Isaac Newton was also a member of the society. After discovering the location of Alexander the Great's tomb, Leonardo began working on his most famous painting: the *Mona Lisa*.'

'Wow, what a story,' said Boyce, his eyes glowing with admiration. 'I love *La Joconde* even more now. But who is she, exactly?'

'Many believe Leonardo painted himself in female form, arguing that she seems too masculine. And others believe she was the French wife of Francesco del Giocondo. But now that I know the truth about what resides in the *Mona Lisa*, I have a theory of my own about who this person is,' Edna said.

'And who's that?' asked Boyce, leaning forward eagerly.

'I believe Leonardo painted Alexander the Great, but in female form to conceal his identity,' said Edna, looking intently at Joey. 'It was his homage to the general, who many believe was a god. If you cast your eyes over to either side of the figure in the painting, there are two cut-out columns, clear signs of a man who lived as a king in his kingdom. The *Lisa's* hint of a smile is da Vinci's way of teasing the masses.'

'Teasing?' repeated Joey.

'Yes. Leonardo knew the greatest general that had ever lived would never be identified in his painting.'

'Changing the subject,' said Boyce. 'Wasn't Leonardo da Vinci also a gay man?'

Edna grinned. 'Yes, he was, and that's why this project was so special to Leonardo, as Alexander too was known to sleep with both men and women. To understand the importance of Alexander the Great you need to understand what he built and what he achieved for his people at an extremely young age. His loyal army followed him to the edge of the earth, as it must have seemed then – all the way to Asia Minor. At thirty-three years of age, he had created the largest empire in history, and he took care of all his people, even the people he conquered. Instead of destroying their cities, he rebuilt them. His cult loved him for it and constructed in secret a burial chamber in his honor for when his reign ended.'

'I can't believe after all this time they still haven't found it,' said Joey.

'That's because, boys, they are searching for it in the wrong place,' said Edna. Joey and Boyce's heads snapped up at this unexpected response. 'They think it's in Egypt. I don't believe it's there. Maybe it's somewhere close, but not Egypt. I think the background of the *Mona Lisa* is part of the map.'

Joey held up the oil painting and studied it. Boyce also leaned in to take a closer look.

Edna said, 'The weird windy road, the mountains, the bridge which clearly has numbers on it and of course the waterfall have to be part of the location, I believe. Think about it: if this is a tribute to Alexander the Great, there's a very good chance the landscape is also part of the clue.'

Joey took a deep breath. He felt like he was in a history

class, though it was like none he had ever experienced. Perhaps because it involved his own family tree, it was the first history lesson he felt truly fascinated by.

'I know this is a lot to take in,' said Edna. 'But the painting you hold in your hands conceals a clue that people would kill for, especially the Christian churches. The location to the tomb has been hidden for hundreds of years, and, I am sorry to say, it needs to be kept that way.'

'What are you saying?' asked Joey.

'Ask yourself what good would come from finding Alexander's tomb. What I'm saying is that you need to destroy the painting. Throw it in the fireplace right now.'

'Sorry, I can't do that,' said Joey. He laid the painting down on the couch away from Edna's line of sight. 'We've come too far to just destroy it now. And it's the only bargaining chip we have to get your daughter back.'

'In that case, you leave me no choice.' Edna's voice had turned hard and cold. With a speed that belied her age, she pulled out from underneath the couch cushion a gun and aimed it at Joey.

Neither Joey nor Boyce had seen that one coming. Both jerked back on the couch and raised their arms in the air in surrender. It seemed there was more to Joey's future mother-in-law than met the eye.

Chapter 33

'What are you doing?' shouted Boyce in a high-pitched voice.

Joey sat as still as he could, working through his options in his mind as he waited for Edna to respond.

'People stare at the *Mona Lisa* and all they see is its beauty,' said Edna. 'All I see is death. Now stand up and move away from the painting.'

Joey did as she asked and Boyce followed.

'Don't do anything stupid, Edna,' said Joey quietly. 'Remember, we're not the bad guys. I don't care about the tomb or the treasure. I just want to get Marie back, and the painting is the key. She is worth the risk of the secret coming out.'

'You wouldn't even have known about the secret if I hadn't told you,' said Edna bitterly. 'I should never have done it.' The hand holding the gun began to shake.

'So why did you tell us, then?' asked Joey. 'I'll tell you why. You wanted us to know.'

'I thought if I told you, it would convince you to destroy the painting.'

'Come on,' said Joey. 'Put the gun down, you don't have to do this. We're certainly not planning to tell this secret to anyone.'

Edna stared into Joey's blue eyes and said, 'You say you're not the bad guys, and perhaps you won't reveal the secret to anyone, but what if you decided to go and find the tomb, and inside you happened to find documents that suggest my faith is entirely made up? What would you do then?'

'I guess the truth will be revealed in the end,' said Joey. 'People have the right to know the truth either way.'

'No, Joey! That's the incorrect answer. I can't let you destroy what I believe in and what half the world believes in,' Edna said with conviction. 'So that makes you a bad guy.'

'Hang on, Mrs. Martino,' said Boyce. 'Let me get this straight. You want to destroy Leonardo da Vinci's most beloved work to protect what you don't know: what we might or might not find inside a tomb that we don't even know is real. Come on, that's absurd!'

Edna shook her head firmly. 'Too much is at stake,' she answered, and she brought her other hand up to the gun to quell the shaking. 'Now stay there.'

Edna moved in to pick up the *Mona Lisa*.

But Boyce quickly blocked her path, positioning his teenage frame between the old woman and the painting. With a snarl, Edna aimed the gun squarely at his chest. Boyce swallowed hard.

'Now's not the time to be brave,' said Joey quickly, though he admired the boy's courage.

'You wouldn't shoot a kid, would you?' said Boyce.

'You are a brave boy,' she said. 'But also a really stupid boy. Now move!'

'No!' retorted Boyce. 'Somehow I found myself on this journey with JP and now I want to see it through.

Maybe we'll even find this treasure,' he added defiantly.

'Move any closer and I will kill you,' Edna warned.

'Don't be stupid, Boy,' said Joey. 'Let her take it.'

Ignoring Joey, Boyce took a step forward.

'I'll shoot you,' Edna repeated.

Joey could see her aging hand trembling again; she didn't want to squeeze the trigger, but he thought she probably would if he tried to intervene.

Incredibly, Boyce reached for the gun.

It was too late.

Click … She squeezed the trigger.

But nothing happened.

Boyce reacted instantly, snatching the weapon out of her hands and pushing the old lady back on the couch.

'You are one crazy motherfucker,' said Joey, laughing weakly with relief at his fearless friend. 'You're lucky you're not dead.'

Breathing heavily, Boyce said, 'I noticed the de-cocker lever safety switch was still left on and took the gamble.'

'You're lucky you guessed right. How did you know about the safety?'

'I come from the streets, remember? I've seen a few guns before – that may be the one advantage of having criminals for parents.'

'Ah yes, that's right,' said Joey, carefully taking the gun out of the youngster's hands.

Edna sat hunched on the couch, once more the vulnerable old woman she really was. 'Promise me, Joey,' she whispered. 'I beg of you, promise me you'll destroy the painting. The information it contains needs to be kept a secret.'

'Sorry, I don't think I can do that,' replied Joey slowly.

'You can't let it fall into Pierre's hands,' said Edna. 'He's not a Christian man. If there is anything in the tomb that would do damage to Christianity, he would shout it from the rooftops, and there would be cataclysmic consequences. For the sake of peace in our world, it can't be allowed to happen.'

'I can't promise you anything,' said Joey. 'But what I will promise you is your daughter's safety. That's all I care about.'

'I can see that you love her, for that I'm grateful, and I'll pray for her safe return, but I need to know – will you go looking for Alexander's tomb?'

Joey didn't answer. He picked up the *Mona Lisa* and placed it back inside the pillowcase and heaved it over his shoulder.

'Of course we're going to find it,' Boyce said before Joey could open his mouth. 'Imagine the gold we could discover.'

Edna shook her head, her expression one of despair.

Joey sighed at Boyce's comment and replied to her calmly as they walked toward the door, 'Remember, Edna, like I said before; we are not the bad guys. You can trust us.'

Chapter 34

Joey and Boyce left the house; the daylight had disappeared and the sudden cold air hit their faces.

'You drive, Boy,' said Joey.

'But I don't have a license.'

'Have you driven before?'

'Sure, of course, many times.'

'Well then, I don't see the problem. This is a stolen car, remember? Having a license will be the least of our problems if we get caught. Don't worry, we'll be okay.'

They climbed into their stolen Renault and Boyce used the screwdriver to start her up. With ease the old car came to life. He turned on the headlights and with a jerk Boyce accelerated forward, leaving a billowing cloud of dust in their wake. They disappeared down the same overgrown path they had come in on, Boyce following the tire marks that had been pressed into the long grass.

'That was intense,' said Boyce as the neared the main road. 'Where to now?'

'It sure was, my friend,' said Joey. 'But don't ever do anything stupid like that again, you could have been killed.'

'Sorry … I just couldn't let her destroy *La Joconde* in front of our eyes. I had to do something.'

Joey looked over at the kid, who was concentrating on the road. He had put his life on the line to save the painting. Joey wondered if he too could have done such a brave thing.

Joey gave Boyce directions, and they hit the main freeway and drove in silence for a while.

'We need to find a gun shop,' said Joey out of the blue.

'A gun shop … Why?' asked Boyce. 'Are you going to buy a weapon? I always wanted a gun.'

'No, but we can get our infrared goggles from there.'

'Good idea,' said Boyce. 'We can use them to read the secret message.'

'That's right. We have to drive back toward Paris to find one, though. They'll only be in the major centers.'

They were driving once again through flat green sugar cane farm territory. Joey was watching the straight road in front of him, keeping half an eye on Boyce's driving, when he saw a dark Chevrolet pickup truck approach and pass them at high speed. At first he thought nothing of it – it was just another vehicle on the road. But once it had passed them, some instinct told Joey to turn and look back at it, and to his amazement he saw it do a massive –180-degree U-turn. The tires screeched as the pickup regained its grip on the road and was catapulted back in their direction.

'Oh shit! It's Frederic and Lamond,' said Joey, recognizing the two figures in the front seat as they careered toward them. They had found them. With its 420-horsepower engine the pickup caught up with the inferior Renault with ease. 'Go as fast as you can,

Boyce, and try to stay calm,' said Joey, turning in his seat to keep an eye on their pursuers.

Boyce flashed his eyes at his rear-vision mirror every couple of seconds.

Joey identified the shaved head and scar on Lamond's lip. 'Lamond looks pissed.'

'Why?' asked Boyce, and Joey noticed the boy's hands were shaking as they gripped the wheel.

'I killed his brother. We need to lose them somehow.'

White-knuckled, Boyce tightened his grip on the steering wheel. 'He's going to ram us,' he said, his voice wavering.

The sound from the beast behind them had increased. The headlights blinded them. A blur of black flooded the rear-view mirror, then the truck hit them with a loud *Voooooom*!

The impact forced Joey and Boyce forward in their seats as the front end of the Chevy nudged the Renault, as though they were in a Daytona race. The car wobbled uncontrollably, hitting the dirt patch on the side of the road. Somehow Boyce regained traction and careened back onto the highway.

'Don't let him hit you,' said Joey, bracing himself against the dashboard with one hand and clasping the grip handle above the window with the other.

'Easier said than done,' said Boyce, who began ducking and weaving to try to avoid the monster behind them.

Joey turned again in his seat to see Lamond grinning. He was clearly enjoying this way too much. It was obvious he wanted revenge, and if they continued on this route, they would eventually succumb to the superior size, speed and weight of the pickup.

'What's he doing?' asked Boyce.

From the passenger seat of the pickup, Frederic climbed out of his window and entered into the Chevy's cargo box at the back of the vehicle.

Joey relayed this to Boyce. 'Oh shit, this doesn't look good.'

When he reappeared, Frederic was holding a Heckler & Koch M27 IAR machine gun in his hands.

'He has a machine gun,' said Joey flatly.

'We're fucked! Ah, we're fucked!' gibbered Boyce, who sounded on the verge of tears.

As he spoke, a tongue of machine-gun fire was let loose. Bullet sparks exploded all around the small vehicle.

Bratatatat!

The back window shattered, showering the inside of the car with glass. Joey and Boyce ducked for cover in their seats and protected their faces as best they could.

'Keep cool, Boyce. I'm thinking. Just concentrate on driving.'

Boyce struggled to keep the car on the road as it veered to one side. 'They shot out one of our tires,' he reported. The car began to wobble and slide, losing speed as the rims scraped against the road. 'We just lost another,' shouted Boyce. 'Oh my God, we're going to die, this is it.'

'Hang on,' said Joey, 'change of plan.' He reached over and grabbed the wheel with his right hand and yanked it hard to his right. The Renault skidded off the express road and into a field of sugar cane. 'Hit the gas!' Joey yelled. Boyce put his foot flat to the floor.

Whump ... Whump ... Whump ... The sound of the

cane leaves pounded like thunder on the hood as they plowed through the greenery.

'I can't see where I'm going,' said Boyce anxiously.

'I'd rather take my chances through here than on the road with those guys,' said Joey, turning again in his seat to see glimpses of the headlights from the Chevrolet fast approaching.

Lamond was coming in at high speed.

Then, all of a sudden, just like that, the sound of the sugar canes hitting the car ceased and they emerged into an open field. Visibility was low, but when they reached the end they saw they faced a treacherous hill in front of them. It was a death trap: very steep, and it led all the way down to the freezing lake below.

'Turn left!' shouted Joey, his heart pounding as if it were going to burst right out of his chest.

'Shit!' screamed Boyce, hooking the steering wheel. The battered Renault skidded and in spite of his seatbelt Joey's body jerked forward toward the dashboard, his forehead colliding with the windscreen. The back tires felt the lip of the hill as the car skimmed along the edge.

In the nick of time, they had avoided the cliff. Joey glanced out his window to see no solid ground, only the lake that sat below. 'Get us out of here, Boy,' he said.

They seemed now to be on an old dirt track that skirted the edge of the extremely steep muddy hill that dropped away from them to their right. It was their only option, so Boyce continued along it as the damaged vehicle bounced in and out of potholes.

'What do we do now?' said Boyce, sweating with the effort it took to steer the car with two flat tires on an uneven, muddy road in the darkness.

Joey scanned the track behind them in the hope that Lamond would not be as lucky as they'd been. But Lamond was no amateur. Joey's heart sank as he spotted the truck in the distance and saw that it was picking up speed at a great rate.

And that was Lamond's downfall.

Even with the Chevy's larger tires, he managed to anchor himself deep in the mud. The more he pushed it, the more the car wasn't going anywhere.

Joey laughed with relief, realizing what had happened. The fact that the Renault had two flat tires was a godsend in disguise. It allowed Boyce to traverse the mud more successfully than he ever could have with tires filled with air.

'They're stuck,' reported Joey, patting Boyce affectionately on the back of his head. 'Just keep going. There's got to be a way out of here somewhere.'

Boyce pushed the Renault on along the narrow path.

'Hang on,' said Joey. 'We're not out of this yet. Frederic's on foot.'

'Don't worry, he won't be able to catch us …' replied Boyce, then stopped.

A red-and-black sign appeared up ahead, to the left of the hill.

It read: *DANGER ne pas entrer.*

'You were saying?' said Joey mildly. In front of them was nothing but the end of the muddy track. The land dropped steeply away all around them. There was nowhere to go. The lake below was ink-black in the dark. Joey could see the lights of a small town across it. 'Okay. Plan B.'

'What's Plan B?' asked Boyce quickly.

'I have no idea,' said Joey. He sat still for a moment, thinking. 'Okay,' he said finally. 'We need to get down this hill and try to get across into that town.' When Boyce tried to interject, Joey continued, 'We have no choice, if we stay here we die.' Joey knew he had to act fast. Frederic was armed and heading their way. They had to take the risk.

'Are you out of your mind?!' said Boyce fearfully, tapping his thumb on the steering wheel and clearly trying to stop himself from hyperventilating.

A bullet ricocheted off the car's metal frame, then another hit the side window. 'We have to go, Boy,' said Joey. 'We need to try to drive down this hill right now!'

'Sorry, I can't,' said Boyce. 'That's suicide, it's too steep!'

'We have no choice,' said Joey, checking over his shoulder again. Frederic had made up a lot of ground. 'There's no other way,' begged Joey. 'He will kill us both if we don't.'

The bullets rained down on them more vigorously this time. Frederic was close. Joey and Boyce ducked instinctively in their seats.

'Do it now!' shouted Joey. 'Now!'

Chapter 35

The Renault looked like it had been on an Afghan battlefield. Bullet holes riddled the white frame and most of the windows and tires had been shot to smithereens. Joey grabbed the *Mona Lisa* in its pillowcase and sheltered it as carefully as he could with his arm, then he and Boyce held on tight, preparing themselves as best they could.

'Hold on,' said Joey grimly, 'it's gonna be a bumpy ride.'

The car moved slowly forward and then tilted at a precipitous angle. The sky was gone in a flash and they saw nothing but black.

'Ahh ... SHIT!' yelled Boyce.

Joey gritted his teeth as he felt his stomach sink.

The car dropped on a sharp thirty-degree angle, and then picked up speed alarmingly as it descended the hill. Boyce grappled with the steering wheel, but it was no use. He slammed his foot down on the brakes, but the wheels just locked and lost all traction. The car continued to gain speed. The front tires bounced along the steep terrain while the back tires scraped along and dug into the hill, ripping up everything in their wake, aquaplaning wildly out of control.

The one undamaged side window now shattered

as they plowed through the uneven terrain. The hood sprang open and the front tires snapped from the impact. Then the terrain became rocky as they neared the lake's edge. The car's passage formed a mini-rockslide, which seemed to carry the vehicle along with it.

'We're not stopping, JP!'

'Brace yourself,' said Joey, shaking in his seat.

'We're heading for the lake,' Boyce shouted, his voice trembling. 'The painting is going to get wet!'

At that moment they free-fell off a ledge, and the three-second drop felt like an hour as they nosed into the rocky terrain below. Miraculously, the car remained the right side up, but now they had another problem to face at considerable speed: the lake.

'Shit, we're going in.' Joey grabbed the painting, thankfully still in its pillowcase, and lifted it up high. It touched the inside roof of the car. He felt this was the only way he could protect it, short of throwing it out the window, which was sure to shred it. He prepared for the cold impact that was now only moments away.

Frederic reached the point at which the Renault had nosedived off the hill. The probability of the American surviving that fall was slim, but he didn't care about that. The idiot had condemned the painting to destruction. 'Fucking Generation Y,' he muttered to himself as he waited to see what would transpire.

Chapter 36

The Renault, damaged beyond repair, was headed straight for the water. But its speed was drastically reduced as it bounced off the rocky obstacles in its path, so that it ended up entering the lake almost gracefully, as if it were in a James Bond movie.

The fog surrounded them as the car drifted forward at a steady pace, as if it were a small boat traversing its waterways. Joey and Boyce both broke out into relieved laughter.

'Holy shit! I can't believe we made it,' said Joey jubilantly. 'What a ride.'

'Oh my God, the car is floating,' said Boyce, straining to see through the shattered windscreen. 'I can see the other side. Do you think the momentum will take us across?'

Water had started to trickle into the vehicle from below. Powerful mini-jets of spray shot in through the network of bullet holes and cracks.

'It's not going to stay afloat for long,' said Joey.

'If only it were winter – this lake would be completely frozen over and we could have just walked,' said Boyce.

'And frozen to death while we were at it,' said Joey, although the water now gushing all over Joey and Boyce's jeans and creating a deep puddle at their feet was almost unbearably cold. Ice might have been preferable, Joey thought. He continued to hold the painting up high, away from the incoming water that was entering from everywhere. He saw that they had glided about halfway across the small lake, but were now facing another challenge as the car slowly began its dive into the abyss.

Frederic set off down the steep hill. His sidestepping and concentration showed him to be a man who had dealt with this type of terrain before, and even worse situations. He kept a close eye on the Renault as he went, and was surprised to see two moving figures in the wreckage. So Joey and the kid who was with him had survived, he thought, but they now had to deal with a sinking car.

Frederic reached the slippery rocks at the lake's edge and set off purposefully toward the car. The return of the *Mona Lisa*, undamaged, was Frederic's top priority now. If it meant having to help the two men, then he would. Until he got the painting back. Afterwards was a different story.

'It's filling up quick,' said Boyce, now waist high in cold water. 'We need to get onto the roof.'

'Yes, quickly,' said Joey, gasping with the cold. 'I'll pass you the painting when you're up there.'

Boyce climbed out first through his driver's-side window and stood on the roof, which sank closer to the lake's surface with each passing moment. Joey snaked the painting out of his window and passed it upward, avoiding the lake's crystal-clear water. When the teenager had it safely in his hands, Joey followed him onto the roof, and that's when he spotted Frederic in the distance. If anything happened to the painting, he knew Frederic would make him pay. And Marie, too.

Then, all of a sudden the vehicle jolted against something in the lake. Boyce lost his balance and flung the painting at Joey before he fell overboard, back first into the water. When he surfaced, blue-lipped and shivering, Joey felt panic bloom in his chest. The water was dangerously cold, and he knew that sooner rather than later they would both be swimming in it.

Chapter 37

At the edge of the lake, watching with worried eyes, Frederic spotted several large broken timber pylons. He knew the object that had hit the car was part of an old bridge that used to run right across the lake. Strong winds had caused landslides that had crushed the bridge, and it had never been rebuilt. Looking around, he saw a half-broken hexagon-shaped wooden strut that had once been part of the bridge. He rolled it to the waterline and pushed it into the lake, where it floated, as Frederic had hoped.

'I'm coming to help you,' shouted Frederic in English, entering the water with the giant piece of wood.

'Shit,' said Joey to Boyce, who had climbed back onto the roof and stood shivering, rubbing his hands together to try to get warm. 'Frederic's coming.'

'I'm a good swimmer, Joey. Give me the painting. I can hold it above the water with one hand as I swim to the other side.'

'I'm also a good swimmer. But it's too risky.'

'We're running out of options.'

The roof of the car was inches away from being completely submerged. They both stood, feet apart, and surfed the car as it plunged downward.

'Okay, Frederic, stop!' shouted Joey. 'Stay there.'

'I am trying to help you,' Frederic shouted back, continuing to come toward them.

'No! You're trying to save the painting,' said Joey. 'You don't give a damn about us.'

'Don't be stupid, Joey.'

'Just push over that piece of wood.'

'Joey!' shouted Frederic in dismay.

'I don't care if the painting is destroyed,' said Joey. 'Don't tempt me, just push that strut in our direction, we're running out of time.'

'Make sure you keep the painting above the water,' said Frederic, who pushed the wooden piece as hard as he could over to the sinking vehicle.

'Okay, here's the plan,' said Joey, facing the teen. 'When that log reaches us, I'll grab it with my left arm and keep the painting above my head with my right. Your job is to swim and push us to safety. Can you do that?'

Boyce nodded his head and they both turned to face the wooden strut that was making its way over, just as the Renault submerged completely and the cold water lapped at their ankles. Boyce took off his shoes and dove in to retrieve the strut, which he then positioned carefully for his American friend to grab hold of.

Joey also took off his heavy shoes and seized the log in front of him. Before he attempted to abandon the car, he turned to look at Frederic one last time. The Frenchman had already swum back to shore and picked up a walkie-talkie. He faced the hill he had just descended. When Joey followed the direction of

Frederic's gaze he saw, to his horror, a glistening object up on the hill.

He knew then and there it was Lamond. The other Frenchman had set up a rifle on a tripod and could easily take them out.

Chapter 38

Joey entered the icy water slowly, like an old lady about to enter a swimming pool. He tucked the large wooden strut under his left arm, while he held himself as high as he could above the water, the pillowcase in his other hand. His aim was simple: to keep the painting preserved and dry, despite what he'd said to Frederic.

Boyce positioned himself on the opposite side of the piece of wood, facing Joey. He dragged the strut as if he were a lifeguard rescuing a damsel in distress.

Two minutes into the swim Boyce started gasping for breath. Joey knew their body temperature would be dropping rapidly. The young boy's body would be protecting its core by cutting the blood flow to his muscles.

'My legs hurt,' Boyce said.

'Mine do too, Boy. I'm so sorry I pulled you into this shit,' said Joey, his breath visible in the cold air as he helped kick toward dry land. 'We need to get across this lake before hypothermia sets in. Keep pushing, we're not far now.'

Joey quietly thanked his lucky stars that the lake was still tonight. There was no swell or wind, just the chilly water that would freeze to solid ice in a month or two. Glancing at the lights of the town on the lakeshore, he saw that they were close, one hundred and sixty feet or so away from dry land.

'Hey ... so do you have a girlfriend?' asked Joey out of the blue, fighting the urge to let his right arm drop down into the water.

'What kind of question is that?' Boyce replied, his teeth chattering in the cold. 'My legs hurt.'

'Humor me,' said Joey, hoping to distract the teenager from the pain. He knew this was a mental game as much as a physical one.

'No, I don't.'

'Have you ever had a girlfriend?'

'No!'

'So you're still a virgin?'

'If you're trying to make me feel better, stop, because you're not,' said Boyce. 'I'm only fifteen.'

'What's that supposed to mean? I had slept with plenty of girls at your age,' joked Joey.

'Shut up!'

'Don't stop kicking, man,' said Joey. 'You don't want to die a virgin, do you?'

Boyce grouched, 'All I can say, JP, is you'd better make it up to me when you buy me my new boat.'

'If we get out of this,' said Joey, 'I promise, I'll look after you.'

'What do you mean *if* we get out of this?'

Joey sighed, checked over his shoulder and said, 'What are we going to do when we reach the edge?'

'We run free,' said Boyce, slightly confused. 'What do you mean?'

'Those men we're running away from are soldiers,' said Joey.

'So?'

'When we get out of the water and the painting is on dry land, they'll take us out. Lamond is up on the hill and he's armed. He's not going to hesitate to pull the trigger, because I killed his brother.'

'Fantastic!' said Boyce sarcastically, trying to stretch out his blue fingers. 'If we don't get out of this water we'll die. And if we get out, we'll also die.' Suddenly the strut wobbled as their feet found solid ground.

'Relax, Boy. One thing at a time. Let's get out of the water first.'

'How can I —'

'I have a plan.'

'What plan, what is it?'

'Simple ... we use the *Mona Lisa* as a shield. We need to stick together. If we separate, we die. Make sure we stand united as one and walk backwards into the village.'

Chapter 39

Lamond readjusted his telescope and dug his feet into the mud. This was the moment he had been waiting for. 'I have a shot,' he said through his earpiece.

'Not until the *Mona Lisa* is safe on dry land,' said Frederic. 'Wound them in the leg first before you take the final kill shot. Remember, Lamond, our mission is to save the painting first.'

'Roger that,' the big Frenchman said, readying himself to reap his revenge and end this.

At the edge of the lake, Lamond saw Boyce and Joey trembling from the cold as they staggered through the shallows, standing close together, the pillowcase-covered painting held protectively between them. He tightened his finger on the trigger, ready to squeeze when the men were clear of the lake. But then his mouth dropped open when he saw Joey remove the *Mona Lisa* from the pillowcase and, quick as a flash, hold it up in front of them. It covered their faces as they backed away from the water in unison.

'What is this?' said Lamond, his tone agitated. 'They're using the painting as a shield.'

'Smart boy,' said Frederic in Lamond's earpiece. 'He must have seen you. He knows you're there.'

'Do I aim low? Do I still shoot them in the leg?'

'No! It's too risky. If you hit the painting, it's all over. Let them go.'

'Fuck … Fuck … Fuck …' screamed Lamond. He wanted that shot. He needed that shot. His finger continued to hover over the trigger. 'I can —'

'Back away, soldier, that's an order,' said Frederic. 'I know you want revenge, but now is not the time. Let them go.'

'I have a message for you, Joey,' shouted Frederic from across the lake. 'You have until midnight tonight to return the painting or your girlfriend dies. Do you hear me?'

Joey and Boyce continued to walk backwards until they could duck behind some trees and away from danger. Now safe, Joey shouted back, 'I know about the secret in the painting. I know about the secret tomb the *Mona Lisa* is hiding. You're not going to kill anyone, Frederic, or I will destroy this painting and no one will ever be able to find it. You go back and tell Pierre that.'

Frederic turned away to gather his thoughts, pacing up and down for a moment before returning to see that Joey and Boyce had disappeared from sight.

'The secret tomb the *Mona Lisa* is hiding,' he repeated to himself. 'What the hell is he talking about?'

Chapter 40

The soft rain that had been falling when Pierre Savard left Paris had turned into a heavy downpour by the time his black AS350 Eurocopter landed in the church's empty parking lot late that evening, blowing away loose sand around its skids. Pierre looked through the windscreen at the church-house he had visited on many occasions. The pilot was first out of the helicopter with umbrella in hand, holding it low enough to avoid hitting the slow-turning blades above.

Pierre stepped outside into the cold rain. His expensive Italian leather shoes touched the wet pavement of rocks. He stood there for a moment in his long three-quarter suit jacket and took in the impressive site of the church in front of him.

He gave the hint of a smile when he saw fresh imprinted tire marks to his right. *Someone had been here*, he thought. He then approached the porch to see muddy footprints: two sets with slightly different shoe sizes.

He knocked three times on the wooden door with a black leather-gloved fist. 'Open up,' he said in French in a loud voice.

No one answered.

The rain continued to pound on the arched roof and formed puddles in the driveway. Pierre sniffed the cold fresh air and cracked his neck, tilting it to one side. He then said once more, 'Open the door, Edna, I know you're inside.'

Still no answer.

'Are you still playing hard to get?' he said with a bitter smile. 'After all these years.'

He reached into his back pocket and pulled out an old 1892 French revolver, commonly used throughout World War II. It was one of the many weapons he'd collected over the years and kept on his gun wall.

The pilot who had escorted Pierre to the door moved over to one side. Pierre could tell he was scared. The gun could backfire, being an antique. But one thing the young pilot did not know was that all Pierre's weapons were cleaned and lubricated on a regular basis.

Pierre aimed and shot two eight-millimeter rounds at the lock on the door.

A female voice inside whimpered.

Pierre kicked the door and it swung open. The timber flooring of the old church creaked as he stepped in. He peered around at the remodeled layout for a while, then he spotted a familiar face hiding behind a couch near the fireplace.

'Well, well, well. It sure has been a long time,' he said, holding the pistol loosely in his hands while indicating to the pilot that he should wait outside.

'What do you want, Pierre?' said Edna, her voice filled with hatred and dread. 'You are not welcome in my home.'

'Please sit,' said Pierre with a friendly gesture toward

the couch she crouched behind. He watched her move to take a seat. He scanned her up and down, then said, grinning, 'What ... can't I visit an old girlfriend?'

Edna sighed. 'That was a long time ago.'

'Yes, it was, but it feels like it was only yesterday,' said Pierre. A silence fell on the room before Pierre shook himself and continued, 'Now, the reason why I'm here. It seems you've had visitors. I need to know exactly what you told them.'

'I don't know what you're talking about,' said Edna somberly.

'Don't play games with me, Edna,' retorted Pierre. 'I know you better than that. You never were the best liar.'

Edna's expression hardened and Pierre felt a shot of anger surge through him. He was a man who got what he wanted, and Edna was not being straightforward with him.

Her eyes on the gun in his hand, Edna said, 'They told me you kidnapped my daughter.'

'Yes, it's true,' said Pierre, clearing his throat. 'Her boyfriend has something I want back. I think you know what I'm talking about.'

'Let Marie go, Pierre. I mean it, or I'll ...'

'You'll do what?' he said scathingly. 'You know how important the *Mona Lisa* is. We've spoken of her importance in this room countless times, with and without Bernard.' He readjusted his tie and waited for her response.

'Haven't I suffered enough?' she said quietly. 'You killed my husband, and now you are holding my daughter hostage. She looked up to you like an uncle. Don't do this.'

Pierre cracked his neck again. Then in a loud voice he replied, 'Your husband worked for me, he was my best friend. I trusted him to keep the truth about the *Mona Lisa* a secret. She was his to restore. He had free rein to make that painting the best it could be. Then one day, out of the blue, he decided he wanted to out me. Why? Why did he turn on me? We were supposed to be friends.'

'You're surely not that stupid,' said Edna, her face reddening. 'I can't believe you still don't know.'

'Know what?'

'The day you had Bernard shot was the day I told Bernard about our affair,' said Edna, stopping to take a breath. 'I had never seen him so upset in my entire life, but I never expected him to do what he did. He would never have tried to destroy his life's work for any other reason – he did it to punish you, I'm sure of it.'

'But I asked you, after his death, why he did it,' said Pierre, squeezing one hand into a fist. 'And you told me you didn't know why.'

'Of course I did! You were responsible for his death. I was pregnant and scared for my life, so I pretended I didn't know.'

Pierre moved his hand over his head, thinking fast. 'So you're telling me this whole thing could have been avoided if you'd just kept your mouth shut?'

'I will die knowing my husband was killed because of my stupid actions, so you can say and do what you like.'

'You don't realize what I and my father have gone through these last hundred years, keeping a lie as big as this a secret. And yes, doing what needed to be done to eliminate any possible threat to our jobs, to the

Louvre's reputation. But there's more to it than that, isn't there? Edna, you of all people should understand the importance of what's at stake. I know you're a devoted Catholic and don't want this find to question your faith.'

'The contents of Alexander the Great's tomb are a matter of pure speculation. Nothing could change the way I feel about my god,' she said firmly.

Pierre felt a flare of anger. 'Tell me you didn't tell Joey and his friend about the tomb. Tell me you didn't!'

'Sorry, Pierre, you're too late. I told the boys everything.'

Pierre's face flushed red. 'Why the fuck did you do that?' He stood up and kicked the coffee table in front of him three feet away. Edna jumped.

'Because the truth always comes out in the end,' she said, swallowing hard. 'It always does. I wanted them to know the truth, so they could keep the *Lisa* safe and away from you.'

'Well, it's all out now,' said Pierre bitterly. 'Does it make you feel better, are you happy now?'

'Please, I beg you,' pleaded Edna. 'Let Marie go.'

'If I were you, I wouldn't be worried about what I'm going to do with her right now.'

Pierre moved his pistol, aiming it at Edna's chest.

'I see … After all we've been through, you're going to end my life, too,' she said. 'But before you pull the trigger, there is one more thing you probably should know.'

'And what's that?'

'The next time you are facing my daughter, I want you to look into her eyes.'

'Why?'

'Because they're yours.'

Pierre froze. 'What?'

'This is why Bernard hated you so much,' cried Edna. 'It wasn't just our affair. I was pregnant with your child. Bernard couldn't live with that knowledge. That was why he did what he did.'

Burning rage hissed through Pierre's body as he darted his eyes up at the church ceiling. He felt like a volcano about to erupt. He was wired with too much information and could not deal with it anymore. He lifted his revolver to Edna's head.

Edna closed her eyes. 'Oh, Lord,' she prayed. 'Forgive me for all my sins.'

'Sorry, my love,' said Pierre. 'God's not going to save you this time.'

He pulled the trigger.

Chapter 41

Safe and away from harm for the moment, Joey and Boyce entered the small town that began at the lake's edge and disappeared up into the Jura Mountains. They were bedraggled and drenched to the bone, and made a strange sight as they wandered barefoot up the old cobblestoned street.

The cold that had seemed mild at first now numbed their faces and crept under their wet clothes. Boyce folded his arms across his body and tried to brace himself against the cool wind that had sprung up.

The way Boyce's teeth were chattering, and the fact that he had spent more time in the freezing lake than Joey told Joey that both of them, but the boy especially, were in desperate need of a change of clothes and a hot drink. After a short walk that felt like forever, they made it into the heart of the small town, which was deserted, quiet and dimly lit at this late hour. All the old homes in the distance were lined with carved smoking chimneys.

Then, out of nowhere, a speeding vehicle skidded to a halt feet away from where they stood. It was a yellow Swiss Post van. The driver was middle-aged, bald and had a beer belly. He climbed out, leaving his door open, and hurried into some nearby bushes holding his crotch.

Joey immediately saw the opportunity and yanked Boyce by the arm. 'Let's go,' he whispered, carrying the poplar wood panel in his right hand away from his wet clothes.

They stepped inside the twelve-seater van and the first thing Joey felt was the warmth. The air-conditioning had been left running; it was like being back home in California. 'Quick,' said Joey. 'Down here.'

Boyce ducked down behind the last row of seats and curled himself into a ball. Not long after they had entered, the driver climbed back in and set off again, unaware he had two passengers hiding inside.

Boyce glanced over to Joey, who was keeping time on his watch, which, being waterproof, had thankfully survived the river. After a seventeen-minute drive up a winding road, they reached a town that a sign informed them was called Vallorbe. The driver parked, locked the van with his key and left the two stranded inside.

'The coast is clear,' said Joey, peeping out the window to see the driver disappear into an establishment that seemed to be a pub.

After unlocking the car from the inside, they stepped outside and the cold, crisp air hit them in the face again.

'I need to get out of these clothes,' said Boyce, beginning to tremble uncontrollably once more.

They might have escaped from Frederic and Lamond, but Joey knew that finding shelter was now a matter of life or death. He reached into his wet pants to pull out his wallet. The bills inside it were all stuck together and beginning to disintegrate.

'Hang on,' said Boyce, digging into his own pants with a shaky hand. 'I still have your credit card. I forgot to give it back to you at the hotel.'

'I wonder if it still works,' said Joey, taking it back. 'There has to be an ATM here somewhere.'

Vallorbe was the complete opposite of the town they had just come from. It was a party town with music playing in each venue. All shops big and small were open for business, even at 10 pm, as well as cafés, restaurants and bars.

As they wandered down the busy wet strip, a thundering noise pounded from up high on the hill. Joey glanced up and savored the moment with a grin. It was the first genuine city sound he had heard all day. It was a train arriving at the Vallorbe train station.

His eyes then fell on an ATM further down the street. A sign depicting a green arrow pointing to the left hung on a building. It was a BCV Automatic Teller Machine positioned just outside the Banque Cantonale Vaudoise. The bank seemed designed to have the same look and feel as its surrounding buildings, which were all beige.

'Now, let's pray my card still works,' said Joey, with a bounce in his stride for the first time since getting out of the lake. He entered his credit card into the terminal. After he selected his language of choice and entered his four-digit PIN, he was surprised to see that it was still operational.

'How much are you allowed to take out?' asked Boyce.

'I don't know,' said Joey, entering nine hundred euros into the keypad. A warning message appeared on the screen: *Limit Exceeded. Try again.* With a shaky hand, Joey keyed in eight hundred euros and waited.

'Come on, please,' he begged. He needed this money to purchase new dry clothes, something warm to eat and lastly train tickets back to Paris. After a nervous thirty-second wait, eight hundred euros was delivered through the slot. Joey sighed with relief.

The next hour went by exceedingly fast. Joey and Boyce had a bite to eat and went on a shopping spree. They purchased new clothes and shoes and obtained a waterproof dark-blue carry bag to conceal the *Mona Lisa* from prying eyes.

Now, warm, fed and dressed, they were ready to head home when out of the corner of his eye Joey spotted a bright light. Further down the street, away from the commercial hub of the town, was a bar. Joey paused to think. He was mesmerized by the large neon lights that lit up the place like a Christmas tree. 'Red neon lights,' he murmured out loud.

'What about them?' asked Boyce curiously.

'Maybe we could use the neon lights to read the map.'

'I thought you said it needed to be under infrared lights,' said Boyce.

Joey gave the teen a sidelong glance. 'Well, it's got me thinking ... In da Vinci's letter he said the text must be read under red light. I think he could have meant that literally: under a light that was red. No matter how advanced da Vinci was, he was unlikely to have developed a direct equivalent to infrared four hundred years before anyone else.'

'I guess there's only one way to find out,' said Boyce. 'Let's go, there's no harm in trying.'

The rest of the town silently slipped away as they

walked down the quiet street. The only light now came from the bright neon lights in front of them.

'Why is this place so far away from town?' wondered Boyce, moving out of the way as a group of three males heading in the opposite direction approached, struggling to walk straight while singing completely out of tune.

Reaching the bar, they stood facing the bright neon lights as the music belted around them. Men could be heard cheering inside the club. That's when Joey realized that he'd seen no females down this end of the road. Now, seeing the red bulb hanging in front of the building, to the right of the bar, he understood why. It was a double-storied structure with a red door. The door was in fact a glossy black, but the red globe that hung above it made the door glisten a bright Ferrari red. Joey pressed his lips tight to keep from smiling.

'How are we going to read the map without looking suspicious?' said Boyce, clueless to the goings-on around him.

'I have a plan, Boy,' said Joey with a wide smile. 'Oh do I have a plan.'

'What do you mean?' asked Boyce.

'You'll find out. Come with me.'

Joey waited until nobody was in sight, then approached the red door and used a terracotta pot found resting against the building to step up and unscrew the bulb from its fixture.

'What are you doing?' asked Boyce in a strangled voice.

'Shut up, man,' Joey replied, stepping back down and placing the red bulb inside his sweater.

That's when the front door opened.

A young European beauty wearing black spandex and high heels, her hair piled up on her head, was there to greet them both. '*Hallå*,' she said in a seductive tone. '*Du letar efter en bra tid?*'

'Um … um …' Boyce replied, not able to put two syllables together.

'Yes … *Ja*,' answered Joey, flashing a smile, loving the fact that his virgin friend was as nervous as hell.

'What are we doing here, Joey?'

'Relax. I have a plan. Wait here and I will be right back.'

The gorgeous blonde led Joey up a staircase that was also framed with red neon lights. Joey enjoyed the views in front of his face. The girl was smoking hot, with a killer backside. At the top of the stairs, five similar, blonde-haired girls stood waiting. They all appeared to be Swedish, and they wore hardly any clothing; each one was hotter than the next.

An older woman in her fifties, who appeared to be the proprietor of the establishment, came forth and introduced herself to Joey, and he asked her if she spoke any English.

'I speak a little,' she said with a strong Swiss accent.

'Excellent. I need a room to make an important phone call.'

'Yes, pick a girl,' she said with an open hand at the five standing nearby.

'No girl,' Joey said. 'I just need a room.' He mimed making a phone call in case she hadn't understood.

With a puzzled expression the woman agreed, but indicated that he needed to be quick. Joey nodded and was ushered to a private room that was dimly lit and decorated in earthy shades of red and brown. There was a bathroom off to one side, and an open shower in the corner of the main bedroom, separated by a big sheet of glass. In the center of the room was a king-sized bed surrounded by mirrors, which also included the ceiling, presumably for maximum viewing pleasure.

Joey thanked the girl who had escorted him and shut the door behind her. He went quickly into the bathroom. It wasn't huge, but it wasn't small either. The floor-to-ceiling tiles were all in white and the towel racks were hung with red-and-brown towels to complement the earthy color scheme in the room outside. Joey took out his red light globe and used the steps that led to a bathtub to swap the bulbs in the light fitting above his head.

All of a sudden the white room transformed to a vibrant red. Joey took out the *Mona Lisa* from his carry bag and laid it face-up on the sink basin. Staring at the painting, he waited for something to show. Then, out of nowhere, beautifully written white cursive writing appeared just underneath the *Mona Lisa's* arms. It was just as Mrs. Martino had said it would be. The *Mona Lisa* did have a secret.

A smile took over Joey's face. 'It's real,' he said to himself.

Bending over to examine it more closely, Joey read the words, which were written in Italian, luckily a language Joey had been taught from a very young age. To Joey's surprise, Leonardo da Vinci had not used his common mirror-writing technique this time. Joey had to read the passage several times to be certain he understood it, as the language was in an archaic form he wasn't familiar with.

It read:

The great son of Zeus was buried with treasures not just of wealth, but of information. But be warned of what you might find. Start your journey at the sacred place of Cyprus and continue past the winding road that will lead you to the goddess of love and beauty. The baths will take the quest to an underwater cave. In it you will find the answers you seek.

After committing the passage to memory, Joey turned off the light, leaving the red bulb in place. He put the *Mona Lisa* back in the carry bag and left the room, heading down the hallway. As he went, he spotted a chair outside another of the rooms, over which some clothes had been thrown. A cell phone protruded out from the pocket of a pair of jeans. Joey quickly swiped the phone and left the establishment in a hurry.

Chapter 42

The underground chamber door opened and the light came in with it. Marie listened to the footfalls that descended the stone steps and were heading her way. She immediately put down the broken frame she was using to break the wall around the rusted bars. She stood quietly and waited, her toes at the mercy of the cold floor. To punish her, Frederic had removed her shoes and let her dread the rodents that would be lurking at her feet.

The figure advanced toward Marie, grabbing a battery-operated torch at the bottom of the stairwell. She could see the beam of light coming her way in the small indented alcoves that lined the walls. She had been left here to rot, alone in the darkness with nothing but the smell of the disintegrating oil paintings piled up around her.

As the figure drew nearer, she recognized the aging face of the man whom she'd once called Uncle, and judging by his expression, something was upsetting him. A tremor of fear coursed through her. What was wrong?

'So ... did you get what you're after?' asked Marie in English, both her hands gripping the bars of the cell wall that separated them.

'I did,' said Pierre in an eerie voice. 'I got much more than I bargained for.'

'I'm glad to hear that,' said Marie sarcastically. 'Now can you let me go?'

'No!'

'Why?' Marie asked. 'Can you at least give me back my shoes?'

Pierre moved in close, ignoring her. The light bounced off his face and for a second he looked like Hannibal Lecter. 'Do you know about the map?' he asked softly, reaching through the bars to touch the heart-shaped necklace inside her shirt.

Marie flinched and took a step back. 'What are you talking about? What map?'

'I saw your mother tonight,' said Pierre, shaking his head. 'Can you believe it? It's been decades, and she still managed to floor me. She told me something that I never saw coming.'

'What did she tell you?' asked Marie, wondering where he was going with this.

'She told me the real reason why your father tried to destroy the *Mona Lisa*.'

In spite of herself, Marie glanced up quickly, unable to hide her curiosity. 'Why did he?'

Pierre opened his mouth as though he was laughing, but no sound came out. 'You don't know, do you?' he said with an amused sigh. 'Your mother never told you the truth … I guess she was ashamed.'

'What truth?'

'I'm sorry to be the one to tell you this, Marie, but your mother wasn't faithful to your father. She had fallen for another man, and she told your father about it on the day he died.'

'What!' Marie snapped as a flush of adrenaline tingled through her body. She tried to take in this news, and wondered if she could trust it. Then the puzzle pieces suddenly fell into place. 'It was you, wasn't it?' she breathed. 'That's why my father wanted to destroy the *Mona Lisa*. He restored that painting to protect its secret, but he did it for you. It was a secret he promised his good friend he would never reveal. But then, you weren't a very good friend to him, were you? And so he wanted to punish you, and to make sure the secret remained a secret, you had him killed.'

'I was in love with your mother,' Pierre interrupted sharply. 'We shared everything. I even told her about the map.'

'What map?' Marie shouted, unable now to hold back her rage. 'What are you talking about, and why did my mom bring all this up now?'

'Because I had a gun pointed at her head,' Pierre said smoothly. 'It's amazing what people will say when their life is in jeopardy.'

Marie sighed and closed her eyes, and when she reopened them she asked, 'Did you kill my mother?'

Pierre didn't answer. He stood there with a blank, emotionless face, gazing down at the old stone floor.

His body language told Marie all she needed to know. 'I'm going to kill you!' she exploded. She reached through the bars to grab his suit, but he anticipated her reaction and backed away. 'Why did you have to kill her?' cried Marie, covering her hands with her face. 'You said you loved her!'

'I did love her,' gasped Pierre. 'But I killed her because she's got a big mouth. Your boyfriend now knows more than he should.'

'I don't get it,' said Marie. 'Joey already knows about the *Mona Lisa*.'

'No, my dear, you haven't got the slightest idea what you're dealing with here.'

'Why don't you enlighten me then, shitface. You're going to kill me anyway, aren't you?' said Marie, stepping back into the shadows of the cell.

Pierre flashed his torch in Marie's direction, lighting up the area around her. A rat scuttled away from the light source and hid somewhere in the darkness.

Pierre leaned forward and said, 'You think I'm doing all this because of the *Mona Lisa*? The priceless painting?'

'Why else?' murmured Marie.

Pierre smirked. 'You are wrong, my dear. It's far more important than that, and that's why both your parents were killed. They both knew way too much. Your mother has been reliable up till now, but when you and your boyfriend got involved, I should have known I could no longer trust her. That was my mistake. And now that I know she has blabbed to your boyfriend, he must die, too.'

Marie closed her eyes. The asshole in front of her had killed both her parents and had the balls to tell her that to her face. 'So tell me, what did they know?' she asked steadily, hiding her tears.

'They knew that the original *Mona Lisa*, the one Joey's idiot great-grandfather stole, had a secret map hidden in it showing the location of the greatest treasure mankind has ever seen.'

'You have got to be kidding me,' Marie breathed. 'This is all because of a stupid treasure map? What treasure could be worth killing for?'

'How about the lost tomb of the most famous military general of all time, a man who created one of the largest empires in history?'

'It can't be!' said Marie. 'Are you talking about Alexander the Great's tomb? It has never been found.'

'Yes, I am,' he said with a mirthless grin. 'After Alexander's death in 323 B.C.E. his body became one of the most venerated objects in the classical world. Octavian, who became the emperor Augustus, as well as many other pilgrims, which included some of the most powerful emperors of the ancient world, visited and paid homage at the shrine of the king.'

'Yes, yes, I know all about this, I majored in history,' Marie reminded him testily. 'Alexander's successor, Ptolemy, left his mortal remains for the people to worship as they would a god. But what's this all got to do with the *Mona Lisa*?'

'Do you want to know?'

'Yes.'

'Okay, then shut up and let me explain,' said Pierre. 'You're impatient, just like your mother.' He took a breath before continuing. 'So we know what Alexander the Great did and how important he was. He was worshipped as a pagan god. He morphed from being just a man to a divine being, right into the era of the Roman Empire.'

'Yes … There was a revolution of spiritual beliefs for thousands of years,' said Marie. 'The people of Greece, Egypt and Rome believed in many gods and many cults existed around the known world.'

'You don't understand how refreshing it is to talk to an educated person who knows her history,' said

Pierre with a sly smile. 'It will be a lot easier for you to understand it. It took your father ages. Okay ... You tell me what happened in the fourth century, three hundred years after the time of Jesus.'

Marie thought for a moment. 'That's when the Roman emperor Constantine embraced a relatively new cult: Christianity. He adopted the minority cult and it became the official state religion. Paganism was polytheistic and was banned.'

'Yes ... What's funny about that is that even after being dead for over six hundred years, Alexander was perceived as a threat by the followers of Christ. So a series of decrees banned pagan worship and all structures and temples were closed and destroyed. All polytheistic practices were stopped. And that's when all traces of Alexander's colossal fame and importance simply vanished into thin air.'

'Okay, so we know that at that time paganism was stopped and Christianity was going full steam ahead,' said Marie. 'I still don't understand what you're getting at.'

Pierre smiled. 'That's when Alexander the Great's cult took the initiative and moved their pharaoh's body to a secret burial place among all his treasures. It is said he was laid to rest with many Christian documents from his Library of Alexandria – many documents that were discarded by the church, one of which could have been the gospel of Jesus himself.'

Marie began to see where Pierre was going with this.

'This is where the *Mona Lisa* comes into play,' Pierre continued. 'You see, Marie, the cult of Alexander kept his resting place a secret for centuries, passing it down from stonemason to stonemason, until it reached the secret societies of men in power and knowledge.'

'The Priory of Sion,' she blurted.

'Yes, and into Leonardo da Vinci's hands. Soon after, he went to work on the *Mona Lisa*.'

'Hang on, let me get this straight,' said Marie. 'You're telling me Leonardo da Vinci's painting of *La Joconde* is linked to Alexander the Great?'

Pierre smiled coldly. 'Not as bright as I thought you were, are you? The *Mona Lisa* is not the king's wife Lisa Gherardini, or a self-portrait of da Vinci in female form. It's a portrait of Alexander the Great as a woman. Da Vinci wanted to conceal Alexander's identity, and since rumors circulated that both men had had homosexual encounters, da Vinci disguised Alexander the Great as a woman, as a personal joke and also as a way of keeping his secret. So now do you understand why the *Mona Lisa* that Joey has is so important? It contains the location of the place where Alexander has been left to rest for over two thousand years.'

Marie let out a long breath. 'I have heard a lot of stories in my lifetime, but this one's a first,' she said, thinking hard. 'But finding the tomb can't be about actual treasure for you, you're already rich. And it probably isn't about recognition; you're the Louvre curator, for goodness sake. What the hell are you in it for?'

Pierre's mouth snapped shut and he looked away. When he glanced back, Marie peered into his eyes, and suddenly she knew. 'You're after the religious documents, aren't you?'

Pierre smiled nastily. 'I would do anything to read

such documents if they exist,' he said. 'If the church discarded them, I want to know why.'

'Even if you find them, they might be completely illegible after so long – if they have survived the passage of time in the first place.'

'I'm sure the men entrusted with burying Alexander would have taken exceptional care and preserved the documents in some way,' said Pierre. 'But enough of this. I'm tiring of this conversation.' With a dismissive glance back at Marie, Pierre turned and began to walk away.

'I didn't take you for a religious man,' Marie called after him. She was still reeling from what she'd been told, but talking about it beat being alone and in complete darkness.

Pierre turned back to face her. 'The church is nothing to me,' he hissed. 'I was an altar boy when I was a child. I witnessed terrible abuse of some of the other boys by the clergy, but nobody would listen or believe me when I tried to tell everyone what was happening.'

'Were you abused?' asked Marie, feeling a hint of sympathy for the man.

Pierre didn't respond to her question. His face flushed in the glow of the flashlight, and he turned away again, as if annoyed with himself for making this revelation. 'You asked me if I was a religious man ... No!' he growled. 'How could I follow a religion that allows such terrible things to happen, even to this day? I would do anything to damage that church, and to prove that everything they believe is predicated on a lie.'

'And that's why you want to find Alexander the Great's tomb?' said Marie gently.

Pierre marched back over to Marie and stared searchingly into her eyes, as if he were looking for something. Startled, Marie took a step backwards.

'Your mother told me something else she had kept secret from me,' he snarled.

'What else is there?' said Marie. 'What is it with all these secrets?'

'Your mother was pregnant ... with my —' To Marie's astonishment, a lone tear trickled down Pierre's aging face.

'No ... it can't be,' frowned Marie, her mouth falling open in shock.

'I'm sorry,' said Pierre. 'But it's true. You are my daughter.'

'No!' barked Marie.

'I should have seen it before,' said Pierre. 'You have my eyes, my intelligence, my love of history and art.'

Marie was stunned. 'If this is true, are you going to kill your own daughter?'

A strange expression crossed Pierre's face, as if rage and despair and frustration were at war within him. In a strangled, cold voice he said, 'When I have back what belongs to me, I'm sorry, my dear, you will die.'

Marie spat in his face. 'You're not my father. Get away from me!' she yelled.

Pierre took out a handkerchief and wiped his face clean. Then he turned on his heel and left her to the darkness.

Chapter 43

Thursday, 11:30 pm

Joey exited the establishment with a smile on his face.

'So, tell me,' whispered Boyce excitedly. 'Did you find the secret message? Is the map real?'

'I can't believe I'm saying this,' said Joey. 'But yes … it appears to be true.'

'So … where is it?' asked Boyce as a drop of rain hit his forehead, followed by another as the rain picked up its pace. 'Enough with the water already,' he said, glancing up at the heavens.

'Let's get somewhere dry first. This way,' said Joey, and the pair began jogging up the old cobblestone street as the downpour intensified. After navigating the old town for a few minutes, they found the train station in a heritage building beyond a façade that was adorned with a large clock. Once inside they saw three platforms. With relief Joey realized that the Vallorbe train station sat on the French–Swiss border and had high-speed train services in and out of France. The last train to Paris-Gare de Lyon was leaving at 11:43 pm. Their timing could not have been any better. They purchased the tickets and boarded the train.

Sitting opposite each other in the warm, dry carriage, they both allowed themselves to relax. Their trip would have them arrive in Paris at 3:30 am in the morning. It was time to rest and work out what they were going to do now.

Joey carefully placed the bag containing the painting against the window seat next to him. Like his great-grandfather, he had become the keeper who knew and protected its secret. Resting his legs on the seat in front of him, he leaned back and ran the past couple of days through his head. Since he'd arrived in Paris, he'd been held at gunpoint, he'd jumped off a balcony, fought against some thuggish teens, almost died in combat with a trained soldier, and his girlfriend had been taken hostage. Plus, to top it off, he'd survived what should have been a fatal death drop that had ended in the freezing lake. He needed and deserved a rest, so he shut his eyes.

'JP, are you going to tell me what the painting revealed?' asked Boyce.

'I'm too tired,' Joey pleaded.

'I need to know!'

'Do you realize what I've been through these last couple of days?'

'I thought we were partners,' mumbled Boyce. 'My world was turned upside down when I met you. My boat was destroyed and I've almost died on more than one occasion. I am not a religious person, but I believe you entered my life for a reason. Now that we have discovered this amazing bit of history, you can't deny me the knowledge. I want to share this journey with you now.'

Joey opened his sleepy eyes, leaned forward and looked into the teen's innocent brown eyes. 'Boy, don't be stupid,' he said. 'It's best we part ways when we reach Paris. I've put you in enough danger already. I promise you that I'll have my accountant in the States set you up an account that will cover your boat and all your trouble.'

'No!' said Boyce forcefully.

'It's too dangerous,' warned Joey again. 'These men are going to come after me.'

'That's why you need my help,' insisted Boyce. 'We're a team now. I have no place else to go.'

Joey thought for a second. He felt sorry for the teen, and recognized that they had formed a strong bond. The two of them had endured something out of an Indiana Jones movie and survived. What Boyce was saying was true, though. They had done it as a team, and a good team at that.

'Okay,' said Joey reluctantly. 'But for this to work, you need to do what I say, when I say it.'

'I understand,' said Boyce as a grin spread over his face. 'Now, the tomb's location, please?'

Joey sat upright and took out the cell phone he'd stolen from the brothel.

'Where did you get that?' asked Boyce.

'I stole it,' said Joey, leaning in so no one else in the carriage could hear. He quickly explained to Boyce how he'd switched the light globes in the bathroom at the brothel. 'Under the red light the message appeared in some kind of invisible ink. The writing was in Italian.'

'Could you read it?' asked Boyce.

'All I can say is thank God for Italian school. My

father was extremely strict with me and my brother when it came to church and learning the language. The wording was archaic, but I think I translated it okay.'

'It's like all this was meant to be,' said Boyce. 'What did it say?'

'I memorized it.' Joey recited the passage and translated it for Boyce. 'So you see, it's not very exact. Isn't Cyprus a country?' asked Joey. 'I was never a geography whiz,' he admitted sheepishly.

'It seems you need me more than you think,' joked Boyce, extracting Joey's phone from his hand and bringing up the Google website. 'Okay ... Cyprus is a country. It is smack-bang in the middle of the eastern Mediterranean. Countries such as Egypt, Syria and Turkey surround it. It's had many different rulers over the years, including Alexander the Great. After the division of the Roman Empire into an eastern half and a western half, Cyprus came under the rule of the Byzantine Empire in the fourth century, and in the twelfth century A.D. the island became a target of the crusaders.'

'So we know Cyprus was a country many conquered, including the Knights Templar. I wonder what the hell they were trying to find?' asked Joey.

'Exactly!' said Boyce. 'Cyprus is only a day trip by boat from Egypt; they could easily have moved Alexander's body to a place where no one would have ever thought to look. Perhaps that's why it has never been found. And now ... we know where to look.' Boyce smiled.

'What do you mean? Where?'

Joey tapped the phone. 'It says here that the goddess of love and beauty was the Greek goddess Aphrodite.

In Cyprus, up on a hill in the Akamas region, thirty miles north of Paphos, is the site where she supposedly came to bathe.'

Joey whistled. 'That would explain the stream of water in the painting,' he said.

'That's right.'

The pair sat in silence for a moment, trying to work through the ramifications of what they'd discovered.

'Maybe Pierre will let your girlfriend go when you tell him the location?' Boyce suggested.

Joey didn't like his chances. He wondered how all this was going to end.

Chapter 44

Friday, 3:30 am

Joey and Boyce made it back to Paris. The air was on the warmer side compared to the mountains they had just come from. Joey took out the cell in his pocket and dialed the Louvre. It was the middle of the night, but he knew Pierre would be waiting for his call.

The phone rang three times before Pierre answered it, sounding groggy, as though Joey had woken him up. 'Joey, is it you?' he said.

'I have lost count of how many times you've tried to kill me,' said Joey without preamble. 'And now I know the location to the tomb.'

There was a moment's silence.

Joey knew that Pierre understood what would happen if Joey decided to reveal the true provenance of the *Mona Lisa* that currently hung in the Louvre: it would end his career. But if the world were to find out that the real *Mona Lisa* contained the location of Alexander the Great's tomb, the fallout would be much greater.

'Are you still there?' asked Joey.

'What do you want?' said Pierre, his tone now filled with aggression.

'All I want is Marie. You've pissed me off, and I don't care about what happens to the painting. I should burn it right now.'

'No!' shouted Pierre. 'Don't be stupid. I'll give you Marie. Just don't damage the painting. Please ... Joey, I beg you.'

'It's funny how the tables have turned,' replied Joey, but he took no pleasure in saying it.

Pierre fell silent once more.

'Okay, Pierre, this is how it's going to go down. Listen, because I'm only going to say it once. Meet me in front of your glass pyramid in an hour and bring Marie.'

'You will bring the painting?' asked Pierre.

'I want you to promise me that when you let Marie go she will not be followed like the last time. Keep your soldiers on a leash, or I promise you *La Joconde* will be destroyed. No bullshit this time, do you understand?'

'I understand,' replied Pierre. 'No funny business this time. Make sure you bring me back the real painting.'

The phone went dead.

Immediately after ending the call, Pierre sent Frederic a text message: *It's game time, my office.*

Chapter 45

Frederic and Lamond had searched the village on the lakeshore. To their disappointment and surprise, Joey and Boyce seemed to have vanished into thin air, so they headed back home to Paris, escorted by Pierre's helicopter.

In the wee hours of the morning, Frederic and Lamond made their way into the Louvre. They walked purposefully through the hallways, reminiscing about all the good times they'd had with Thierry. Frederic knew that if Lamond stopped to dwell on his brother's death, his rage would be uncontrollable, and Frederic needed to keep him under his control. He knew his longtime friend well. Lamond was burning inside, wanting nothing more than to avenge his brother's death. Thierry had been Lamond's twin, his best friend and his only living relative. They had fought side by side in battle and would do anything to protect each other, and now he was gone.

The two men viewed the *Mona Lisa* hanging in the *Salle des Etats*. Frederic remembered what Joey had shouted from across the lake. What was the secret tomb he had mentioned? It was an unusual remark and Frederic had yet to ask his boss if it were true.

Frederic led Lamond out of the grand gallery and headed for Napoleon's secret office below ground. The two soldiers, wearing cargo pants and combat boots and strapped with semi-automatic Beretta M9 pistols, entered the darkness of the underground. The door behind them slammed shut as they descended the winding staircase.

Marie woke when she heard the jarring noise of the door closing and grabbed onto the bars in fright. She watched the guards march quickly past her cell, their faces grim. They ignored her and left her in the darkness, pushing open the large wooden doors to Pierre's office. She knew that if she didn't act soon, she would pay with her life.

'I just got the call,' said Pierre calmly. 'He'll be here in an hour. We have no choice this time, we need to let his girlfriend go and swap the painting for her. It's unclear what he might do if we don't.'

'Do you want me to take him out after the exchange is made, sir?' said Lamond.

'Lamond, the painting is of the utmost importance, do you understand?' said Pierre. 'No harm must be allowed to come to it.'

'Yes, I understand,' said Lamond, his expression stony.

'When the painting is safely in my hands, then you can dispose of them however you please,' said Pierre. 'But not a moment before.'

'So what's in the *Mona Lisa*?' asked Frederic curiously. He folded his arms and stood with his feet apart in a commanding pose.

'Why do you ask?' said Pierre warily.

'Joey said he'd found a secret tomb in the *Mona Lisa*. I think you haven't been totally honest with us.'

'That's irrelevant!' said Pierre, trying to sound dismissive. 'It's no concern of yours. You're my personal guard. I'm paying you to bring the painting back to me, nothing else.'

'So there *is* a tomb?' said Frederic. 'This changes everything.' He turned to his right and said to Lamond, 'Don't you want to know what your brother died for?'

'Yes, sir, I do,' answered Lamond.

The towering soldiers peered down at Pierre's shorter frame in his expensive suit. Frederic's folded arms showcased his biceps, which bulged out of his shirtsleeves, the veins protruding from his forearms.

Pierre fixed his gaze on the two men and swallowed uncomfortably. It was imperative that he keep the soldiers on side until he had the painting in his hands.

'Is it true?' asked Frederic again.

'It is true,' said Pierre carefully. 'Inside the original *Mona Lisa*, the one Joey has in his possession, there is a secret text which contains the location to Alexander the Great's tomb. Joey must have found a way to read the text – unless he's bluffing. But if he's telling the truth, he now knows where it is.'

'*Merde*!' exploded Lamond, lost for words.

'See … that wasn't so hard, was it?' said Frederic with a sigh. 'You said Joey will be here soon. I don't want to be tricked again. Is there any way we can determine that the painting is authentic?'

'Yes … there are a couple of things. The back of the painting should have the Louvre's stamp on it,' said

Pierre, rubbing his chin in thought. 'Also the hidden text, or whatever it is on the painting, is said to be revealed under red light. That would also prove its provenance.'

'Red light,' replied Frederic with a smile. 'Too easy.'

'What do you propose, sir?' asked Lamond.

'This is what we're going to do. Lamond, I want you a hundred yards away, out of sight, with a sniper rifle at the ready. This is just a precaution, I hasten to add. Make sure you pick up an X27 thermal clip for your riflescope. I want you to identify the secret text under infrared before we let his girlfriend go. Let's make sure we are dealing with the real thing first. Then when we let her go, I want you to discreetly follow her without Joey knowing. That way we take them both down by surprise. As usual, a snatch-and-grab operation. However, I must have that painting in my hands before you do anything, or heaven knows what Joey will do.'

Lamond nodded his head and left the room. Pierre was now alone with the major.

This was the moment Frederic had been waiting for. He stepped toward Pierre. 'When I first joined the military, we studied Alexander the Great's war victories. I aced the subject. He was the greatest military genius of all time, the man who single-handedly changed the nature of the ancient world in little more than a decade. After his death he was worshipped as a god.'

Pierre flashed a benevolent smile. 'Wow … I would never have guessed you knew that much.'

'Well, you never asked me,' said Frederic in an injured tone, feeling affronted that Pierre only ever treated him as the muscle. 'When we get back the painting, I would like to join you on the quest to find this tomb. I would love to see the remains of the great king.'

'I don't give a rat's ass about his bones,' said Pierre harshly, moving behind his desk and sitting down in his expensive dark leather chair. 'I want what's in his tomb.'

Frederic bit down on his back teeth, making his jawline more pronounced. He hated how this old fart didn't respect the warrior king. 'How can you be so sure the tomb exists, and this isn't some kind of wild goose chase?' he asked.

Pierre opened the first drawer in his desk and pulled out a small notebook. He extracted a torn piece of paper from its center. He handed this to Frederic, who tried to read the inverted Italian text. Then his eyes fell on the signature beneath the writing: the missive was signed by Leonardo da Vinci himself.

'What does it say?' he asked, looking up.

'Without this find we would never have known the map even existed. When read in reverse in a mirror, it reveals that the secret clue was hidden within the *Mona Lisa*.'

'But how would da Vinci know the resting place of Alexander the Great?' asked Frederic, trying to put the pieces of the puzzle together.

'This is a gray area; no one really knows,' said Pierre. 'But what we do know is that Alexander had a large cult following. I believe the secret was passed down over the centuries to men in power, until it eventually reached the secret society, the Priory of Sion, and fell into Leonardo's hands.'

'You realize you're talking about a man who died over two thousand years ago,' said Frederic. 'That's a long time. How could such a cult survive all this time?'

'Looks like you need convincing,' said Pierre with an amused smile, clearly happy to talk history and his obsession. 'Alexander died in 323 B.C.E. and his body was moved to Alexandria, where he lay in his mausoleum for all to worship. Then, in 380 A.D., seven hundred years after his death, the king of the time, Theodosius, placed a series of decrees that banned pagan worship.'

'Is that when his body vanished off the face of the earth?' asked Frederic.

'No. In 390 A.D. the writer Libanius said Alexander's body was still able to be viewed. Therefore, it had withstood the bans for ten years, through the third-century crises of the Roman Empire and the Christian movement. Many believe Alexander's cult moved his body in 392 A.D. and he was laid to rest with Christian doctrines and documents that were considered heretical by the Christian church. This is what I want to find ... the scrolls.'

'How can you be so sure these texts even exist?' asked Frederic.

'Alexander was seen as an Egyptian god, we know that. So for him to have eternal life, he would need to be buried like a pharaoh, with all sorts of valuable possessions to take to the afterlife. I believe the treasure found in Alexander's tomb would make Tutankhamun's tomb look insignificant. I have already achieved my life's work, but being able to bring the church to its knees would be the icing on the cake.'

'What kind of scrolls are you planning to find?'

'Ones that tell the truth,' said Pierre. 'If there's any

text the church wanted destroyed and didn't want anyone to see, I believe it will be in that tomb.'

Frederic considered this. 'Can I ask you a question, sir?'

'Yes. What?'

'Are you a religious man?'

Pierre gave a hint of a smile and said, 'Ask me that question again when we find the tomb.'

Chapter 46

The stars in the sky were still obscured by thick clouds that never seemed to want to go away. Napoleon's courtyard was wet and deserted, but lit up by sizable lanterns strategically placed around the palace walls. The effect gave the structure a yellow glow, showing off the intricate carvings and statues up high on the second level.

This was Joey's first time visiting the square at night and he was blown away by its grandeur and beauty. In the distance, the illuminated glass pyramid stood in all its glory, the focal point of the square and his designated meeting spot.

A screeching sound rang out loudly in the silence of early morning. It derived from an object Joey was dragging, an item he had rescued from a dumpster on his way over. It was a kid's Little Tikes Explorer Wagon, big enough for a young child to sit in and be pulled along.

Aside from the rusted wheels, the toy was in excellent working order. Joey hauled the wagon along with one hand, while in the other he carried the priceless masterpiece under his armpit. Three figures stood outside the Louvre's revolving doors, two male and one female. Even from a distance Joey could tell the woman was Marie being restrained by a heavy hand on her shoulder.

Joey skirted the roundabout where the inverted pyramid lay, then passed by the equestrian statue of King Louis XIV that was to his right. The illuminated glass pyramid rose in the sky. Marie's sad, exhausted face was now clearly visible. Dark circles framed her eyes and her posture was slumped and defeated. Joey felt anger bloom in his stomach.

Frederic knew he needed to be cautious. Joey was up to something, he was sure of it. *Why the toy wagon?* he thought. 'Lamond, you in position?' he said quietly through his earpiece.

'I have a laser target on the back of his head,' said Lamond. 'Give me the order and he's gone.'

'Remember, not until I give the order,' Frederic reminded him. 'Can you see what's in the wagon? He's definitely up to something.'

Lamond was in the bushes of the roundabout Joey had just passed, well camouflaged. From his position, he had a clean shot at the back of Joey's head. But from his low angle, he couldn't see inside the toy wagon. 'No positive ID,' he replied. 'But he's really pulling on that handle, sir; suggests it's something heavy. One thing I can confirm, though: the painting in his hands has the Louvre seal on the back.'

'Okay, good work. Stay alert and wait for my instructions,' ordered Frederic. 'Don't forget we still need to identify the painting, use the scope.'

'Roger that.'

Chapter 47

Joey stopped thirty feet short of the group by the entrance and observed his girlfriend's frightened eyes. He could read in them the worry Marie felt for him, and her fear of the dangers they now both faced. You didn't need to be an expert to know Joey was outnumbered and vulnerable out in the open. He was dealing with mercenaries, trained experts in combat and strategic planning. These men could assassinate a key figure in the morning and go to breakfast just as if nothing had happened. Joey knew that in spite of Pierre's assurances the major would have orchestrated something; the smirk on his face suggested a man who was certain of himself, a man who could handle this situation with his eyes closed and who seemed to have things under control. *Well,* Joey thought, *we'll see about that.*

That's when Joey lit up a match.

Pierre flinched.

Joey flicked it into the wagon's container and in an instant, a flame flared up. The fire logs that Joey had drenched in spirits ignited on contact with the match. The site in front of the famous glass pyramid now glowed as its surfaces reflected the small fire coming from the toy wagon. It was suddenly clear what Joey was threatening to do.

★ ★ ★

Frederic chanced a smile. 'This kid is smarter than I anticipated,' he said grudgingly. 'Stand by, Lamond.'

'What is this, Joey?' shouted Pierre with open hands.

'This is my insurance plan,' replied Joey, holding the *Mona Lisa* high above the fire. 'You didn't think I was thick enough to come here without a plan, did you? I see Lamond is not here. He most likely has a rifle pointed at my head right now, wanting revenge. Tell him if he shoots me, the painting goes up in flames.'

'*Ne pas faire feu!*' said Frederic through the earpiece. He knew Lamond would love nothing more than to squeeze the trigger, and Joey's provocation would only make things worse. '*Ne pas faire feu!*' he said again. He was beginning to like this kid's style, but he wasn't going to let him dictate the proceedings. He lifted his Glock and forced it up against Marie's temple. The woman let out a whimper of fear.

'Joey!' she cried, shutting her eyes.

'It'll be all right, Marie, I have this under control,' said Joey, watching Pierre's eyes as he spoke. Pierre's gaze was fixed on the painting in his hands. 'Oh, that's right, Pierre, I forgot,' he said lightly, 'this is the first time you've actually ever laid eyes on the real *Mona Lisa*.'

Joey flicked the canvas carelessly around in his hands. Over and over he spun it, as if it were a toy; one slip and it was toast. 'The portrait of Alexander the Great and the clue to his resting place,' said Joey. 'I'm sure you don't want it to burn to a crisp before you have a chance to find it?'

'No, I don't,' said Pierre gratingly, his expression pained.

★ ★ ★

Lamond clipped on the X27 clip and changed the dials to infrared mode. Then he scanned the painting while Joey continued to flip it in his hands. What he saw made his mouth drop open. 'The *Mona Lisa* is real,' he shouted, his words tripping over themselves in his astonishment. 'I repeat, real. I can see the hidden text under infrared. The map is real.'

Still holding the gun to Marie's head, Frederic turned to Pierre and murmured, '*La peinture est reel.*'

Pierre's eyes widened.

'Of course it's real,' said Joey, who was watching the men carefully and seemed to have understood Pierre's reaction.

Watching the red flames come close to the board's surface, Pierre saw a hint of glistening text appear. It was where da Vinci had described having hidden the clue. The text must also be legible in the reddish light from the flames, he reasoned. Excitement rushed through his body.

'What are you going to do when the flames die down?' said Frederic, always thinking ahead.

Joey smiled as if he wasn't the least bit concerned. 'These fire logs have a burn time of up to two hours,' he said confidently. 'So I'm good, and ah, yes, there's something I forgot to mention. You're not the only one here with a rifle. My own man has one pointed at the curator's head right now.'

Both Pierre and Frederic peered around the perimeter of the courtyard, searching for possible vantage points, but it was dark and the shooter could be anywhere.

'This is what's going to happen,' said Joey, once again in a commanding position. 'Let Marie go like we discussed on the phone.' Joey turned to face his girl. 'Marie, run to your left under the passage and head toward the Seine River. I have a plan for you.'

'But ... what about you?' she replied.

'I'll be fine, trust me.'

Joey lowered the painting toward the heat of the fire. The toy wagon was just big enough to allow the entire board to be engulfed by the flames, if Joey let it drop.

'Stop!' said Pierre. 'Okay ... Let her go, Frederic.' He turned to Joey. 'I will do as you wish.'

Pierre gave Frederic a nod. The big French guard reluctantly let his hostage go and nudged her forward with his Glock.

Marie stepped forward, stopping halfway between them all and focusing her eyes on Joey. She then looked down at his hands, which were trembling. On the surface, he was like a lion waiting for the right moment to pounce, but she knew Joey was playing it tough.

Joey rotated the face of the masterpiece in Marie's direction. She stared into the *Mona Lisa's* eyes and thought about the conspiracies that had been associated with this portrait for centuries. She took in the brilliance of the sfumato technique, and one thought flooded her mind: this was probably going to be the last time she would ever see it again.

Chapter 48

Marie took a deep breath and made a run for it across the plaza, past the equestrian statue and the castle walls. Her tennis shoes, which Frederic had thankfully given back to her, splashed in the puddles on the wet pavement. She disappeared through the arched Denon Wing passage and out of the large black-gated doors that were decorated with gold spikes on the pointy ends. Within minutes she was out of sight, but the adrenaline continued to pump in her veins. She knew that no matter what Pierre had agreed to, Lamond would not be far behind, and there was no way she was going back to that dank cell in the Louvre without a fight.

Then there were three. Joey stood in Napoleon's outdoor courtyard under a somber and starless sky, his knees feeling the warmth of the fire at his feet. He gazed upward and hoped the rain would hold off. The rain was the one thing out of his control; he could not afford to damage his only bargaining chip. All he could do was pray that it stayed dry long enough for his plan to work.

'You got what you wanted. I let Marie go. Now it's your turn,' said Pierre, stepping closer. Frederic also moved in, his gun now by his side while his finger touched his ear and he said something into his earpiece.

Frederic was getting dangerously close, and the thought of him leaping over and snapping Joey's neck was not something Joey wanted to contemplate. Joey had held the *Mona Lisa* in both hands this whole time. He now let his right hand drop, and the left wobbled under the twenty-pound weight. The fire below was still burning strongly as he grasped the painting over it. 'This is my weak hand,' he said as he lowered it slightly. 'Stop moving and put your gun down, Frederic.'

'I should just shoot you in the head,' said Frederic, aiming his nine-millimeter between Joey's eyes. 'All I need is one killer shot and you could miss the fire entirely.'

'That might be true, but are you willing to take the gamble?' said Joey, knowing he would not.

'I haven't decided yet,' replied Frederic aloofly.

Joey lowered the painting a little more.

'Stop it, stop playing games,' said Pierre, palms forward like a cop halting traffic. 'Frederic, put it away.'

'Yes, Frederic, listen to your boss,' said Joey smugly. 'Throw your weapon in the pool. I need to know that when you get what you want, no harm will come to me.'

'Of course, you have my word,' said Pierre, who nodded his head in an upward direction to suggest to Frederic to do as he was told.

Frederic obliged and tossed his weapon into the shallow pool of water near his position, one of three triangular reflecting pools designed around the transparent structure, complete with fountains and lights that shot upward at the glass triangle. The gun made a loud splash and sank down to the dark tiles.

'Okay, Joey, it's your move,' said Pierre. 'You hold all the cards in your hands.'

Joey sighed. 'A couple of days ago I came to Paris with the knowledge that I had acquired the real *Mona Lisa*. I was going to return it, and all I asked was to be acknowledged for this deed, so I could clear my family's name.'

'But it can't be —' said Pierre.

'Shut up and let me finish,' interrupted Joey. 'Since we met in Napoleon's underground secret room, when you threatened me and took my girlfriend hostage, I have climbed and jumped off a five-story building. I have fought with a gang of thugs. I have been relentlessly chased and shot at. I have been in a boat accident. I have fought a marine and nosedived a car off a cliff. And during all this James Bond shit, I find out that the painting in my possession contains the location of a tomb that has been sought for centuries.'

Frederic laughed and replied sarcastically, 'Welcome to Paris.'

'Thanks, Frederic, but it's not really the Paris trip I had imagined.'

Pierre frowned. 'Why are you giving us this speech?'

Joey watched Pierre, who could not take his eyes off the *Mona Lisa*. She was much richer in color than Raphael's *Mona Lisa* in the Denon Wing. Even in the dark night with the outside yellow lights and the fire burning, its purity was unquestionable. There was only one word to describe it: she was *magnificent*. Pierre gave a ragged sigh.

'This is not the way I'd envisaged all this happening,' said Pierre. 'I'm so sorry for what you have been through, Joey, but now you must realize the importance of the piece of art you hold in your hand. She is not just a renaissance masterpiece. She is a secret that until now has been protected and preserved.'

'Yes, and because of it, I have a target on my back,' said Joey, keeping his eyes on Frederic.

'Have you read the inscription?' asked Pierre.

'You mean the location of the tomb, the text that can only be read under red light?' said Joey lightly.

'Did you read it?'

Joey smiled.

'Where is it?'

'I'm sorry, but this is where it all ends,' said Joey, shaking his head. 'Edna was right; the painting needs to be destroyed. Some things were never meant to be found.'

'Don't believe anything that bitch said,' said Pierre. 'She was the reason why Bernard was killed. Did you know we had an affair? When Bernard found out, he tried to destroy me by destroying the painting.'

'So you fucking killed him?' said Joey incredulously. 'People like you don't deserve to know a secret like this.'

'I need that painting, Joey.'

'No, you just *want* it. Nobody needs this. Nobody should have lost their life for this.'

'Don't you even think of dropping it in the fire,' said Frederic. 'If you do I'll take my time with you and kill you slowly.'

Joey swallowed hard; the threat was real. He found himself in a predicament. He had hopefully saved Marie, but he knew that if he handed over the painting it was all over for him. Lamond was still out there somewhere, and once the painting was out of his hands, the kill shot would come. 'Just remember, if I accidentally dropped the painting in the fire the secret stays with me. Tell trigger fingers that.'

From out of nowhere, sirens wailed in the distance. As he'd hoped, the security cameras must have caught the fire in front of the Louvre and the police were coming to investigate.

'Police,' said Frederic. 'It looks like our little friend wants to get arrested.'

'Did you think I would trust you, after what you've put me through?' said Joey. 'I'd rather get arrested and take my chances with the police.'

'Smart boy,' said Pierre with a wide grin. 'The police will keep you safe. Now hand over the painting. It's over.'

'But I told you: you don't deserve to know.'

'Enough of this.' Frederic moved in.

'Take one more step,' said Joey, lowering the canvas. His arm was trembling with the effort of holding the painting's weight. The smoke fumes from the fire glided off the glazed surface.

'Stop, Frederic, no!' warned Pierre. 'Wait.'

Frederic paused, only feet away now.

The police sirens sounded closer. Joey turned to *La Joconde*; the real *Mona Lisa* that had been in his family for decades. The portrait he knew now was of Alexander the Great. He took it all in, exhaled one last long breath, and did the unthinkable.

Chapter 49

Marie found herself running east along the Voie Georges Pompidou, which ran alongside the Seine. The early-morning air was crisp and a thick fog hovered over the entire riverbed. The visual was something out of a horror movie. There was no one around. No cars, no movement; just desolate walkways and bridges that could be seen in the distance, looming through the dense fog.

Marie's heart pounded as she continued to run, turning her head every few steps to make sure she was not being pursued. She had never felt so alert as she did now.

Then, from out of nowhere, a boy jumped into her path from behind a slender tree trunk. Marie's heart seemed to leap into her throat and she screamed, 'No!' Her body was shaking uncontrollably and would not obey her attempts to flee. Her eyes wild with fear, she scanned the stranger. His figure was short and slender. The way he put up his arms suggested to her right away that he meant her no harm. He was just a teenager. A moment later something clicked in her mind.

'I know you,' she said, scrabbling to get herself under control. 'Aren't you the boy from the bridge?'

'Yes, I am a friend of Joey's. My name is Boyce,' said the teen, who then reached out and grabbed her hand. 'This way. We must be quick.'

'What's going on?'

'I'll explain later, but for now you need to trust me.'

They both proceeded to jog down the road until they reached the Pont des Arts pedestrian bridge. This bridge crossed the river Seine, linking the Institut de France and the central square of the Palais du Louvre.

At the edge of the bridge Boyce stopped and turned back to face in the direction they had just run from. He stood as if waiting for something to happen.

'What are you doing?' Marie asked. 'Why did you stop? We need to keep running!'

'You need to trust me,' he replied.

Marie felt like she was going to be sick.

'Here he comes,' said Boyce. 'Just as planned. He has seen us.'

When she saw the male figure heading their way, Marie felt panic set in. 'Oh my God,' she breathed. It was Lamond.

'Okay, now move!' hissed Boyce.

They pounded across the wooden boards of the thirty-six-foot wide bridge, passing a sea of padlocks, each supposed to represent a couple's commitment and love. In a tiny corner of her mind, Marie promised herself that if she survived this ordeal, she would one day return and contribute to this work of art by putting up a padlock for her and Joey.

Halfway across the 170-yard-long bridge, Marie glanced back over her shoulder to see the silhouette of a man's shape reaching the pedestrian bridge.

Lamond ran like a man possessed; a man who wanted his brother's death not to have been in vain. At this pace, he would catch up to them by the time they exited the bridge.

'Oh shit!' Marie panted. 'He's gaining on us.'

Beside her, Boyce seemed calm and in control. 'Run, Marie,' he said, and Marie redoubled her efforts. Their lead was diminishing, but Lamond was still a fair distance away. Once they reached the other side, they quickly disappeared into the fog.

Boyce took Marie by the hand, and with his other hand put his finger to his lips, indicating that she should be as quiet as possible and follow him. They turned left and ran down a flight of stairs that took them below the level of the bridge, where a cobblestone walkway ran along the riverbank, which was lined with houseboats. The impenetrable fog made excellent cover. The other side of the river was barely visible; nothing but gray.

Lamond reached the end of the bridge. He stopped for a moment and closed his eyes, listening. His heartbeat was loud in his ears, but it slowed with each breath. He began to hear sounds around him; the wind, the birds flying overhead and the ones that landed in the river below.

Then he heard a boat's engine start.

His eyes flashed open and he turned to his left, chasing the sound down the concrete steps to the cobblestone path below. He flipped forward the M16 machine gun that was strapped to his back. The safety switch was turned off and it was cocked and ready to be used. Lamond let the M16 lead the way through the dense fog to a small timber boat that had just left the jetty. It pulled out sixteen feet, then thirty-two feet.

It was game time. In a flash Lamond was down on one knee and a tongue of machine-gun fire exited the muzzle of the gun, raining down upon the boat that was getting away. Wooden fragments flew everywhere, then one of his last remaining bullets hit the engine.

KABOOM!

The boat exploded in a billowing smoke cloud.

Some of the timber pieces floating in the river remained alight, causing a bright reflection on the surface of the dark water. Lamond, feeling a sense of satisfaction for the first time since his brother's death, stood up and smiled.

Behind Lamond, Marie stepped out of a houseboat, armed with a sawn-off shotgun that Boyce had thrust into her hands. She squared off, ready to fire.

Turning to go, Lamond saw her and stopped short.

'Drop it!' she shouted. 'It's my turn now.' She cocked the gun.

Lamond let go of the empty M16, which hit the ground with a clatter that echoed along the river. He smiled and began to reach slowly for the nine-millimeter pistol that was wedged in his front belt buckle.

'Don't even try it,' she warned.

Lamond did not listen.

Marie knew this was what he lived for. She knew he would go for the quick turn and shoot.

'Do you think you're faster than me?' she said.

'We will soon find out,' replied Lamond.

But Marie wasn't stupid. She knew she had seconds,

at best. She pulled the trigger. There was no missing with the shotgun. She had seen enough movies to know that hesitation would be her downfall. *Just shoot and kill the bastard*, she told herself, and that's what she did.

Lamond's torn body fell backwards near the edge of the river. Blood spouted from his mouth as he inhaled his last breath of air and then he lay still. After a moment, Marie approached his dead body and gagged as she removed the communication earpiece from his ear.

Boyce stepped out of the houseboat to see the damage she'd wrought.

Turning to him, Marie said, 'How did you know there was a shotgun in that boat?'

'That's my friend's boat,' said Boyce, watching the timber continuing to burn. 'He showed me the gun one day. He had it to protect himself from the shady element he was dealing with. He's going to have a breakdown when he finds out what happened to his boat.'

Marie flashed him a smile, and hesitantly put the earpiece in her own ear. Then, with Boyce's help, she rolled Lamond's prone form into the dark river. His body glided into the water and floated for a second or two, then disappeared into the murk, just as his brother's had.

Chapter 50

Joey threw the painting in the fire.

The face of the renaissance masterpiece hit the flames and immediately blackened. The flammable oils used by Leonardo da Vinci caused the fire to flare up and double in size and intensity. There was no going back. The priceless painting was burning before their eyes.

'NO!' screamed Pierre, his distraught eyes gleaming with hatred as the smell of wood smoke drifted in the air around them. He immediately went to recover the painting, but the fire was too strong, too hot. He kicked the wagon with fury, and its contents fell all over the paved wet ground. The combustion logs, still lit, rolled to a stop. With his aging hands, Pierre batted ineffectually at the fire. The French *La Joconde* was now unrecognizable. The fire had eaten away all its layers of pigment, leaving nothing but the remnants of a burned-out poplar board.

Joey moved to one side and watched the curator live out his worst nightmare. The sirens were blaringly loudly now, and he turned to see a small white-and-blue Peugeot speed up and park along the Carrousel du Louvre. Two tall uniformed officers stepped out of the car. Even from a distance, Joey could see they were armed with batons and standard nine-millimeter pistols in their holsters.

Joey sighed with relief. His escape plan was working. He knew the 24/7 surveillance cameras in the Louvre's courtyard would be closely scrutinized. He knew the French police would not go easy on him, but it beat the alternative: his death. While he waited for the officers to approach, he wondered if Marie and his young sidekick's escape had gone to plan. Then, he lifted his head to see a fuming Frederic towering over him. The Frenchman's eyes were narrowed, rigid, cold and hard, and he wasn't smiling.

Joey thought fast.

Frederic was a man who hated to lose. It would be unacceptable to him that he had been outsmarted, Joey thought. And indeed, Frederic gritted his teeth and attacked with the speed of a lunging snake, putting his body between the police and Joey to disguise his movements and grabbing Joey by the neck. 'You little shit!' he hissed, and squeezed with the force of a death grip.

Joey struggled to breathe. He lifted both hands to try to loosen the vise-like hold Frederic had on him, but he simply wasn't strong enough. His felt his lungs begin to collapse as his windpipe was being crushed. Desperately, he tried to move his head to see where the police officers were, but there was no sign of them.

'No, Frederic,' warned Pierre hoarsely. 'Let him go. He's the only one who knows the tomb's location. We can't kill him.'

With a groan of frustration and rage, Frederic obliged, and let go of the American.

Joey fell to his knees like a bag of heavy potatoes, and gasped for air. He wanted to talk but couldn't. Finally, out of the corner of his eye, he saw the police officers approaching. He raised his hand, but still nothing came out of his mouth.

The first officer, a well-built man with a trimmed mustache, seemed to be the more senior of the two men. His partner was much thinner and more athletic looking and stood slightly behind the first man, his hand hovering over the firearm tucked into his holster. The senior officer said something in French. Joey suddenly realized that he hadn't considered the language barrier.

'You speak *Anglais?*' asked Joey quickly.

'*Non*,' replied the officer.

Shit, thought Joey.

As Frederic stepped purposefully in front of Joey, Pierre stepped toward the officers, smiling reassuringly.

'Hello, officers, my name is Pierre Savard. I'm the Louvre curator and this is my head of security, Frederic. We have a slight situation here, but we are dealing with it. We're sorry to have caused any disturbance.'

'I know who you are, Monsieur Savard, but a fire so close to the Louvre is not what I call a slight situation.'

'We've caught the perpetrator,' said Pierre, pointing down at Joey.

'Thank you for your help, but we'll take it from here,' said the mustached officer, who stepped forward and looked down at the timber logs on the ground, which were still smoldering.

'What's your name, Officer?' said Frederic in his calm voice.

'Officer Donat.'

'Donat, I was a sergeant major in the French army and served with your chief of police. We're good friends. I need you to do me a favor and walk away. Let me deal with this arsonist my way, and I'll personally give you and your partner a recommendation.'

The officers glanced at each other with bewildered eyes.

'Don't listen to whatever they're saying,' said Joey, climbing awkwardly to his feet. 'He wants to kill me.'

'Shut up,' said Frederic, frowning.

'Please arrest me,' begged Joey, folding his wrists as if he were wearing handcuffs.

The two officers looked at each other, but Pierre was relieved to see that they didn't understand what Joey was saying.

'Ignore him,' said Frederic back in French. 'He just wants attention.'

In a flash, Joey did something that caught everyone by surprise. He turned to the thinner of the two officers and punched him squarely in the face.

Blood poured out of the officer's nose. With flaring nostrils, he tackled Joey to the ground over the burned-out logs, twisted his arms behind his back and clapped on a pair of handcuffs before forcing Joey to his feet.

'Sorry, but after that little stunt he's coming with us,' said the officer. 'Nobody hits a police officer and gets away with it.'

Neither officer noticed the look of pure relief that flooded Joey's face.

Frederic stood frozen. He couldn't believe he had been outplayed yet again. The rage he felt was uncontainable.

With lightning speed, Frederic moved, positioning himself behind Donat. Lifting his arms, he cradled the officer's head and snapped it to the side. The mustached officer didn't even have a chance to react. There was a loud crack and he fell to the ground like a ton of bricks.

The second officer, who had been trying to stem the blood that was rushing down his face, was momentarily unaware of his partner's sudden death. He only had time to yelp before Frederic ended his life with the same deadly maneuver.

'What have you done?' said Pierre shakily. He pointed up at the surveillance cameras around the courtyard. 'There'll be no getting out of this.'

'You wanted Joey, didn't you?' snapped Frederic. He grabbed Joey roughly by the shoulder and forced him to his knees so he couldn't run off. 'I wasn't going to let him get arrested. You said yourself that you've been after the location of Alexander's tomb all your life. Joey will tell us that location tonight ... then I will kill him.'

'Only after he speaks,' said Pierre quickly. 'He's the only one who knows the location now.'

Frederic shook his head. 'He's not the only one. That kid he was with in Switzerland knows.' Frederic adjusted his earpiece. 'Come in, Lamond, did you complete your mission? Come in, report.'

There was silence for a moment, then the static picked up and a voice could be heard. 'I'm sorry, Lamond can't come to the phone right now, he's at the bottom of the Seine,' said Marie cheerfully. 'He messed with the wrong bitch.'

Frederic felt his face contort in fury. He was as angry as a baited bull. His cheeks flushed and he shot a death stare at Joey. 'Fuck!' he screamed, clenching a fist and directing a full-force kick into Joey's rib cage.

Joey winced in pain and confusion.

Frederic had lost his entire team to this dumb American. He pressed his earpiece one more time and hissed, 'You think you've won, but you haven't. You've just killed your boyfriend.'

Frederic removed the earpiece from his ear and threw it to the ground, breaking it in two. Then he turned and put his fist into Joey's face as hard as he could, and the American collapsed, out cold.

Chapter 51

Joey struggled to open his eyes as he regained consciousness. His head buzzed and his ears rang as though a train had just passed through them. He was not outside the Louvre anymore. He was lying on a cold surface somewhere indoors. Frederic's boots came into view, and then he felt a tug on his hair, which hurt. Having no choice but to bear the pain, he tried to take the pressure off by pulling himself to his knees.

Joey now realized he was at the top of the spiral marble staircase underneath the glass pyramid in the Louvre; the awe-inspiring entrance he had walked down only a couple of days ago. Without any remorse, Frederic adjusted his grip on Joey's hair and dragged him down the stairs with a clear objective: to cause him harm. It was too late to stop the momentum. Joey knew it was time to pay the price for Thierry's death, and it was going to hurt.

Because his hands were still handcuffed behind his back, Joey's shoulders, chest and chin hit the marble with each step. After a seemingly endless descent to ground level, Joey's aching body pitched forward into something cool and soft. Turning his head to see what it was, he recoiled in horror: he'd hit the two dead bodies of the police officers.

★ ★ ★

Pierre stood in the shadows, rubbing the stubble on his chin with his right hand. He knew Frederic's decision to kill the officers had not been the smartest one. The guard had snapped in the heat of the moment and not considered the consequences of his actions. There was no going back for him, but Pierre thought he might be able to salvage the situation for himself. He would need to cut all ties with Frederic after tonight, that went without saying, but first he needed Frederic to flush out the location of the tomb from Joey's head.

Chapter 52

At the bottom of the staircase, Joey struggled to stand. He stepped over the dead policemen and fixed his gaze on Frederic, who was standing there grinning almost manically, clearly pleased with himself. Joey felt a rising trepidation. Frederic's presence was strong; he had served his country at the top of his profession. He was a leader who always got his way and now he wanted his own revenge for the humiliations Joey had made him suffer.

'Where's the tomb?' asked Pierre, stepping into the moonlight that had broken through the cloud cover and now shone through the glass ceiling above. 'Before you answer, let me remind you that the doors are locked and we're the only ones inside.'

'I'm not that stupid,' said Joey. 'It's the only reason you haven't killed me yet. If I give you what you want, I'm a dead man.'

Frederic smiled, moving in and out of the shadows in the dark and barren subterranean foyer. The place had an almost crypt-like atmosphere. Joey shivered, watching the big Frenchman with fearful eyes.

'No, Joey, you're going to die either way tonight,' said Frederic. 'It's too late for you now. It just depends on how painful you want it to be.'

'Screw you, Frederic,' said Joey, his jaw tense. 'Who made you king?'

Pierre entered Joey's line of sight.

'If I were you, Pierre, I would be more careful who I conspired with,' said Joey. 'You didn't order Frederic to kill the police. He did that on his own. He's a loose cannon.'

Pierre didn't answer.

With lightning speed Frederic stepped right into Joey's personal space, his eyes piercing as he flung a quick jab to Joey's chin. 'Shut up, you're bothering me,' he said after connecting.

The punch brought Joey to his knees. Once again the blackness crept across his vision and the buzzing sound filled his head, and it seemed to stay longer this time. When he came around, blinking his bruised eye, he saw Pierre's shiny black leather shoes standing next to him.

'Why not make this easier on yourself,' said Pierre calmly. 'Tell me the location. You owe it to me, after you destroyed the one painting I have been searching for my whole life.'

'I don't owe you shit,' said Joey, spitting out some blood that had pooled in his mouth. 'You don't deserve to know.' He struggled to lift himself up and searched for Frederic, who had disappeared again into the darkness.

'You owe me more than you think,' said Pierre, his voice harder now. 'Do you even realize what's at stake here? Alexander the Great's tomb would be the most wondrous find in history. In it there are treasures unimaginable.'

'So this is all about money? Fame? Haven't you got both already?'

'No ... it's about something much more than that.'

'Ah yes ... the manuscripts. Edna told me.'

Pierre gave a wry smile. 'If they exist, I need to find them.'

'She also mentioned that she hated your guts,' said Joey mockingly.

'Just think for a moment,' said Pierre, ignoring his last comment. 'Imagine the manuscripts do exist and have been sealed away with this pagan god, waiting to be found. What might they reveal about the past? Tell me the location and let's find out the truth.'

'Edna was right,' said Joey, shaking his head. 'This secret is bigger than all of us.'

'No,' interrupted Pierre. 'It's the biggest cover-up in human history. Don't you want to find out the truth?'

'Edna wanted to keep it a secret so much that she nearly destroyed the painting herself, and would have sacrificed her own daughter for it. That's the reason I destroyed it. It has caused enough death and heartbreak already.'

'And like Edna you will die,' said Pierre in an even voice.

'Fuck you!'

Suddenly Pierre smiled. 'That's no way to talk to your future father-in-law.'

Joey stared stupidly at the older man. 'What are you talking about?'

'Didn't you know? Marie's my daughter.'

For a moment Joey was floored. That was unexpected. The comment was so out of character. Joey just stared at Pierre, open-mouthed. His brain formulated no thoughts other than to register what he had heard.

'One last chance,' said Pierre, moving over to the dead policemen and bending down. When he stood up he lifted his hands to show Joey the small key to the handcuffs. He had removed it from the policeman's pocket. Pierre came forward and unlocked the handcuffs, letting them fall to the ground. 'I'm not a monster, Joey. Consider this a gesture of goodwill. If you tell me the location, I'll let you go. It's up to you.'

'I can't believe you're Marie's father,' said Joey, playing for time. 'I thought her father was Bernard Martino.'

'That was a lie,' said Pierre. 'Edna kept it a secret. But she told Bernard on the day he died.'

Joey shook his head sadly. 'That explains why Bernard wanted to destroy the *Mona Lisa*. It was the one possession he knew meant the most to you. I would have done the same thing myself.'

Pierre nodded toward the shadows, and Frederic re-emerged, cracking his knuckles.

'Are you ready to speak?' he said in a deep voice that echoed in the open foyer. 'Or would you rather feel the pain?'

Joey took a step back, trembling as adrenaline raced through him. He bumped into something hard and, putting his hands behind him, realized that it was a stainless-steel pole, the type with a circular base and a retractable band that showed museum-goers where to queue.

Joey quickly unhooked the black strap from the pole and took hold of it as if it were a baseball bat. He began to swing it around like a crazy man. It wasn't the best weapon, but it was better than nothing.

Frederic casually extracted his Beretta M9 pistol. 'Enough of this crap,' he said.

When Joey saw the pistol, his eyes widened. Without thinking, he tossed the pole as hard as he could at Frederic's armed hand. The heavy end knocked the pistol to the ground, and even in the shadows Joey saw Frederic's face turn crimson.

Joey made a run for it down the dark Denon Wing.

'Bastard,' Frederic shrieked. 'I'm going to kill you.'

'Relax, Frederic he's trapped. I'll turn on the lights,' Joey heard Pierre say. 'Remember, I'm the curator. I know every inch of this place. He has nowhere to go.'

With these words ringing in his ears, Joey ran along the arched corridor, feeling all the eyes from the renaissance masterpieces following him as he went. He was shut in. Once the lights were turned on, he was as good as dead. He needed to find a way to call for help.

In no time at all, the large lights above the Denon Wing were switched on, one after the other. It was like watching a synchronized light show heading his way.

Joey immediately turned to a Caravaggio. 'I'm so sorry,' he said as he grabbed the gilded frame and tried his best to remove it from the wall.

He had seconds.

The lights beamed directly above his head.

Pierre spotted him and pointed. '*Merde*, he's trying to trip the alarm.'

Frederic began to sprint toward Joey. The closer he got, the harder Joey heaved the masterpiece toward himself, until finally it tore from the wall and landed on the floor.

Instantly, an alarm rang out and a large iron security

gate fell nearby, followed by another one, barricading the entrance and stopping Frederic in his tracks.

'I'm going to kill you,' Frederic yelled, staring through the gate and watching Joey hide behind a marble column. 'You're going to pay for what you did to my men, that's a promise. You will be dead soon!'

Chapter 53

Moments later, police sirens wailed outside. Joey peered out around the Corinthian column he was hiding behind and breathed a sigh of relief. He knew the police would need to come in and investigate. It would no doubt get him in no end of serious trouble, but it was the only way out of this sticky situation, and he was going to take it.

Pierre stood perfectly still as the alarm buzzed piercingly around him. 'If you think you're getting any help, you're wrong,' he shouted down the cavernous corridor. 'All you've done is delay the inevitable. Scream as loud as you want, they won't be able to hear you.'

Pierre's body language belied his frustration. Fires of fury and hatred smoldered in his narrowing eyes. He turned to Frederic, who was clenching and unclenching his fists, trying to control his own rage. 'Frederic, this is the hundredth time you have let me down. I'm sick and tired of all this shit. Now we have the police force to deal with again.'

'It's just a setback,' said Frederic in a tight voice.

'Setback my ass. I asked you to do one simple thing and you failed.'

Frederic took a deep breath. 'What do you propose?'

'We move the bodies to the cells. After I deal with the police I'll deactivate the gates and Joey is all yours. Your one and only job now is to extract the location out of his head. Can you do that?' His eyes bored into the big guard. 'Is that too much to ask?'

'No, sir,' said Frederic, giving him a sidelong stare, as if not liking the tone of his voice. But he grabbed the feet of one of the dead officers and began sliding him across the marbled floor.

The sound of a loud knock on the Louvre's glass doors above vibrated down into the empty foyer. Pierre composed himself as he took the elevator up to greet the three police officers, who were waiting outside in the rain that had begun to fall. All the men were armed, just like the two dead souls that had just been moved out of sight.

'Hello, officers,' greeted Pierre, opening the door with a friendly smile. 'Come in, get out of the rain.'

The three policemen entered the glass structure and looked around. Pierre thought they had probably been inside the pyramid before, but it was hard not to be awed anew by its grandeur and beauty.

'I know you,' said the youngest-looking of the officers. 'Aren't you the curator?'

'Yes, I am,' said Pierre. He hoped his relative celebrity would help him in this situation. 'Sorry for the inconvenience, gentlemen, it's just a false alarm. My electrician triggered the alarm by accident, but it's nice to know that the police response time is so good. I'll make sure your captain is aware of how well his officers responded.'

One of the older officers nodded his head understandingly. 'Okay, fantastic, it seems everything is under control here.' He had a florid complexion and a pregnant-looking stomach. He was no doubt delighted he would not have to chase anyone. 'My ears are hurting. Can you please go and turn off that dreadful alarm?'

'I will,' said Pierre.

'Okay, we'll leave you to deal with that,' said the fat man. He then turned to one of his fellow officers and said, 'While we're in the neighborhood, there's that great patisserie around the corner. It should be opening soon ...'

'Thanks again, officers,' said Pierre. 'Sorry about the inconvenience.'

Two of the men stepped outside, but the youngest officer hesitated. 'Just one more thing. Have any other officers come to see you tonight?' he asked.

'Why do you ask?' Pierre replied.

'There's a police car parked outside, at Place du Carrousel. I was wondering where the crew is. They've left their door open and it's raining.'

Pierre's instinct was to avoid the policeman's eyes, but he forced himself to meet his gaze.

'Sir,' the policeman whispered, locking eyes with the old man. 'Wink if you're in any trouble.'

Pierre's eyes darted to the floor while he thought. He knew Frederic's stupid mistake earlier could come back to bite him in the ass if he didn't handle it carefully. He needed to put all the blame on Frederic and find another way to get the location out of Joey. So he lifted his head and winked.

'Rémi, Destin, how about I catch up with you guys

later?' said the young officer before they left. 'I'm going to hang around and wait for the other officers from that patrol car to turn up.'

'Okay, suit yourself,' said the leader. 'Give us a heads-up when they do, we won't be far.'

Now alone with the young officer, Pierre quietly asked, 'What's your name?'

'Etienne,' he replied, then put a finger to his lips to suggest Pierre speak softly. 'How many are there?'

'Two.'

'Are they armed?'

'Yes.'

'You lead the way. Go turn off the alarm.'

Etienne took out his nine-millimeter pistol from its holster and kept a safe distance away from Pierre, who took the elevator while he discreetly took the stairs.

At the information desk in the foyer, Pierre booted up a computer terminal and entered his personal access code. With his level of access, he could control the entire Louvre complex. Within seconds the alarm was switched off and the lights in the other two wings came on. The iron security gates began to retract. Even as silence fell, the ringing was still loud in their ears.

From his hiding place behind the column, Joey saw a policeman approaching down the Denon Wing, his gun held at the ready.

The officer called something in French in a commanding voice, and even though Joey didn't understand the words, their meaning was clear. He immediately showed himself. He was safe. He approached the officer in navy blue, and then he saw

Pierre appear at the far end of the corridor, and stopped.

'This is not what it looks like, officer,' warned Joey.

'Put your hands up!' the officer said in English, and Joey felt a rush of relief that this one could understand him.

'Pierre is the criminal, don't trust him,' said Joey, raising his hands.

'Keep walking and shut up.'

Then, suddenly, Frederic came running down the corridor. When he saw the policeman with his weapon drawn, a look of shock and surprise flashed across his face.

'You, stop!' demanded the police officer in French, turning to face the well-built guard. He swung his weapon between the two men, then said to Frederic, 'Show me your hands.'

'Pierre, tell the officer who I am,' said Frederic as he came to a stop.

'Who is he?' asked Etienne.

Pierre took a deep breath. This was the moment where he burned his bridges. 'He used to be my head of security,' he said. 'These two men are trying to rob the Louvre. They have me hostage.'

'What the hell are you doing?' said Frederic menacingly. 'I've been loyal to you for years. Why are you betraying me?'

'He killed the two officers from the police car outside,' Pierre told Etienne. 'Watch him, he's dangerous.'

'He's lying,' said Frederic, stepping closer.

'I need you to stop,' warned Etienne, keeping his gun trained on Frederic while he took out his radio with his other hand.

'Don't do that,' warned Frederic, coming even closer.

'Stop!'

Frederic's demeanor changed. He was wired, and Pierre saw that he had begun to shake. He would not be able to control himself for much longer.

Etienne pressed the radio's talk button. 'I need assistance.'

'Coming in, over, is that you, Etienne?'

'Yes, I —'

Chapter 54

Before the officer could say another word, Frederic lashed out with his right hand. He had retrieved his pistol that was wedged in his back belt and fired off a single bullet with perfect precision, right between the young officer's brown eyes.

The policeman's body fell backwards, hands flailing as they hit the ground, his radio and pistol skittering away across the marble floor. He'd been killed instantly and now lay still, eyes wide open. Frederic turned his angry gaze on Pierre.

'I'm so sorry, Frederic,' said Pierre, back-pedaling. 'I had no choice, you have to understand that.'

'No, boss, you always have a choice,' said Frederic with a sigh. 'You just picked the wrong one.' Frederic trained his weapon on his longtime friend, his hand now rock-steady. 'So it seems you will never get to see the inside of Alexander the Great's tomb after all.'

'No, Frederic, don't be stupid. I made a mistake.'

'Yes, you did,' replied Frederic, and with no remorse emptied his gun's chamber.

Chapter 55

Fourteen bullets entered Pierre's chest inches from each other. The momentum drove him off his feet and he fell backwards. His spine bounced on the hard floor as blood began to flow out of his wounds, blooming like flowers against his white shirt and forming a pool of crimson around him. With his hands pressed hard up against his chest, his breathing became fast and shallow and his complexion paled as the life drained from his body. He glanced over at the young American who was never going to tell him the secret he longed to hear. He then turned his head to the side, and saw an angel in the distance.

Situated at the end of the Denon Wing, carved completely from marble, was the eight-foot-tall winged headless Greek goddess Nike. Pierre took in the gray sculpture, which he had passed many thousands of times, and felt a strong compulsion to let go. He closed his heavy eyelids for the last time.

As he watched the curator take his last breath, Joey's heart raced. He stood there alone with Frederic, a murderer who had just executed a man he had once called his friend. Joey stood frozen to the spot, waiting for Frederic's next move. He hoped for a miracle.

Frederic stared at Pierre's body for a moment, then turned his cold, intimidating eyes on Joey. He raised the Glock once more.

This is it, thought Joey; he was going to die like the rest of them. Tomorrow's headlines would read: *The curator, three policemen and an American tourist gunned down inside the Louvre.*

Desperate, he raised both hands in the air. 'Wait … Wait …' he pleaded. 'I'll tell you where the tomb is.'

'I don't care about the tomb,' said Frederic.

'You should,' said Joey. 'You'll be a wanted man soon.'

'I've been trained to disappear,' said Frederic. 'That won't be a problem.'

'That's true, but you could be a rich man on the run. In Alexander's tomb, we're talking about millions in gold, emeralds and diamonds,' Joey invented, hoping he sounded genuine. 'It's is said his tomb would make all other tombs look petty. I can tell you the location, but you have to let me go.'

Frederic lowered his gun. 'Okay, Joey,' he said, nodding his head. 'Tell me the location and I will not kill you, but first help me drag these bodies down to the cells.'

'Why?' asked Joey.

'Because I said so, that's why!'

It was clear Frederic was acting on emotion and not thinking clearly. There was no hiding what he had done, but Joey decided he didn't have much choice but to obey, so he took hold of Pierre's legs, while Frederic grabbed Etienne's. They dragged the bodies through to the Egyptian section, past the yellow stone walls that displayed many carved Egyptian hieroglyphics. Joey recognized the same dead end he and Marie had come to when they were first taken to greet Pierre in his secret underground room.

After Frederic touched the button inside the cartouche, the door opened, just as it had the first time. The memorable damp, musty smell hit Joey in the face. Joey felt his heart sink as he dragged Pierre's dead body down the spiral staircase into the cold dark underground. Frederic had promised him his life, but Joey knew he wasn't out of the woods yet.

At the bottom of the steps, Frederic picked up the two dead bodies and stacked them up on top of the other two dead officers inside one of the cells as though they were pieces of meat. When he'd finished, he turned and put a heavy arm across Joey's shoulder. A chill ran down Joey's spine.

'Step inside,' Frederic ordered.

'What are you doing? You said you were not going to kill me.'

Frederic pushed him inside and slammed the cell door shut. 'Where is the tomb, Joey?'

'If I tell you, what guarantee do I have that you'll let me live?'

'You don't,' said Frederic. 'But since you've been a worthy adversary I promise you I will not shoot you.' He released the empty clip from his nine-millimeter and cocked out the one and only bullet left in the chamber. He then threw the useless gun deep inside the cell among the scattered paintings. 'Where is the tomb?' he asked.

Joey sighed, his heart racing as he frantically thought about how he was going to convey this information.

His gaze fell on the mountains of moldy paintings piled up behind him. Turning back to Frederic, Joey stepped forward and grabbed the cell's bars. 'Actually, the painting didn't give me the location Pierre said it would.'

'What do you mean?' said Frederic, eyes narrowing.

'It gave me only half the clue. But it did say where I could find the other half.'

'I'm listening.'

'Not many people know this, but Leonardo da Vinci painted two *Mona Lisas*. *La Joconde* and the Isleworth *Mona Lisa*. She was the prequel to his famous *Mona Lisa*. She's a much younger version and is now owned by a Swiss consortium. She has spent forty years in a bank vault in London.'

'What's in the painting?'

'If you carefully examine the real *Mona Lisa* you'll find numbers and letters. The letter S is found in the left eye and the letter L in the right eye. A number 72 is also found under the arched bridge in the background.'

'So what?' said Frederic. 'What's that got to do with anything?'

'In the Isleworth *Mona Lisa*, in the same places, you will find two other letters and two other numbers. Do you see where I'm going with this?'

'GPS coordinates,' blurted out Frederic.

Joey smiled. 'Put all those numbers together and you will find the tomb.'

Frederic couldn't believe it had been so easy. The American had been a pushover after all. Armed with the knowledge his boss would have dreamed to know, Frederic now dug his hand in his pocket and took out a box of matches. It was time to silence the troublesome American once and for all. Apart from anything else, Joey knew too much about what Frederic had done in the past few hours, and it was imperative that Frederic remain undetected. He had spent too many years evading the authorities to be caught now. He knew he would not have been clearly identifiable in the footage from the surveillance cameras outside the Louvre. It was dark, and the bright lights that shone out from the pyramid were at his back, which would have cast him in silhouette. But these deaths at the Louvre would bring down greater scrutiny than he'd ever been associated with before. He hoped that with the death of Joey his name wouldn't reach the ears of anyone in government, who would love nothing more than to bring him in.

'What are you doing?' said Joey, suddenly realizing the gun wasn't the only way he could be killed. He'd been a fool. If Frederic flicked a match onto the hundreds of oil paintings in his cell, the fire would burn unstoppably. It would spread to the other cells, creating the deadly carbon monoxide that would ultimately end his life, if the flames didn't get there first. 'Stop! You're going to burn down the Louvre.'

'No, I won't,' said Frederic as he watched the match come alive between his fingers. 'The fire will not be able to penetrate the stone walls down here.'

'Please don't.'

'See you in the next life, Joey.'

Frederic flicked the match inside the cell, and Joey found himself in a scene from hell.

Chapter 56

Before Joey could do anything about it, the mountain of canvases burst into flame, and as he had anticipated, the fire spread along the corridor of cells with shocking speed. Holding on to the bars, Joey kept a safe distance away from the heat of the fire. Frederic disappeared into his dead boss's room and emerged a few moments later carrying a small notebook that must have belonged to Pierre.

'*Bon voyage*,' he said with a nasty smile as he bolted upstairs, shutting the only exit door. Then Joey heard a loud jamming sound, and realized that Frederic must have destroyed the door's opening mechanism. Frederic had made sure that no one was coming in or getting out anytime soon.

Joey knew he didn't have long. As thick smoke began to fill the air, he dove to the floor and searched the dead police officers' pockets for anything he could use. Frederic must have taken their weapons; their holsters were empty. Joey paused to rip off a piece of fabric from an officer's jacket to cover his nose and mouth from the toxic fumes building in the air.

Returning to his search, he found a tactical LED rechargeable flashlight hanging from one officer's belt; it was 6.5 inches long with a solid aluminum alloy-housing frame. He snatched it up and shone it around the edges of the bars, looking to see if there were any weak points. To his surprise he saw a small hole in the wall, and chip marks in the sandstone. He wasn't the first person to have tried to escape this way, he realized. He would have to succeed where they had failed. Using the flashlight as a pick, Joey chipped feverishly at the hole. The gap wasn't big enough to escape through, but with a bit of hard pounding it might loosen up the crumbling walls around the bars enough to slide between them.

Chip … Chip … Chip … The flashlight hit the wall and small pieces of sandstone flew in every direction. Joey coughed into the material protecting his nose and mouth as the dust mingled with the acrid smoke in the air.

His eyes now streaming and his muscles burning with the effort, he forced himself to keep pounding the wall harder and harder. It was get out or die. Then, to make matters worse, the flashlight's head broke off and rolled away outside the cell.

The blazing hot flames were encroaching. Joey was weak, injured and exhausted. He let the piece of material covering his nose and mouth fall to the floor. He would rather die of smoke inhalation than be burned, he decided. He inhaled the smoke and blinked rapidly as ash stung his eyes. Slumping against the wall in the corner of the dingy cell, he waited for the fumes to work their magic.

Then he saw it.

As if an angel had put it there for him to see, in all its shiny, silver glory.

Three feet or so outside his cell was the single bullet that Frederic had cocked out from his gun's chamber. The same gun that he'd thrown somewhere within Joey's cell. Joey's eyes darted to the raging fire, crackling and devouring everything in its path. He needed to find that weapon.

Adrenaline surged through him as he pushed himself away from the wall and approached the blazing heat of the fire. He used his feet to kick paintings out of the way while he rummaged frantically through the burning detritus. Sparks ignited, and he shielded his face from the veil of choking, noxious smoke. Sweat cascaded down Joey's face, and his cough worsened with every breath. The carbon monoxide that had built up in the room must have been at near fatal levels, he thought. He had minutes, at best, or it would be all over. It was either find that gun or die trying.

Seconds later, among the inferno, he found it.

Frederic's nine-millimeter pistol was lying there, the flames reflecting off its shiny black surface. He picked it up and felt the heat in his palms. There was no time to spare. He dove back to the cell bars and reached out for the bullet, but even with his arm fully extended, it was still inches out of reach. Looking around desperately, Joey grabbed the broken flashlight and, holding it between his fingertips, managed to knock the bullet close enough to grab hold of.

In seconds he had loaded the weapon into its chamber and fired it at the cell lock, breaking it in two. With frantic speed, he opened the cell door and hurried into the corridor, where he considered his next move. He couldn't get out through the broken door into the Egyptian section. He would have to try his luck in Napoleon's secret room. He might be able to call for help and alert the authorities from there, too. The sizable, stone-walled room would buy him some time until the help arrived.

Keeping low to the ground he moved, barging open one of the giant-sized wooden doors and slamming it shut behind him. The air was fresher in here, and he gulped some deep breaths before instinct kicked in once more. With a sense of urgency, he ripped down some of the old decorative curtains that hung around the room and wedged them under the door to block out the smoke. He knew it wasn't the fire that would kill him; it was the toxic smoke. His barricade helped a little, but wisps of smoke were still getting in through the smaller holes and cracks in the old timber doors.

Joey sprinted to Pierre's desk and picked up the phone, but there was no dial tone. He hit the receiver a couple of times to check, but got no response. Frederic must have cut all communication lines.

'Fucking hell,' breathed Joey. 'I'm going to die in here.'

Panic rose in his chest, but he knew that if he didn't stay calm, he would have no chance of surviving this ordeal. He took a breath and tried to slow his galloping heart. He had ten minutes or so before Napoleon's room was consumed with fumes, he reasoned, if the wooden doors didn't ignite during that time. That would exponentially speed up the process of his death, as a deadly billowing smoke surge would come rushing in.

He had to act, and he had to act now. Joey began to search the room as meticulously as he could. Then, to his astonishment, he saw something peculiar and unexpected.

The trailing lines of smoke that had entered the room were drifting toward the south wall. Joey immediately approached the wall, where an enormous, ten-by-six-foot tapestry hung. It depicted Napoleon on a horse with his army marching through the Arc de Triomphe in victory. With both hands, he yanked it off the wall, taking the hooks with it.

In front of him on the stone wall was an exquisite carved image of an eagle in side-on profile. It possessed a bright red eye on top of which were two scepters running across each other: a sign of authority and power.

The smoke seemed to be drawn to the edges of the carving.

'Napoleon built an escape route,' said Joey to himself in wonder, and began trying to push on the stone. 'If the smoke can escape, so can I.' After several fruitless attempts to move the stone, he remembered how he had entered this underground chamber in the first place: by simply pressing on the cartouche. The eagle's red eye now caught his attention. *Could it be that simple?* he thought.

He pushed it.

The three-by-three-foot piece of stone that sat underneath the eagle scraped backwards and moved to the side, revealing a narrow path. Joey let out a relieved bark of laughter. He couldn't believe it, but he wasn't going to waste any time thinking about it.

Joey snatched one of three battery-operated lanterns he found on Pierre's desk and, switching it on and bending low, he stepped into the darkness of the tunnel. After about sixteen feet, he exited into a vast underground chamber where he could see the original foundations of the castle walls.

The musty smell of damp was in the air, but it smelled sweet to Joey, who was just happy to be away from the poisonous gasses and smoke of the fire. He held the lantern up high in the underground crypt, illuminating the brick walls. He remembered reading that the fortress dated back to the reign of Philippe Auguste, the French king who had paved the streets and built the walls of Paris. After a short walk along one wall, Joey's lantern shone on a picture he recognized; another eagle with two scepters. Without hesitation, he pressed his thumb into the bird's eye once again. And just like that, another secret door opened and he was miraculously inside the Medieval section of the Louvre, where the lights were all still on.

Leaving his lantern on the ground, Joey hurried through the lower level of the museum's Sully Wing, following the path through to an archway of steps that led him from the Medieval Louvre back into the Egyptian collection. He approached the exit in a hurry.

He decided that this time he would exit through the north end, and jogged across the underground Carrousel du Louvre shopping center that exited onto Rue de Rivoli. He ran up the escalator and passed a red-and-white vertical banner which read *Carrousel*.

At the top, he took a moment to catch his breath, then proceeded to the glass doors that led to the outside world. To his surprise they were left wide open. He thought that was strange, but didn't care, he wanted to get as far away from this place as he could.

He exited the doors with haste.

Then, from out of nowhere, he was ambushed.

Chapter 57

A dozen or so commandos wearing bulletproof vests and carrying M16 machine guns circled Joey. They looked to be the equivalent of the Paris SWAT team. They came in hard and they came in screaming.

'On your knees!' yelled someone in English.

Joey had no more fight left in him. He dropped to his knees, blinded by the incoming flashlights. Frozen, he raised his hands in surrender and laced his fingers behind his head.

'On the ground!' a deep voice commanded.

Joey obliged and dropped to his stomach. Lying there on the cold, wet surface, he felt a knee dig into his spine. His hands were pushed behind his back and handcuffs slapped tight against his wrists.

Joey was taken to a dark BMW four-wheel drive that had been left parked on the curb with its motor still running. His head was nudged down to avoid hitting the car's metal frame and as he sat up in the back seat, it immediately sped away.

Gazing out the window at high speed, everything was a blur. The dark streets of Paris were empty and the heavy fog was slowly drifting away as dawn neared. After about ten minutes they reached their destination.

Joey saw a sign reading *Rue Saint-Dominique* before the BMW drove through two giant green doors in a building of textured stone. The armed men on either side of the doors appeared to be military soldiers. The vehicle drove inside and parked where two other armed soldiers were waiting.

Joey's handcuffs were removed and he was escorted into a towering fortified building. The letters DGSE were mounted above the front reception desk. He had heard about this: it was the General Directorate for External Security, otherwise known as the French intelligence agency. In spite of his exhaustion he felt a frisson of fear. He might well have got into serious trouble in the last few days, but he was no threat to France.

On the third floor of the establishment, he was guided to a corner office and told to wait. The room was presidential with an attractive outlook over the city. A large antique desk was on one side, accompanied by a wall of shelving units in the same color scheme. Two expensive fabric couches faced each other atop a blue rug that seemed to be the centerpiece of the room. It was like being in the Oval Office, Joey thought. Instead of the White House seal, though, was the blue logo of the DGSE. It was designed to look like a globe of the world cut up in pieces, with a stand-out red section that represented France.

Hung on the walls were many photographs of influential people Joey could identify such as Nelson Mandela, the former pope John Paul II, and the Minister of State for Antiquities Affairs in Egypt, Zahi Hawass. Joey remembered his face from watching documentaries about ancient Egypt on the Discovery Channel. There were many others with a Middle Eastern appearance whom he didn't recognize, but he knew they were probably important people. Also on the walls were war medals and two old rifles from World War I, but what caught Joey's eye was an unusual framed papyrus image of the sun. The ornate yellow image had sixteen separate pieces forming the sunrays, which each extruded outward to a sharp point. It was a strange arty piece compared to the other decorations in this office, Joey thought.

'Sorry to keep you waiting, Joey,' said a man's voice in accented English, and a man of about seventy stepped into the room. He had thick snow-white hair and a distinctive scar on his temple. If it hadn't been for that mark on his face, he would have been an attractive man for his age. His posture was strong and he was clearly in excellent condition. Joey could tell from the way he carried himself that this was a man of power.

'I am the general in charge here. My name is Julien Bonnet.'

'I'm sorry, sir,' said Joey, trying to keep his voice steady. 'I think there's been a misunderstanding.'

'Relax, son, you're not in any trouble,' said the general, moving behind his desk and taking a seat in his high-backed leather chair.

Joey was a bit taken aback by this. 'If I'm not in trouble, why am I here?'

Julien rolled up his long shirtsleeve to reveal a tattoo on his wrist. It depicted a picture of a lion with wings and a sun shape that hovered above the lion's head. It was the same sun shape that was up on his wall.

'You are here because of Major Frederic Dubois.'

Joey gave a sigh of relief and worry when he heard that name.

'Until recently we thought he had been killed with his team five years ago in an operation you are not classified to know about. Then we identified one of his men, who was found dead in suspicious circumstances in the Seine River.'

'Are you talking about Thierry?' said Joey quickly.

'Yes, and we just got word from the police that another body has been found up river, a body with a remarkable resemblance to that of his twin, Thierry. Any idea whose it is?'

Joey's eyes found Julien's. 'Please tell me my friends are safe.'

'How do you think we knew where you were?' said the general, planting both hands on his desk. 'Once your friends reached the police department we were instantly notified, and here we are.'

'Thank God,' gasped Joey. Relief washed through his body. 'So why am I here?'

'Look, Joey. As soon as we're done here a car will take you to your friends and you're all free to go, but first, would you happen to know where Frederic might be going? Any intel that helps us catch him would be much appreciated. We have reason to believe he might become a security risk and want to do harm to his country.'

'Sir … I just watched him kill three police officers and the Louvre curator as if they were worth nothing, but if I may, Pierre Savard is to blame for all this. He was the reason why they were after me. He was after a painting, I —'

'I know,' Julien said, cutting him off. 'I was informed of these goings-on by your girlfriend, Marie. And rest assured, we will be looking into everything, in time.'

'I was lucky to escape,' said Joey, his voice raised.

'Did Frederic tell you where he was going?'

Joey stared at the old man warily, but then nodded his head. 'He didn't tell me, exactly, but I have a good idea he might be going to England to see the Isleworth *Mona Lisa*. He thinks he'll find letters and numerals in the painting like in the *Mona Lisa* and together they will form GPS coordinates showing the location of a lost tomb.'

A smile erupted on Julien's face. 'Whose tomb?'

'Alexander the Great's,' said Joey, and he watched as the general's eyes widened and he shook his head in stunned surprise. Then he regained his composure and said, 'GPS ... I can't believe Frederic of all people fell for that.'

'I was desperate, sir,' replied Joey with a smile. 'I remembered my girlfriend telling me something about the Isleworth *Mona Lisa* one day and it stuck in my head.'

'You have put yourself in grave danger, though,' said the commander, the smile fading from his face. 'What do you think he's going to do when he finds out GPS was invented in the late 1960s? He will come back for you.'

Joey swallowed hard at the thought and shrugged. He hadn't had a chance to think that far ahead.

The general picked up the phone on his desk and spoke quickly into it in French. Joey heard him mention Frederic and the Isleworth *Mona Lisa* and gathered he was ordering Frederic's capture.

'What now?' asked Joey after Julien dropped his phone back on its dock.

'With any luck Frederic will be obtained and you will be safe, but let's talk off the record now, like two old friends.' Julien clasped his hands together in front of him. He had a way with words, Joey acknowledged. Joey felt quite comfortable and at ease, though he knew he should remain on guard. It confirmed why Julien had so many influential relationships around the world.

'Okay,' said Joey. 'What do you want to talk about?'

'God knows how you survived these past few days, and if I've put the pieces together correctly, it seems it has all been because of a conspiracy theory. Do you know yourself where this tomb is, and most importantly, do you believe such a tomb exists?'

Joey forced a smile and said, 'I didn't until I reached Paris.'

'Do you know what I believe?' said the general, leaning in on his desk.

'What's that, sir?'

'I believe some things are never meant to be found. They are fairy tales passed down through generations, to tease treasure hunters and art historians like the curator.'

'I think you're wrong, sir,' replied Joey with a confidence he hadn't known he felt until now. 'I think it does exist, and somehow I'm involved because of what my great-grandfather did back in 1911. If none of this were true, why would my family spend a century protecting that painting? You said it yourself, I was lucky to have survived. But I believe I survived because it's my destiny to get to the bottom of this secret.'

'So it seems,' said Julien with a hint of a smile. Then

he stood up, sauntered around his desk and offered his hand. Joey shook it, startled by the general's strong grip.

'I wish you well on your journey, Joey, but be warned, if you do find what you seek, then remember this: to sit on the throne of the great king, you need to bow down and worship his pagan symbol, the sun god.'

'Sun god,' repeated Joey in some confusion. Perhaps the old man was a bit past his prime after all. Then, just like that, after a quick wave of the old man's hand, two commandos stepped in and took Joey away.

Sitting in the car, Joey watched as the gray light of morning bled through the Paris streets and the first orange-hued rays of sunrise kissed the cobblestones. He was dropped off in front of a familiar hotel. He smiled, exited the vehicle and spared a glance at the awning that had saved his life when he'd jumped off the second-story balcony.

The commandos escorted him up to his penthouse, where another soldier was standing guard in front of the door. He nodded when he saw them and let them enter.

Inside, two worried eyes stared at him as if they had seen a ghost. Marie's hands trembled as she ran into Joey's arms. Joey squeezed his girl tight and closed his eyes. 'One thing is true,' he said in her ear.

'What's that?' she asked, hanging on like she was never going to let go.

Joey grabbed her shoulders gently and gazed into her hazel eyes. 'Paris will definitely be a city I'll never forget.'

Marie laughed and cried with tears of joy.

A cheerful voice behind Joey now shouted, 'JP!'

Joey turned to see Boyce, who was also waiting with open arms. 'Yeah, we survived,' he joked.

Overjoyed, Joey embraced his young friend. 'Thank you,' he said. 'I couldn't have got through that without you.' Even though Boyce did not know it yet, Joey was going to make sure he never needed to worry about money again.

Marie interrupted them, her eyes searching for something. 'Hey, hang on, where's the *Mona Lisa*?'

Joey had forgotten; she hadn't seen what he had done to the painting. He desperately tried to hide how fearful he was about sharing the news. 'I'm sorry, babe, I had no choice,' he said, trying to control the tremor in his voice. 'I threw it in the fire so they would not get their hands on the secret. It was the only way.'

'You did what?' Marie clenched her fists, her eyes bright. 'I can't believe you did that,' she said, her voice betraying her despair. 'Leonardo's legacy is gone.'

'That wasn't da Vinci's legacy, I understand it now,' said Joey, reaching over and placing his hand on her shoulder to comfort her. 'His legacy was the location of the greatest tomb that has never been found. Don't you want to be the one to find it? It was fate that handed me the painting and that's why I'm going to finish what my great-grandfather started. I want you both to come with me. Let's find out for ourselves if this tomb really does exist. Who's in?'

Chapter 58

Pierre's Rolls-Royce pulled up at the airport hangar and parked near his jet plane, which was resting under the enormous curved roof of corrugated iron. In the vehicle, Frederic flipped through the pages of the notepad he had stolen from Pierre's office. An old document fell out onto the leather passenger's seat, but he paid it no attention. He was searching for a particular page he had seen before. Then his hands fell still. He'd found it: a hand-drawn image of the *Mona Lisa* with writing all over it. It was this page that he had suddenly recalled when Joey had first mentioned the GPS coordinates.

On the *Mona Lisa's* right eye was written the letter L, and on her left eye the letter S.

Under the arched bridge in the background were the numbers 72.

Frederic assumed the letter S in the *Mona Lisa* stood for south, so that meant the L probably stood for Latitude, because latitude ran north and south. Now that he was halfway there, he was hoping to find in the Isleworth *Mona Lisa* the other half that gave the longitude coordinate, which would be either east or west.

Scanning the notepad, he read some of the other

notes Pierre had scribbled over the years. Leonardo da Vinci had been fascinated by religion and mysticism. One of Pierre's notes suggested that the number '72' was significant, as it was found in the Kabbalah, a form of Jewish mysticism, and also in Christianity. Even when considered separately, '7' was full of symbolic associations in both Judaism and Christianity, for example the creation of the world in seven days and the number of God, and the number '2' may have been a reference to the duality of the male and female. Frederic laughed. Only he knew the numbers' true significance.

Tossing the notepad onto the seat, Frederic climbed out of the car and approached the Eurocopter AS350 waiting on the helipad. The pilot stood beside the open door and welcomed Pierre's right-hand man, who stepped inside and sat in the copilot's seat.

'I need you to take me to London ASAP,' ordered Frederic, clipping on his seatbelt.

'Will Monsieur Savard be joining us, sir?' asked the young pilot, moving his headgear into place.

'No, it's just me today. How long will it take?'

'Just a little over an hour, sir.'

'Okay. Let's move.'

The blades began to beat in the air. The single-engine French-built helicopter lifted off and they were on their way. Frederic watched as the pilot competently guided the chopper to a smooth altitude. He appreciated the fine machinery, familiar with its capabilities, having flown many of them in his prime.

The picturesque landscape of Paris came into view as the sun shot through the gray clouds. The iconic Eiffel Tower towered above all. The Arc de Triomphe and its colossal roundabout dwarfed the ant-sized cars trying to circumnavigate it. The Obelisk of Luxor, the Tuileries Garden, the glass pyramid of the Louvre, the Notre Dame Cathedral and the long Seine River with its many small offshoots could be seen from far above as well.

Thirty minutes into the flight the clean-shaven pilot asked, 'So why are you going to London, if you don't mind me asking?'

'Pierre has me looking into some GPS coordinates,' said Frederic, still focused on the land below. 'He claims to have found some in a painting.'

'Wow, that sounds interesting,' said the pilot, keeping the joystick steady.

'Speaking of coordinates, where are we now?' asked Frederic.

The pilot pointed to the coordinates on the GPS dashboard navigational system, which read 50°55'37.5" north and 1°45'56.0" east.

'In my line of work, I don't know what we would have done without GPS,' said Frederic, slowly shaking his head as he remembered some close calls. 'The number of times we were surrounded by the enemy and airlifted to safety …'

'Yeah, thank God for Roger Easton.'

'Who's Roger Easton?'

'He was the man who began the satellite tracking systems in the late 1960s.'

Frederic paused, his frown lines becoming more pronounced as he took in the information he had just learned. Then he asked a question he already knew the answer to. 'So a Renaissance painting could not have —'

'Pardon?' repeated the pilot.

Suddenly, Frederic went as red as a beetroot, clenched his hands into fists and let out a mouthful of fury. 'Motherfucker!!!'

The pilot looked alarmed. 'What's wrong, sir? Is it something I said? I didn't mean to be disrespectful.'

'I've just been outsmarted,' retorted Frederic. 'No one outsmarts me and gets away with it!'

The helicopter had now reached the English Channel separating southern England from northern France. Frederic glanced out the window at the waves crashing violently against the base of the crumbling cliffs.

'Stop the helicopter,' commanded Frederic.

'What do you mean, stop?' said the pilot in confusion.

'Hover the chopper low over the ocean and jump out,' ordered Frederic.

'What! Are you out of your mind? Why?'

Frederic didn't like repeating himself. He took out his nine-millimeter and aimed it at the pilot's head. 'You have ten seconds.'

The pilot froze when he saw the barrel of the weapon pointed his way. 'Please don't,' he begged. 'I have children.'

'If you want to see your kids again, jump. I'm giving you a choice to live. So if I were you, I would take it.'

With shaking hands, the pilot took his headgear off and hovered the aircraft low enough to cause the water to ripple. 'I'm going to die from hyperthermia.'

'Come on, I don't have all day,' said Frederic. 'Jump or the gun goes off.'

The pilot opened his side door and the cold air of the sea filled the cabin, blowing their hair all over the place.

'You have five seconds,' shouted Frederic over the noise of the rotors.

'Three … two … one.'

The pilot jumped feet-first into the freezing water.

Frederic glanced down at the dark ocean below and after a couple of seconds, he saw a head pop up for air. Alone in the fifty-degree-Fahrenheit water and fighting the swell, the pilot began to swim toward the mainland as his hijacked helicopter banked right and headed back toward France.

Chapter 59

'Is it true? Pierre is dead?' asked Marie.

'He is,' replied Joey. 'The bastard got what was coming to him.'

'What about Frederic?' said Marie. 'I'm not going anywhere if he's still out there.'

'No, that's been taken care of,' said Joey dryly. 'The DGSE will be waiting for him when he lands in England.'

'And why is he going to England?'

''Cause he thinks the Isleworth *Mona Lisa* holds the final clue to the tomb's location,' said Joey.

Marie gazed into Joey's blue eyes and sighed with glee. 'Clever boy.'

'See, when you talk history, I do listen.' Joey chuckled. 'One thing's for sure. When he lands, he's going to get the surprise of his life.'

Marie stood there in thought, her gaze drifting across the room to young Boyce, who was emptying out the bar fridge. These last couple of days had been hell, but with Frederic taken care of a massive burden was lifted; they had no one to run from anymore. Pierre, Lamond and Thierry were all dead, and Frederic was about to be arrested by the DGSE.

'We're in the clear, Marie, let's do this,' said Joey.

'Come on, let's make history together. You in?'

'Okay,' she said, nodding her head. 'Let's do this.'

'Hey, Boy, you in?'

'Of course,' said Boyce, grinning widely. 'I was in the day you blew up my boat.'

Using the computer terminal located within his penthouse suite, Joey booked accommodation in Cyprus and three tickets on a flight leaving the following morning at 9 am.

'Larnaca,' read Marie off the screen. 'Now that's somewhere I've never been.'

'It's in Cyprus,' said Boyce, standing behind her and taking a large bite out of a Mars Bar.

'Ah yes, Cyprus,' said Marie. 'The small Greek island in the middle of the eastern Mediterranean Sea, close to Turkey, Syria and Egypt.'

'So you do know of it?' asked Joey.

'I do,' she replied.

'How long is the flight?' interrupted Boyce.

'Three hours and twenty minutes to Athens for a quick stop, then one hour forty minutes from there,' read Joey from the flight itinerary in front of him. 'How about we all get some rest today, because tomorrow we're going on a treasure hunt.'

'There is just one small problem,' said Boyce.

'What's that,' asked Joey.

'I don't have a passport.'

'You could have told me this before I booked the tickets! Was it destroyed in the boat?'

'No, like I said it's a small problem. I just need to contact my father in prison and find out which safety deposit box he keeps all our valuable items in, including my passport. I just need a couple of hours to go pick it up. It's still early Friday morning, all the banks are open. Trust me I'll be right back.'

And to his word, he did just that.

Chapter 60

Saturday, 9 am

Inside the Airbus, Joey and Marie sat together on the right-hand side of the plane, looking out over the plane's wings. Boyce occupied the two seats behind them and was busy touching anything that could be moved. He opened and closed his tray, pressed the buttons on the TV in front of him and moved his chair seat backwards and forward like an inquisitive toddler.

Marie grabbed and squeezed Joey's hand and smiled. He squeezed right back as the plane took off along the runway and they sat in companionable silence as they ascended to 30,000 feet.

'I can't believe Alexander's tomb is in Cyprus,' Marie said after drinks had been served, taking a sip from her coffee cup and placing it back in the indentation of her seat tray. 'Tell me again the clue you said you found in the painting?'

Joey had memorized it.

'The great son of Zeus was buried with treasures not just of wealth, but of information. But be warned of what you might find. Start your journey at the sacred place of Cyprus and continue past the winding road

that will lead you to the goddess of love and beauty.
The baths will take the quest to an underwater cave. In
it you will find the answers you seek.'

'Wow, that's so *Da Vinci Code*,' said Marie. 'I get
shivers just thinking about it.'

'Tell me more about this country,' asked Joey, turning
in his chair to face her. 'You said before you knew of it.
I didn't even know it existed until yesterday.'

'Well, Cyprus is an extremely small country, but has
lots of history. It's been invaded and ruled by everyone
from the Egyptians in the sixth century B.C.E to King
Richard the First of England in 1191. It was he who
later sold the land to the Knights Templar. Alexander
himself ruled Cyprus during the Hellenistic period.'

'So who does it belong to now?' asked Joey.

'After an invasion by Turkey in 1974, the island is
now divided into the Greek southern side and a Turkish
northern side, but the majority of it is Greek, who are
Christian Orthodox.'

'So it makes sense that the tomb of Alexander the
Great might be there,' said Joey. 'He once ruled it, and
its close proximity to Egypt may have meant it was
relatively easy to move his body there.'

'Yeah, Cyprus is only a day's boat ride from Egypt
and yes, it was ruled by Alexander the Great, but I can't
help thinking that something doesn't seem right,' said
Marie. 'I guess we'll soon find out.'

Chapter 61

The Aegean Airline flight landed at Larnaca International Airport. It was 3:00 pm Cyprus time, an hour ahead of the French time, and the weather was slightly warmer but still gray. After hiring a Mercedes-Benz E-class with Navman from the airport rental car service, they set off for the island's far west, to the town of Paphos.

The small villa they had booked perched on a hillside. It was a charming traditional Greek home with smooth white rendered walls and blue-painted window frames and doors. The area was ironically called Aphrodite Hills. It would have been the perfect little place to stay during the summer season, being so close to the beaches and attractions, but on the positive side it was dirt cheap in the cooler season. The interior, much like the outside, was Mediterranean in style and décor, with white rendered walls and blue doors and architraves. A feature painting of the Greek Island of Santorini was up on the wall. There was no sea view, but the backyard backed onto a large farm, giving the place a relaxing and rural setting.

After sleeping the night and having a continental breakfast, they headed into Paphos, where they stopped at a local scuba-gear shop and picked up some supplies for their adventure.

Boyce, who had not said much since they'd entered the country, sat back in his seat and stared out the car window, seemingly awestruck by everything the island had to offer. His mouth dropped open in amazement when they reached the wild, uninhabited Akamas region north of Paphos, with its spectacular landscapes.

Marie extracted a tourist map from the glove compartment and began to read aloud for all to hear. 'This area is named after Akamantas, an Athenian warrior and son of Theseus, who arrived here after the Trojan War.' She skipped a bit, and then started up again. 'Almost all the geological formations of Cyprus can be found here, from narrow deep valleys to caves, islets and gorges. The "Baths of Aphrodite" is an area in the Akamas between Polis and Cape Arnaoutis. Its name derives from a small grotto shaded by an old fig tree, in the waters of which, legend has it, the goddess Aphrodite used to bathe. According to mythology, this is where she met her lover Adonis. The site is on the Aphrodite Cultural Route, and that's where we're going, people.'

Indeed, road signs to Aphrodite's baths began to appear, and they followed them. Eventually, Joey turned into a gravel parking lot and the tires crunched as he pulled into a bay near the entrance to the site. Exiting the car, Marie and Boyce stretched their legs while Joey opened the trunk and took out a backpack. He put the car keys inside the bag's front slip and shouldered it onto his back.

Sharing an excited smile, the three followed the walkway that led to an impressive sight. A large restaurant was perched on the cliff top overlooking the crystal-clear waters of the ocean, and it appeared that several nature trails, including a 4.6-mile trek for the keen, also started at this point.

Boyce led the way. Joey and Marie followed, and soon the steep gradient of the incline began to take its toll on them. Boyce laughed at the oldies struggling to keep up and stopped for them to take a short break. The ocean views were breathtaking, the expanse of water like an endless oil painting.

Finally they reached the site they'd come to find. Three other tourists were standing around appreciating the natural grotto, so they stood quietly, taking it in. It was atmospheric; the bath itself was a spring in a rocky cleft, surrounded by greenery, with a small waterfall that continued to fall.

'Is that it?' whispered Joey, unimpressed. 'I was hoping to find an enormous waterfall.'

'Shut up,' said Marie teasingly, prodding an elbow into his stomach.

They approached an aging wooden fence. Joey stood in the middle, with Boyce on his left and Marie on his right. He took in the murky green water and the distant rocks, which were covered in green algae. 'I can't believe I have to go in there,' he said.

'On the bright side,' said Boyce, 'it sure beats swimming across that freezing lake. This should be a walk in the park for you.'

Two men dressed in bright orange and red long-sleeved running gear left the baths and continued with their jog. The remaining tourist, a male wearing a tracksuit and a blue baseball cap, was walking up the steps they had just climbed. He seemed to be obsessed with the ocean, stopping several times to take in the view.

'Let's wait until this guy leaves and then you can go in,' suggested Boyce.

Nodding, Joey scanned the cave that disappeared into the hill and pinpointed potential entrances. He would need to check them out when he got into the water. Two large "No Swimming" signs, both in Greek and English, were strategically placed. Joey couldn't help but smile. Swimming was the least of the misdemeanors he was about to commit. He waited patiently as the gray clouds above massed across the sun, and eventually asked Boyce discreetly, 'Is that man still there?'

Boyce turned his head to check and froze where he stood.

Marie also turned and instantly sighed.

A familiar ominous voice spoke up right beside them. 'I'm still here,' he said.

Joey felt ice creep up his spine. He knew that voice. He turned around slowly and the hairs on the back of his neck stood up. *It can't be*, he thought.

But it was.

Frederic had no gun, but his triumphant smile was all he needed.

Chapter 62

Joey was stunned. Frederic was supposed to be in England, 2234 miles away, and in the custody of the DGSE. How could the Frenchman possibly have known where they were going?

'You didn't think you could outsmart me, did you?' said Frederic, facing the three down as though he were a giant and they were his to command.

'How did you find us?' asked Joey.

Frederic flashed a mischievous grin. 'I installed a tracking device in your girlfriend's sneakers.'

Marie glanced down at her feet. 'Oh no, how could I have been so stupid?' Marie all but spat the words. 'They took my shoes from me when I was in the cell,' she explained to Joey. 'I wondered why at the time; I thought it was just a way to punish me. I should have known they had some other motive.'

'You could never have known,' said Joey, looking back at Frederic and shaking his head in disgust.

Joey stood helplessly, fearing what this crazy man was planning to do to them all now. This time there was no getaway car at hand or a river to escape on. All that was between them was a hair's breath of cool fresh Mediterranean air.

'I've got to say, you almost had me convinced,' said Frederic, staring into Joey's troubled eyes. 'I was on my way to England when I worked out your bullshit lie. That's when I decided to track you down. I should kill you right now!'

'Why don't you?' said Joey. 'What's stopping you?'

In one quick movement, Frederic pulled Marie to him and flashed out a razor-sharp blade, which he held against Marie's cheek. She gasped and her eyes opened wide in horror as she tried to pull away from the object.

'Stop,' said Joey, holding up his hands in surrender.

'If I'm going to kill anyone, Joey, you'll be the last. Do you understand?'

Joey nodded.

'Now, this is what's going to happen,' said Frederic, moving his blade from Marie's face and resting it point-first on Joey's athletic chest. 'I assume this shithole is the site. You're going to enter the baths and find me the entrance to the tomb.'

'Why do you want to find Alexander's tomb all of a sudden?' asked Marie, her voice quivering. 'This was Pierre's obsession, not yours.'

'Because of your boyfriend, I need to disappear, and to do this I need money. Pierre told me that if found, Alexander the Great's tomb would make Tutankhamun's look insignificant. He said it would contain gold, emeralds and diamonds, valued in the billions in today's currency.'

Frederic's eyes glittered as he continued. 'Listen … all I want is the money. Either you help me find it or I'll kill you all right now and search for it myself. Do you understand?'

Joey swallowed hard. There was no getting away from Frederic this time. He thought he could try the element of surprise and throw a sneaky punch, but it would be too risky with that blade so close to Marie. Frederic looked like he could take a few. He was trained for combat; he'd killed the guards in the Louvre without even breaking a sweat. And if they did somehow get away from him, where were they going to run? They were on a deserted hillside with no one around, and a good distance from the car.

Joey sighed. 'Okay, Frederic, have it your way, but if we help you find the gold, you have to let us go free.'

Frederic didn't respond. He lowered his knife and tucked it into the back of his pants, out of sight. 'Where do we start looking?' he asked.

Joey turned to the green murky water and pointed inside the cave. 'The clue I found in the *Mona Lisa* has led us here, to the baths of Aphrodite.'

'I don't get it,' said Frederic. 'Why is it in Cyprus? I thought Alexander was said to have been buried in Egypt.'

'I have no idea,' replied Joey. 'Maybe that's why no one has found it.'

Frederic turned to Marie, who seemed to be deep in thought. 'You're the historian and art expert. What's the connection?'

She shook her head and shrugged. 'I really don't know,' she said. 'Cyprus was one of the many countries Alexander took as his own. Something must have happened here.'

'How about we go find out what's down there. Joey, you go first,' said Frederic, clapping him hard on shoulder with a meaty hand. 'Remember, you try anything and I'll slit your girlfriend's throat. Got it?'

Joey nodded his head and Frederic let him go.

Joey took off his shoes and shirt and dug into his backpack, extracting a snorkel mask he had purchased in Paphos. Placing the goggles over his eyes, he climbed over the small wooden perimeter fence and entered the murky springwater.

The water was cold, but Joey walked straight in until he was knee deep, then dipped down to his shoulders. He swam in a breaststroke motion, keeping his mouth above the water. He passed the falling waterfall from above and thought of the Greek goddess Aphrodite bathing here, in a time when the springwaters were said to have been crystal clear.

They sure weren't now. Normally Joey would never have chosen to swim in water that was so muggy and thick. Glancing back at Marie, Boyce and Frederic on the hill above, Joey reluctantly dove his entire body under and began his hunt around the cave's perimeter. He searched for any holes or entry points into the hidden cave, but could hardly see through the gloom, let alone find anything. Along the walls, overgrown tree branches with large root systems had run down into the water and created a wall of their own.

'I can't see anything,' he said as he surfaced.

'Hang on,' said Frederic, who proceeded down the steps where they had first seen him and plucked a reasonably sized duffle bag out of some bushes. He'd come prepared. In the bag, taking up most of the space, was a mini-scuba tank, designed to get you to the surface in the event of an emergency, yet small enough that you would hardly know you were wearing it. After this Frederic pulled out professional-looking military snorkel gear, two Princeton Tec underwater flashlights, flares, a rope and a handful of underwater LED flash sticks used in night dives.

'Here, use this,' said Frederic, tossing an anti-fog snorkel mask and one of the underwater flashlights into the water.

Joey caught the items and took off his cheap mask, replacing it with Frederic's. He switched on the flashlight and went under again. The difference was remarkable. The strong glow of the flashlight cut through the murk, making everything much clearer.

Joey began to scan the rock wall for the second time. About five minutes into the search, his attention was caught by a shape he did not expect to see in this natural setting: low to the ground on the northern side of the wall was a hole that was square cut. It was undoubtedly man-made; too perfectly square to be there by chance, but had been obscured by tree roots. Shining the flashlight through a gap in the root system, Joey discerned a narrow tunnel that disappeared downward into the darkness.

Running out of air, he came up to the surface.

'I think I've found an opening,' he said, moving the goggles to sit on the top of his head. 'There's a tight entrance in the wall, definitely man-made, but there are too many tree roots in the way. I'll need help to cut them back.'

'Okay, everyone in the baths,' ordered Frederic.

'What? I'm not going in there,' said Marie. 'There could be snakes, and the water looks filthy. God knows what else is in there.'

'I said in the baths!' Frederic grabbed the back of her neck and began to squeeze.

'Let her go,' yelled Joey.

Boyce, his hands up, went to collect Joey's backpack. 'Okay, okay, no need to lose your cool,' he said. 'Come on, Marie, it'll be all right.'

Frederic let go of Marie's neck and Boyce helped guide her away from the psychopath, passing her one of the snorkels they had purchased.

They all took off their shoes and Boyce removed his shirt. Behind them, Frederic looked almost comical in his high-tech gear. He carried a blue rope around his neck and wore a belt that housed his sharp knife, a flashlight, and a group of clip-on LED light sticks. And to top it off, a cone-shaped waterproof mesh backpack was strapped around his shoulders.

Climbing down the bank, they entered the water. Marie took great pains to keep her head above the surface to avoid anything entering her mouth. Joey could see her peering fearfully downward as if she were wondering what could be lurking underneath her feet.

They approached Joey, who went straight to work, tugging on the tree roots, which were twisted tightly together. He braced his feet against the wall and yanked at them, tearing some of them out, but it was back-breaking work. The roots and branches were interconnected and overlapped each other like a giant underwater spider web. He managed to break some free and fold other more flexible roots back on themselves to keep them clear of the opening.

When Joey went up for air, Frederic dove under,

flashlight in hand, to search for the hole Joey had said he had found. He wanted to make sure this wasn't another one of the American's little tricks. He'd fooled him once; he wasn't going to fool him again. Checking back over his shoulder, he saw six legs treading water as he continued his search.

Then he saw it.

The hole was barely big enough for a large man like Frederic to squeeze through. It looked about three feet wide by three feet in height, a perfect square. There were still several thick roots growing over it, which Frederic dispatched easily with his knife. Then he shone his flashlight inside to see the cube-shaped tunnel that seemed to run on a downward angle. He unclipped one of his LED light sticks from his utility belt and cracked it on. The water around him turned emerald green. He tossed the stick down the hole and studied the drop, wanting to know how far they would need to swim to reach the other side. The green light drifted down the hole, illuminating the stone walls for about twenty seconds, then disappeared into the darkness as it fell out of the tunnel and dropped out of sight.

Above the water, waiting for Frederic to return to the surface, Marie quickly said, 'We can't trust him. When he gets what he wants, he's going to kill us.'

'Listen, right now we have to do what he says,' warned Joey. 'We have no other choice. If we run, he'll catch us before we can reach the car.'

'I have a bad feeling about this,' said Boyce, spitting out dirty water. His eyes now darted to the small bubbles at his side.

Frederic surfaced and removed his face mask. Clipping his flashlight back onto his belt, he stared at the three wary pairs of eyes. Then, without a word, he pulled out his knife.

Chapter 63

'What's that for?' asked Joey nervously, staring at the blade.

'It's a reminder for you that nobody messes with me,' said Frederic. 'Don't make me want to use it.'

'Did you see the entrance?' Joey asked, trying to change the subject. Joey knew what Frederic was doing. He had seen his father put the fear of God in a man many times before. Joey knew there was nothing a person wouldn't do if he or she was threatened with losing their life. He had to try to keep Boyce and Marie as calm as possible if they were to have any hope of getting out of this alive.

The silence grew around them as Frederic spat water out of his mouth. 'Yes, I saw the hole,' he said. 'It goes down on a forty-five-degree angle and is just big enough to swim through.'

Joey agreed with a nod.

Frederic gestured to Boyce. 'The teen goes first.'

Boyce's eyes opened wide in terror. 'Me ... Why me?' he squeaked.

'Because I said so,' replied Frederic. 'And you're the smallest.'

Boyce turned to Joey, panic written all over his face.

There was no denying it, he was petrified. 'What if the path leads nowhere and I run out of air?' he said, his voice shaking.

'There's an opening at the other end,' said Frederic. 'I threw a light stick down there and after several feet it dropped out of sight. The main tunnel should lead you to an open underwater area, and from there you should be able to get into the cave.'

'I don't know,' whined Boyce, his white, pinched face looking stricken. 'Who knows what's down there?' he added. 'So I have to hold my breath down a descending tunnel, to a place that may or may not have any kind of air pockets to breathe in?'

'Look ... like it or not, you're going down this tunnel,' ordered Frederic. 'Take Joey's flashlight and mask. Here ... take a flare and a couple of my light sticks, too,' he said, unclipping them from his belt with ease. 'Light them up when you're through to the other side.'

Frederic lifted the blue rope up and over his head. 'Lift up your leg,' he said to Boyce.

'What's that for?' Boyce asked.

'It's for when you get through. Tie the rope somewhere inside and give us three strong tugs to indicate you're okay. Do you understand?'

'You mean if I'm still alive,' said Boyce darkly, placing the two flares he'd been given in his shorts pocket. He put the snorkel mask on last and allowed Frederic to tie a handcuff knot to his right leg, a knot Joey knew was used by search-and-rescue operations.

'You'll be okay,' said Joey, clasping his shoulder. 'You can do this, Boyce, just stay calm and hold your breath.'

Boyce gave Joey a worried smile. It was the first

time Joey had called him by his full name. Marie swam over and patted the French teen on his back for encouragement. Then Boyce took three long, deep breaths before diving head-first through the tight opening and into the tunnel.

Boyce plunged deep into the tunnel and tried not to think about the creatures that might be lurking in this darkness. His kicking feet did most of the work as he held the flashlight in front of him. It felt like it took an eternity to reach the end of the tunnel, but as Frederic had said, it emerged into an open area. Now freed from the narrow tunnel, Boyce's lungs began to burn, and he swam upward in search of air. His feet and his free hand working overtime, he clawed through the water, praying that this would not be where it all ended. Then, like a dolphin breaking the surface, Boyce emerged out of the water and gasped for air.

He sensed he was in a vast internal space but he couldn't get a good look with the flashlight still in the water. Floating on his back, he propped the flashlight on his chest and took in what was around him. Amazingly, the first thing he saw were columns – large Greek-style columns. As he turned himself around in the water, he saw more columns. They were everywhere, circling the pool.

Wanting a better viewpoint, he swam over to his right to a small stone ledge into which three stone steps had been cut. Pulling himself up out of the water, he took out his only single flare and fired it above his head into the open air.

The dazzling incandescent flare burst to light around him, revealing an enormous circular space like the top dome of a church. The perfectly aligned columns circled the room and continued to drop deep into the water below.

'Wow,' Boyce breathed.

Boyce then cracked a light stick and tossed it on the ground, lighting up the place an emerald green. He then cracked open his last light stick and used it as a guide to walk around the perimeter of the pool to the opposite side. The water in the center of this chasm now looked completely black.

'What is this place?' Boyce asked himself. His eyes drifted to twelve spherical stone tablets that also circled the ledge. They were strategically placed and perfectly alike, rising about eight inches from the ground. Boyce roamed around the circle, taking in the deeply chiseled drawings on each of the tablets' faces.

They were all different and beautifully carved.

He saw images of a trident, bolt of lightning, dove, owl, lyre, skull, war helmet, caduceus, peacock, lion with sun shape, columns and lastly a bow and arrow.

He felt like Indiana Jones in *The Raiders of the Lost Ark* seeing something that had been hidden for God knows how long. As he walked around the underwater crypt the rope around his ankle snagged on a tablet and tugged on his leg, which reminded him that it was time to tell the others that he had made it to safety.

Boyce removed the rope from his leg and tied it around one of the thick columns, then pulled it with three strong tugs to signal to the others.

Minutes later, one by one, Joey, Marie and finally Frederic appeared in the cave, using the rope as a guide. As each emerged they looked stunned, their eyes widening and their mouths falling ajar as they gazed upon the green-lit dome they had just entered.

'Holy crap, what a cave,' said Joey as he climbed onto the ledge.

Marie was more concerned with getting out of the water and away from Frederic, who was right behind her. Joey reached down to help her out of the water and she hurried up the stairs. Joey followed and so did Frederic, his knife held tightly in his mouth.

Frederic did not seem to share the others' excitement. 'Where's the tomb? And where's my gold?' he demanded.

'You didn't think it was going to be that simple, did you?' said Marie. 'Alexander the Great's tomb and treasures have been hidden for thousands of years. If you were expecting to find his fortune after a short dive, you were mistaken.'

Frederic shot her an angry look, but before he could do anything, Boyce spoke up.

'Marie, check out these tablets,' he said, indicating the round stone carvings. 'I counted twelve of them, and each one is carved with a different image.'

Marie walked over and studied the nearest one. 'Impressive,' she said appreciatively.

'What do they mean?' asked Frederic.

'Unless I'm mistaken, they're pictures that depict the pagan gods,' said Marie.

Everyone stopped to listen.

'You have to remember, this was long before the time of Jesus Christ. The Greeks believed in many pagan gods, like the God of the Sea and the God of the Sun.'

'I don't give a rat's ass about Greek gods,' shouted

Frederic. 'If you don't find me my gold, you will all die in this shithole.'

Frederic flashed a menacing grin, then stopped to gaze into the dark water as something else occurred to him. 'The light stick,' he said in a whisper. 'It's deeper than I expected.'

'What did you say?' asked Joey.

'The light stick I threw in earlier, where is it?' mumbled Frederic. 'I can't see it.' He unclicked another from his utility belt and cracked it open. The cave had been lit up by the green flare before, but now the glaring green of the light stick took over. Frederic tossed the stick into the water and they all stood and watched it drift slowly downward, lighting up the columns that ran all the way down as it went. The green light faded away to a small dot as it continued to fall, and then it was gone.

'Far out, that's a deep hole,' said Boyce. 'It's like there's no end to it.'

Frederic grinned and unclipped his mesh backpack and placed it on the sandy floor. The sound of metal echoed as it hit the ground. The Frenchman opened the top drawstring cord of the bag and lifted out the small scuba-diving canister. 'Unless you can think of something else,' he said, 'someone is going to have to go down there.'

The three others all stiffened.

'That's suicide, man, that canister only holds ten or so minutes of air,' said Joey. 'You saw how deep this hole is. Come on, we're not equipped to go down today. I suggest we come back tomorrow with larger tanks. And you don't need Marie and Boyce. I promise you, I'll come back with you and together we can go searching for the tomb.'

'No!' said Frederic, kicking sand into the water. He dropped the yellow mini-tank in front of Joey's feet and retrieved his razor-sharp blade again. 'Grab the tank and find me my gold, before I start slicing up your girlfriend's pretty face.'

Joey had no choice. He turned to face Marie and they looked wordlessly at each other. One of them would have to go; they knew they had to spare Boyce.

Joey took a moment. But what he did next shocked everyone.

He kicked the canister into the water. There was no way of retrieving the canister from the dark water below.

Frederic's rage was visible for all to see: it boiled in his eyes. Without hesitation he lunged at Joey and aimed a powerful jab that hit him square in the nose.

Marie screamed as Joey dropped lifelessly to the ground.

First there was only blackness, and the ringing noise came afterward. Joey found himself on the ledge, his feet touching the water's edge. Blood was pouring from his nose. He pinched the bridge of his nose as he struggled to stand up. No sooner had he found his feet than Frederic planted a strong kick into his stomach that winded him. He fell to his knees.

'Stop it,' yelled Boyce, placing his smaller frame in front of his friend. Frederic smiled and in a single move seized hold of the teen and threw him up against a wall of columns. Boyce had his hands up and they took most of the brunt, but then he fell awkwardly backwards onto a stone tablet.

His back arched as he rolled over it. His eyes shut and his mouth fell wide open in shock, but at first no sound came out. Then, with an agonized cry, Boyce screamed, 'AHHH, it hurts ... fuck it hurts, my back!'

Marie and Joey looked with concerned eyes at the poor kid in excruciating pain.

And they noticed that the tablet Boyce had hit had moved down a little.

Chapter 64

Marie ran over to Boyce and dropped to her knees to comfort the teen, who now sat slumped against the nearest column. Boyce was arching his back and crying with the pain.

With one hand on Boyce's shoulder, Marie's eyes darted back to the stone tablet that he had just moved. On its face was the picture of a trident: the symbol associated with the pagan God of the Sea, Poseidon. The tablet had moved downward, leaving a small indentation inches from its base.

Frederic stormed over to Marie, his fists clenched. 'If there's no gold, there's no point keeping you all alive,' he said, grabbing Marie's long brown hair and pulling her to the edge of the platform.

Marie squirmed and cried out.

'Stop it!' Joey shouted. 'Let her go.'

Frederic forced her around to face him and slapped her across the cheek.

Enraged, Joey struggled to get up, and tried to charge over to Frederic, but the bigger man had anticipated his move and came in with another killer blow to his head. Joey fell to the ground, bleeding and disoriented, and watched helplessly as Frederic turned back to Marie.

'The tablet,' blurted out Marie, her hands up, ready to protect her face from another possible blow.

Frederic grabbed her hair again and forced her head backwards.

'It moved!' she cried out.

'You're lying.'

'They're not just there for decoration. They're some kind of test,' said Marie, her voice a mere whisper as her head was forced further and further back. 'If we push down on the correct one, the entrance to the tomb might be revealed.'

'Yeah, right, or maybe it's a death trap,' said Frederic, but Marie seemed to have sowed a seed of doubt in him. Abruptly, he let her go. 'Okay, Marie, since you seem to know more than all of us, I hold you responsible. You have ten minutes to find an entrance in this godforsaken place, or one of you will die.'

Still woozy and bleeding, Joey lay where he'd fallen and observed his girlfriend studying the twelve tablets. Boyce did the same from where he sat, his face a mask of pain.

'The twelve Greek gods of Mount Olympus and their symbols,' she said out loud. 'Okay, the trident is Poseidon, the brother of Zeus and God of the Sea.'

She moved on to the next tablet picturing a bolt of lightning. 'That's Zeus,' she said to herself. 'The King of all the Gods.'

'Dove, is Aphrodite the Goddess of Love and Beauty.

'Owl, is Athena the Goddess of Wisdom.

'Lyre, is Apollo the God of Music.

'Skull, is Hades the God of the Underworld and the Dead.

'War helmet, is Ares the God of War.

'Caduceus, is Hermes the God of Travel.

'Peacock, is Hera the Goddess of Marriage.'

She came to the tenth symbol and paused. This one seemed to have taken her by surprise. She hovered over it a moment, considering. 'What are you doing here?' she murmured.

'What is it?' asked Joey. He hauled himself to his feet and walked over to her, with Frederic close behind. Joey looked down at the stone tablet and blinked. 'This can't be,' he said with a puzzled look on his face.

The picture depicted a lion with wings, with a sun shape directly above its head. 'I know this image,' said Joey. 'I've seen it before.'

'You have?' asked Marie. 'Where?'

'It was tattooed on the wrist of the DGSE commander,' whispered Joey, not wanting Frederic to know he'd been in contact with the general.

Marie didn't reply, but she nodded to show she had understood.

'I have a bad feeling about this,' whispered Joey.

From behind them, Frederic said, 'Hang on, doesn't the sun shape represent Alexander the Great?'

Marie nodded her head. 'It does.'

'What about the lion?' asked Joey. 'What's the connection?'

'Archeologists have found coins in Egypt that pictured Alexander the Great's face,' explained Marie to the two men standing behind her. 'They depict the king with the lion's scalp on his head. The Macedonian lion in that time was a sign of power. It's been documented on many mosaics with pictures of nude Macedonian warriors wearing the traditional hat, the *kausia*, hunting the lion.'

'So this must be it,' said Joey. 'The sun and the lion are both symbols for Alexander the Great.'

Marie examined the last two tablets she had not yet seen, which were symbols for Hestia the Goddess of the Home and Architecture and Artemis the Goddess of the Hunt and nodded. 'This is the only tablet that has nothing to do with the known twelve Greek gods. It has to be it,' she confirmed.

'Step on it,' said Frederic. 'And let's find out.'

Joey took a breath and placed all his weight on the stone, but it didn't move.

Frederic watched on, played conspicuously with his knife.

'Hang on, Joey,' said Marie. 'Move over and we'll try together.'

She grabbed Joey's hand and they both stood on the stone, but once again there was no movement. 'Let's jump on it,' she said. Together they jumped, and on their third attempt there came a loud grinding noise. It sounded like two solid objects colliding with each other, and then the tablet they were standing on began to subside into the ground. As it submerged, the sound of stone on stone echoed inside the cave. After countless years of inactivity, the stone now lowered all the way down until it was flush with the ground.

At that point, another loud moving object could be heard, as if they were in a gigantic puzzle and the pieces were realigning themselves. It was coming from behind them. They all turned and faced the sound, including Boyce, who was still on the ground.

One of the columns pushed inwards, and as it went, dust clouded the air.

'You found it,' chirped Boyce. 'I can't believe you found it.'

Chapter 65

Joey picked up the flare Boyce had left on the ground and ignited it. Approaching the indented column, he saw a narrow cavity in the wall to his left. He sidestepped through and broke the built-up spider webs with his flare, hoping there was an opening up ahead. The tight tunnel was slick and wet and a dripping noise echoed inside it.

Marie and Frederic followed, leaving the injured Boyce to sit alone on the ledge, still holding on to his back. He wasn't going anywhere.

As soon as the three adults had disappeared from sight, Boyce didn't waste any time. Without a sound he swiftly entered the cold water and put the pain he was feeling out of his mind. He knew that if he didn't take this opportunity, he might not get another. He took in a couple of deep breaths and under he went, pulling himself along the rope that led outside into Aphrodite's baths. He reached the entrance to the narrow tunnel, glanced back one last time, and then pulled himself through and out toward the daylight.

Boyce broke the surface and gulped in air. Scrambling up the hillside, he dug into Joey's backpack, which they'd left on the ground near the wooden fence, and extracted the keys to the Mercedes. Slipping his feet into his shoes and pressing his hands against his injured back, he jogged awkwardly down the pathway of steps to the empty parking lot. Despite being dripping wet, he jumped into the Mercedes-Benz with urgency and gunned the engine, then sped away, leaving nothing but dust clouds in the air.

Chapter 66

Joey was the first to enter the open space. It was nothing like he had anticipated it to be. He'd imagined it would be a vast underground crypt filled to the brim with gold and items of immense importance, like Pierre and Edna had described.

Instead the room was small, perhaps ten feet wide by thirteen feet long. It was empty except for a large gold throne that sat up high on a pedestal. No sarcophagus, no treasure, no scrolls of papyrus – nothing but this gigantic feature that touched the nine-foot-high ceiling. Joey stepped up to the throne. This, at least, was worthy of a king. It must have weighed a ton, and the artisanship of its carvings was simply astonishing.

Marie exited the tunnel behind Joey, her eyes scanning left and right and then settling on the only shiny object in the room.

'What the hell is this?' said Frederic, the last to enter. 'Is this a joke? Where's the gold?'

'You're looking at it,' said Joey, peering around at the room's four walls, which were rendered smooth and curved at the corners. He noticed that to the right and left of the throne, there were hundreds of small coin-sized holes in the walls. What was their purpose?

he wondered, and walked around behind the throne, which was when he spotted two skeletons clinging to the back of the throne. Joey froze. Who were they, and what had happened to them?

'Frederic, I think this throne belonged to Alexander the Great,' said Joey slowly.

'It doesn't matter who it belonged to,' said Frederic. 'There's no way of getting it out of here. What a disappointment.'

Walking back around to the front of the throne, Joey pointed to the throne's back support, onto which was carved the same symbol of the lion and the sun they'd seen on the tablet.

Marie ran her eyes down the throne's armrests, which were carved with hundreds of pigeons, overlapping each other. The craftsmanship was impeccable, clearly the work of a master craftsman. It was, in fact, da Vinci–like.

'Hang on, there's an inscription on the seat,' said Marie, 'but it's in Greek.'

Frederic moved in closer.

'Babe, can you read it?' asked Joey.

Marie shook her head.

Frederic sighed and pushed Joey over. 'Move, let me try.'

'I didn't know you could read Greek,' said Joey.

'You never asked,' said Frederic smugly. 'My father was Greek.'

'Can you read it?' asked Marie.

Frederic gazed at the throne that could have belonged to the greatest general that ever lived, the man many worshipped as a god. Translating as he went, he read the inscription: *'In honor of our great general, and the exchange that secured his final resting place.'*

Chapter 67

Marie took in the words Frederic had spoken and glanced over to Joey, whose face remained blank. She lifted her hand across her face and took in a hidden breath. Maybe Frederic and Joey had no idea what that phrase meant, but she certainly did.

'What does it mean, Marie?' asked Frederic, stepping up onto the pedestal and taking a seat on the throne. 'What exchange is it talking about?'

'The tomb of Alexander the Great, the tomb filled with gold that we've been looking for, doesn't exist,' she said. 'This is a clue to how to find his bones.'

'Who cares about his bones?' said Frederic angrily.

Joey and Marie exchanged a quick glance. They knew the danger they were in. They had no way of predicting what Frederic would do next.

'I'm sorry,' Marie said. 'But it's not like you found nothing. At least you found this ornate throne. It could be worth a fortune.'

'What good is it to me?' said Frederic. 'I can't carry it out of this place.'

'I'm sorry,' said Marie again, her shoulders slumping.

Joey wondered what to do now. If he didn't think of

something quick, Frederic was going to end both their lives. He looked around discreetly. That's when he noticed many small, razor-sharp objects on the ground near the skeletons. At first he'd taken them for pebbles. There were hundreds of them.

Frederic sat back in the deep throne. He looked like a small child sitting in a large chair, a child whose feet couldn't reach the ground. He shook his head in disappointment. 'It's probably better that Pierre didn't live to see this day.' He smirked. 'All his years of searching would have come to nothing. A dead end ... nothing but a stupid throne.'

Joey turned back toward the tunnel they had come in from and saw the enormous circular boulder that had rolled out of the way earlier, allowing them to enter this secret room. If by any chance something went wrong and it rolled back in place, they would all be stuck in here and left to suffocate. That was most likely how the two dead bodies on the ground had died.

Joey had always been in awe of the engineering of the ancient Greeks and Egyptians, which had allowed them to build astonishing and monumental structures such as the Pyramids of Giza and the Colossus of Rhodes. But one thing ran through Joey's mind inside this man-made cave: the elements holding certain chambers and doors in place were extremely ancient and could possibly crumble at any time.

'Hang on. Don't touch anything, just in case,' said Joey out of the blue.

'What's wrong?' asked Marie.

'Did you notice the skeletons? Ask yourself how they died,' he said, and pointed to the bones behind the throne.

From his high position, Frederic didn't even bother looking. He rested his hands on the armrests and said with a smug smile, 'Right now you should be more worried about how you're going to die.'

Marie and Joey swallowed uncomfortably.

'Don't be stupid, Frederic,' said Marie. 'We have money. We can come to an arrangement.'

As they spoke, something tugged at Joey's memory. It had something to do with the interview he'd had with Julien in the DGSE building. He thought about the framed image of the sun he'd seen on Julien's office wall, and about the image tattooed on Julien's wrist, an image that was also carved into the stone tablet that had led them to this room. The same image was etched in gold on Alexander the Great's throne. Why did this image keep coming up? He remembered what Julien had said to him: *I believe some things are never meant to be found. They are fairy tales passed down through generations, to tease treasure hunters and art historians like the curator.*

Then, he remembered another comment Julien had said to him. He hadn't thought anything of it at the time – indeed, it hadn't made any sense to him – but now he suddenly understood Julien's last words.

I wish you well on your journey, Joey, but be warned, if you do find what you seek, then remember this: to sit on the throne of the great King, you need to bow down and worship his pagan symbol, the sun god.

Joey's eyes darted down to the floor and then back up to the throne, where Frederic had just pulled his blade from his belt.

'No, Frederic,' said Marie, shaking her head and

taking a step back. 'What good will killing us do?'

'It will give me great pleasure,' said Frederic, slowly lifting himself off the gigantic throne.

'Wait ... stop,' said Joey. 'Don't move.'

Frederic didn't even blink. He wasn't going to listen to anyone anymore. He stood up, his blade ready.

'No!' screamed Joey. 'Marie, get down!'

Whip ... Whip ... Whip ...

Out of nowhere, flashes of brown shot across their faces, making a whistling sound. Marie's hair moved as they rushed by. As she and Joey fell to their knees, hundreds of primitive stone arrowheads hit Frederic's unprotected body. Then a second round was propelled out of the small holes and hit his upper torso. Explosions of blood flared out of the major's exposed forearms and neck, and a dozen or so arrows stuck out from his chest.

He hadn't bowed down to the sun god, and he'd felt his wrath.

Frederic roared in pain and dropped his blade, standing there dumbfounded. Then a gush of blood erupted from his mouth and he staggered forward.

Marie and Joey needed no further encouragement. Both jumped to their feet and dashed to the entrance.

'Go, go, go!' Joey yelled.

Sidestepping through the narrow passageway, they reached the outer room in seconds, but something was wrong.

'Where's Boyce?' panted Marie.

'He must have escaped, and that's what we're going to do, too,' said Joey. 'Let's go, you first.'

Marie dived into the water like an Olympic swimmer and clawed her way along the rope. Joey watched her disappear into the tunnel leading to Aphrodite's baths.

Joey prepared himself to dive in after her. He took a deep breath, but at that moment he was tackled from the side and the air rushed out of his lungs. Speckled with arrowheads and covered in blood, Frederic had somehow made it out of the secret room. Adrenaline coursing through him, Joey grappled with the Frenchman, and both rolled onto the tablet that had been already pushed downward by Boyce. This time the stone carved with a trident was forced all the way to the ground, and then suddenly, bubbles appeared in the water below. Within seconds the ledge that gave access to the water was completely submerged.

Chapter 68

Marie swam out of the tunnel and splashed toward the bank, taking in the fresh air. She smiled as she reached the edge and climbed onto solid ground to wait for Joey. But where was he? She scanned the water impatiently as the seconds turned to minutes. What the hell was taking him so long?

Joey and Frederic, now waist deep in water, had been separated by the up-force of the incoming water. The circular cave was filling up fast, as though they were in some kind of giant plunger. The ledge was now too far down to stand on, so they both kicked their legs to stay afloat. In seconds they would both be completely submerged.

'If I'm going to die in this shithole, you're going to die with me,' shouted Frederic, bridging the distance between them and grabbing onto Joey's neck.

Joey tried to fight off the major's strong hands, kicking him in his chest and breaking free for a second. This gave him time to grab a quick breath.

Their bodies had risen up with the force of the water. The domed ceiling was now only feet away.

Like an unstoppable force, Frederic was right back.

With both hands outstretched, he clung on to Joey, dragging him under once more. Joey knew Frederic's time was limited, but before he died, he was going to try to take Joey with him. Joey looked around frantically for anything he could use.

In the cold murky haze his eye was caught by a blur of green and blue. Joey could barely see the light coming in from the exit tunnel, and fought to stay afloat. His face broke the surface once more and he sucked in a quick breath, but Frederic's grip was strong, and under he went again.

The ceiling was now only eight inches away, within hand's reach.

Four inches.

Joey knew he couldn't do this much longer, and bubbles of frustration came out of his mouth. He needed to act or he would die. Facing Frederic's chest, he could see the small shadows of the arrowheads that were protruding from his body. In desperation, Joey palmed in an arrow that was closest to Frederic's heart, and pushed it in with all the force he could muster.

Two inches.

One inch.

With a cry of pain Frederic let go of Joey and plucked at his wounded body. Under the water, bubbles spewed from his mouth.

Joey didn't waste any time. Half an inch of air remained in the cave. Pushing against Frederic, Joey thrust himself upward and practically kissed the ceiling as he inhaled one last time, a breath denied to Frederic as the water slapped against the ceiling. Then, with all the strength he had remaining, Joey turned and pushed off the ceiling as hard as he could, heading downward.

The cave now was one hundred percent under water.

With desperation fueling him, Frederic watched Joey dive into the murky depths and pushed off the wall, giving chase. He would not allow this American to beat him. He would kill him if it was the last thing he did.

Joey swam toward the faint light source that showed the location of the exit tunnel. The upward water pressure had now ceased and the visibility was improving. He glanced backwards and recoiled in horror when he saw Frederic's bloodied face only feet away, one hand scrabbling to catch hold of Joey's feet. *This lunatic would not die*, Joey thought as he swam frantically forward.

The tunnel was in Joey's sight. He knew it would be risky, as the upward angle of the tunnel would allow Frederic to reach him just as he tried to enter it. His life depended on him entering the tunnel fast.

It was going to be tight.

Just as Joey approached the lip of the tunnel, something caught his eye. At that moment he felt Frederic's hand grab the leg of his pants and slip off. Frederic wouldn't miss twice. Joey had run out of time. But what he decided to do next was either incredibly smart, or mind-blowingly stupid. He ignored the tunnel and continued to swim downward.

Chapter 69

Frederic's eyes widened in horror. This was his last chance to get Joey, but once again, he had been outmaneuvered. Joey was trying to outswim him. Frederic thought for a moment about what was he going to do. Should he continue his chase, or try to make it out alive? He knew he was dying with each stroke, and his lungs were failing. A small, logical part of his brain told him that even if he reached Aphrodite's baths, he couldn't survive this, he was done for. Every cell of his body screamed for oxygen. He needed to take a breath, so he opened his mouth and the murky water poured in. Choking and retching, the stream cascaded into the back of his throat, sending jets of pain through his body. As the water in his lungs suffocated him, his body reached its limits and his heart stopped beating. His flailing hands and feet slowly stilled, and his hunched body hung suspended in the cylindrical cave.

Joey turned once to see Frederic's limp body floating still. His plan had worked. A surge of relief flowed through him, but he continued his downward descent. Even though there was no need to continue, he had spotted four shiny green specks of light in the distance, and an idea had come to him. Miraculously, it seemed the lights were sitting on the base of the structure. Previously, when Frederic had thrown in a green light stick to see how deep the well was, it had disappeared out of sight. But that was before the base had moved upward, forcing the water to fill the entire cave.

The unseen base was now in reach. The lights grew brighter with each stroke, but they weren't the reason he was continuing his descent.

Joey's lungs were burning unbearably. His ears felt like they were about to burst, but he was close and he told himself to keep going. The four green LED lights lit up the base of the cylindrical structure like a Christmas tree.

Then Joey saw it, resting all on its own a few feet from the lights; the reason for this madness.

It was the yellow miniature scuba-diving tank he had kicked into the water earlier on, now glistening green. It was his lifeline, his ticket out of this place. His throat burned as he grabbed hold of the tank. He jammed the scuba regulator into his mouth and exhaled onto the mouthpiece, causing bubbles to flow up over his mask. Then he turned the tank valve and inhaled the hit of air his body so yearned for.

It was bliss. The air entered his body and immediately he felt his strength returning. He took slow, small gulps of air, calming himself. The miniature scuba tank could only supply a few minutes of oxygen, so it was time to leave this place. Who knew what other booby traps the Greeks had built inside these walls? With the bottle dangling out from his mouth, Joey grabbed a light stick to keep the darkness at bay, and as he did so, he saw a sparkling object on the ground. He swam over to it and picked it up, using the light stick to see what he had found.

To his surprise, he saw that it was an old steel war tag engraved with the name *Benjamin P. Fontaine.*

This was a mystery for another time. Joey just wanted out. He placed the chain attached to the tag around his neck, looked up, and with a strong push, began his ascent.

Chapter 70

At the water's edge, Marie watched Aphrodite's baths turn green. She held her breath, almost too anxious to find out who was holding that light stick. It glided up to the surface and to her joy and relief, her man emerged from the water.

Joey swam toward her until his feet found the ground, and then Marie grabbed his hand and helped him out of the water. He fell into her arms and she gave him a passionate kiss. 'Thank God you're safe. I thought we were all going to die.'

'So did I,' said Joey. 'So did I ... Let's get out of here.'

As they climbed up the bank Joey scanned the site, searching for something. 'Where's Boyce?' he asked.

'I don't know. He wasn't here when I got out and his shoes are gone.'

The backpack Joey had carried in earlier was still on the ground. Joey kneeled and unzipped it, finding a dry t-shirt, which he gave to Marie.

'Frederic? Is he dead?' asked Marie while changing her shirt.

'Yes ... he's gone,' said Joey, picking up and putting on the shirt he had thrown onto the ground before he had entered the water.

Watching him dress, Marie reached out and touched the war tag around Joey's neck.

'Where did you get that?' she asked.

'At the bottom of the cave.'

'Whose do you think it is?'

'There's a name on it,' said Joey, turning it over to the engraved surface. 'But it's no one I've ever heard of. Whoever this belonged to, he was here a long time ago. Maybe he has the answers we're after.'

Marie looked at the engraved name. '*Benjamin P. Fontaine*,' she read.

Joey shrugged, then put his shoes on and picked up his bag. Marie also put on her sneakers and they began their descent down the pathway of steps to the car park. All of a sudden a deafening gurgling sound came from inside the cave, and they turned back. Sprays of water came shooting out of the cracks in the rock wall and large bubbles erupted on the surface of Aphrodite's baths. It sounded like something was being sucked down or drained out. Then as quick as it had started, there was a loud bang and it stopped.

'I bet you any money if we were to enter the cave again it would be as we found it,' said Joey, shaking his head.

Marie nodded and said with a smile, 'Or at least until some other poor sucker finds their way in and pushes down the wrong tablet. I wonder what would have happened if we'd pushed down one of the others?'

'I never want to find out,' said Joey.

They continued down the pathway until another thought seemed to strike Joey and he turned to Marie and asked, 'So do you believe my great-grandfather knew about all this?'

'Yes, I do,' said Marie. 'I've been thinking about this. I think he must have been entrusted, just like Leonardo da Vinci was, with keeping the secret safe.'

'What are you talking about, what secret?' asked Joey. 'We found nothing here but a gold throne that might or might not have belonged to Alexander the Great,' he said. 'Wow ... big find,' he added sarcastically.

'You Americans.'

'What's that supposed to mean – you're an American, too!'

'The exchange that secured his final resting place? The lion image with wings?' Marie looked at Joey expectantly.

'I have no idea where you're going with this.'

Marie stopped and grabbed Joey's face between the palms of her hands and stared him straight in his blue eyes. 'The tomb of Alexander the Great, which is supposed to be amazing, filled with gold and emeralds and all his prized possessions like Tutankhamun's, does not exist.'

'Go on,' said Joey warily.

'Joey, the symbol of the lion with wings does not represent Alexander the Great. It represents St Mark, one of Jesus's apostles. This is the reason why we're in Cyprus. This was one of the places the saint came to preach the word of God. I never really understood why Leonardo da Vinci would point us to Cyprus, and now it all makes sense.'

'Well, not to me,' said Joey, 'You're going to have to spell it out for me. What does it all mean?'

'Joey, it's like the inscription on the throne said: it's

the exchange that secured his final resting place.'

'What exchange? What and who are you talking about?'

'Think.'

Joey stopped to think and took in a fresh breath of air. He thought of the lion with wings, the image Marie reckoned represented St Mark. 'Are you telling me the body of the greatest general that had ever lived was swapped with the body of St Mark, one of the apostles of Christ?'

'Yes!'

'Fuck me.'

'Exactly! This place is like a symbol or shrine that tells the true story of something that happened over two thousand years ago.' She gave Joey a joyful smile and let him dwell on the thought as they approached the car park, only to find that their car wasn't there.

Chapter 71

Joey and Marie began the long hike back to their villa along the narrow country road. Around them was nothing but bushland, green as far as the eye could see, but as the time passed and the exertions of the day began to catch up with him, Joey started to hope Boyce had a very good reason for leaving them stranded.

'What's that?' said Marie suddenly, stopping to listen.

Joey heard a dull throbbing sound that grew rapidly louder, and then out of nowhere came two Aerospatiale SA 330 Puma helicopters, which swooped in and hovered overhead, blowing loose sand in the air. Joey's hair parted in the middle and Marie had to keep both hands on her head to stop her long hair from whipping in every direction.

'What the hell is this?' said Joey. Then two black SUVs with impenetrable dark-tinted windows pulled up in front of them. Joey raised his hands and looked on, stunned. Marie instinctively ducked behind his frame. Yes, Frederic was gone; they'd thought all their worries were behind them, but now who was this?

The front door of the first black SUV opened and out stepped a man with an air of authority about him. He was tall, his hair was white and as he turned to face them, Joey saw that a scar ran down his temple. Joey immediately recognized him. His face was unforgettable.

It was the DGSE commanding general: Julien Bonnet.

'What's going on?' shouted Joey as he watched him approach, still with his hands up over his head. The helicopters' spinning blades caused Julien's pants to flap around his calves in the swirling dust cloud. Then they pulled back and landed in the distance with their rotor blades slowly coming to a halt.

'It's okay, Joey,' said a voice as someone exited the second SUV.

Joey felt relief flow through him as he turned to see Boyce's smiling face.

'Thank God,' Marie whispered.

'I went for help,' said Boyce.

'You went straight to the top, I see,' said Joey with a chuckle. 'How did you find the DGSE general?'

'I didn't,' said Boyce. 'As I was driving I saw a helicopter, so I flagged it down and explained you were in trouble.'

'Where is Frederic?' Julien interrupted somberly.

On hearing that question, Joey realized they were safe. They weren't the ones the DGSE was here for. 'Frederic is dead, sir.'

'Don't bullshit me, son,' warned Julien, taking off his yellow-tinted glasses and hanging them on his sleeveless blue shirt.

'No, sir, I wouldn't do that to you.'

'What happened?'

Joey fixed his gaze on Julien, a man who seemed to know far more than he let on, and replied in a manner only the DGSE commander would understand. 'Sir,

Frederic died because he didn't know one vital piece of information. A piece of information someone told me only a couple of days ago.'

'And what's that?' Julien asked.

'He forgot to bow down and worship at the feet of the sun god once he sat on the throne,' said Joey, his eyes now lifting to the scar on the top of Julien's head. How else could he have known? Julien must have been in the secret room at some point and lived to talk about it.

Julien flashed Joey a million-dollar smile. 'Let's go back to your villa, kids, we have a lot to talk about.'

Chapter 72

After a short drive back to the villa and in the comfort of clean clothes, Joey, Marie and Boyce assembled in front of Julien for a debrief.

'So how did you know we were in Cyprus?' asked Joey.

'When we arrested you in front of the Louvre and had you pinned to the ground, I had one of my men plant the tracking device on your shoe,' said Julien with a wry smile.

'Not another tracking device,' said Marie, rolling her eyes.

Joey reached down and flipped over the tongue of his shoe to reveal the culprit. It was a small pinhead shape, unnoticeable unless you were searching for it. He smiled as he sat back up. 'All this hassle to hide a secret,' he said, folding his arms. 'A secret that is really only a cryptic clue engraved on a throne.'

Julien seemed to be repressing a smile.

Marie leaned forward and addressed the general. 'This exchange happened two thousand years ago and has been kept a secret all this time, hasn't it?'

Julien didn't answer.

Boyce looked profoundly confused. 'What throne? What was exchanged?'

Remembering that Boyce hadn't seen the secret room, Marie turned to her young friend and said, 'We found a gold throne inside the cave and engraved on it was some Greek text. It read: *In honor of our great general, and the exchange that secured his final resting place.* Also on the throne was an image of a lion with wings and a sun shape that was directly above its head.'

'The lion with wings ...' repeated Boyce. 'Isn't that the symbol of St Mark? I remember seeing it with my mother. Before she died we had gone to church together a few times. It was a St Mark's church and inside was an enormous mural of the lion that depicted the saint.'

Joey looked at Boyce in surprise. 'Hang on, that's what Marie said. Is it true?' He turned to Julien.

Julien nodded his head.

'So wait a minute, let me get this clear,' said Joey. 'All these secrets, this whole conspiracy, was about hiding the fact that Alexander the Great's body was swapped with the apostle St Mark's?'

Julien nodded his head again.

'When I first heard the inscription on the throne I knew instantly,' said Marie. 'But I was trying to make sense of it all. Then I spotted the armrests. Hundreds of carved pigeons ran down to the feet of the chair. Then I knew it to be true.'

'How?' asked Joey.

'Anyone who has visited Venice would know about the hundreds of pigeons that occupy St Mark's Square,' said Marie. 'It was another clever symbol left on the throne to give us a clue about the location of his tomb.'

Boyce leaned forward. 'The basilica,' he breathed.

Marie nodded, her eyes full of wonder, then

349

continued, 'There have been stories and pictures on mosaics all around the world of the saint's body being wrapped in a blanket and taken to Venice. But I think it's actually Alexander the Great's body that's in St Mark's Basilica. When the laws against the worship of pagan gods began to be a threat to Alexander, his cult must have decided to hide his body, but in a very clever way – in plain view. That would have been the best way to hide something of such significance and keep it safe, as it would have been treated with great reverence if people thought it was the body of St Mark. Since that time millions of Christians have come to pray there. But unbeknownst to them, they were really praying to the great king and general, Alexander.'

Joey gave a long, low whistle of amazement.

Julien put his hands together and gave them all a round of applause. He genuinely seemed to be impressed.

'Who are you?' Joey asked Julien. 'Don't bullshit us now. And why do you have the exact same symbol that was on the throne tattooed on your wrist?'

Julien leaned back in the deep couch. 'I am the last living representative of the old Priory of Sion,' he said. 'The secret has been passed down over the years to many people, one of whom was your great-grandfather.'

Julien had their undivided attention now.

'If it was a secret,' asked Joey, 'why did you let me go in search of it, knowing I knew where to look?'

'I am not getting any younger, Joey, and given that your family has played such a vital part in all this, I felt you deserved to know the truth. Now I pass on this knowledge to you.'

Joey didn't know what to say. 'I'm honored,' he said

awkwardly, 'but I'm not sure what I should do with this knowledge.'

Julien smiled and said, 'Before Christ everyone believed in the old gods, and that's what Alexander was, a god to many. He conquered and created the largest empire known to man. After he died, he continued to be revered; even the most powerful emperors of Rome paid homage at the shrine of the warrior king. Then Christianity rose in popularity and there was a revolution in spirituality, which resulted in the worship of all other gods being banned.'

'I think I read somewhere that they destroyed Alexander's shrine,' said Marie.

'It was said to have been destroyed and rebuilt to make way for St Mark's body in 392 A.D., but this is a lie. It was never destroyed, and Alexander's body was never moved. This is when the secret society of Alexander's cult was formed, their aim being to protect the one true god they believed in: Alexander. Both bodies, Mark's and Alexander's, were said to have been laid to rest in the same tomb, until the Muslims took over Alexandria during the Crusades.'

'Is this when the Venetians stepped in?' said Marie.

'Yes,' said Julien. 'The secret society, represented by two Greek monks, made a deal with the Venetians to return their saint, Mark, who would later become the patron saint of the city. In 828 A.D., they brought Alexander's body disguised as the saint's back to Venice by ship, and hid it in a chest full of vegetables and pork to avoid discovery by the Muslims.'

'But weren't there two bodies?' asked Boyce. 'If Alexander is in Venice, what happen to St Mark? What about the documents Pierre was telling us about, that could expose lies in the Christian churches? Did they even exist?'

'No one really knows what had happened to St Mark's body,' said Julien with raised palms. 'Maybe he was also moved and the documents you're talking about were laid to rest with him in an undiscovered tomb. Maybe our forebears destroyed his body so his skeleton would not be found. I don't know. But what we do know is that Alexander's body was moved to Venice in St Mark's name, and a new church was erected as his tomb.'

'All these years,' said Joey, shaking his head. 'You would think that the Vatican would know the truth.'

'Joey, here's the kicker,' said Julien. 'The Vatican *does* know, but they would never dare reveal it to the world; it would undermine the church. If the people in Italy found out, there could be a revolt and an uprising against the church.' Julien paused, then continued, 'Did you know that the body of Alexander's father, King Philip, has been found?'

Marie nodded her head, but the two males shook theirs.

'In 1977 they found the Macedonian King, Philip II, in a two-chambered royal tomb at Vergina, west of Thessaloniki in northern Greece. A simple DNA test could determine whether the remains in Venice belong to his son. I am currently in discussions with the church to have this done in private. Even if they do agree and we find it to be true, we must respect the church's wishes and keep it a secret. Sometimes no good comes from knowing the truth.'

There was silence for a few moments as they all

digested this news. Then Julien asked them, 'Now that you all know the truth, the big question is, can I trust you to keep this secret? You will join the ranks of many great people such as Leonardo da Vinci, your great-grandfather Vincenzo Peruggia, myself and many others.'

Joey knew their response was critical. If they could not promise to keep the secret, they would not leave this villa alive. The way forward was clear.

'Yes, we can keep this secret,' said Joey formally, and Marie and Boyce followed suit.

'Good,' said Julien with a relieved exhalation. 'That is the correct answer. No one can find out about this, or I will come looking for you. Believe me, you don't want that. Do I make myself clear?'

'Yes, sir,' they all responded together.

'By the way, sir, do you know who Benjamin P. Fontaine is?' Joey asked, touching the war tag wrapped around his neck.

Julien inhaled sharply. 'Why do you ask?'

'I found his war tag inside the cave. Is he still alive?'

'Yes … he's alive,' said Julien, absentmindedly touching the scar on his face. 'We were in the army together and he saved my life more times than I can remember.'

Another piece of the puzzle fell into place in Joey's mind. This Fontaine had been with Julien in the cave behind Aphrodite's baths. Judging from the way Julien touched his scar and stared blankly into his memories, Joey suspected Julien owed his survival from the cave's secret room to his companion.

'So where is Benjamin now?' asked Joey.

'He's in Egypt.'

'I might pay him a visit one day and return him his dog tags,' said Joey. 'They're probably important to him.'

'I have a picture of him in my car. I can give it to you, if that helps,' said Julien. 'If you decide to go looking for him, your best bet would be The Museum of Egyptian Antiquities; he practically lives there. Say hi to him for me, and tell him he still owes me one hundred euros for Le Havre.'

Julien stood up and walked purposefully to the door, and they all followed him outside. As they passed the lemon tree in the front garden, Julien paused and turned to face Boyce. 'By the way, I have been meaning to talk to you, Boyce.'

'Yes, sir?'

'You didn't have the best upbringing, did you, son?' Julien thought for a moment then continued, 'Your mother was a drug addict who died from an overdose when you were little and your father is a criminal currently doing time in jail.'

Boyce hung his head and a tear rolled off his cheek. He dashed it angrily away with his hand.

'I had my men run a background check on you. All those years and no place to go … you had to fend for yourself. You're a fighter, son.' Julien's voice was softer now.

Boyce didn't respond.

'I'm always looking for fighters like yourself to join my special unit team. You can start a new life for yourself. Give yourself a purpose, and I promise you, you will learn things about the world we live in today that you wouldn't believe. Things that people have been searching for their whole life.'

Boyce looked up then, and turned to his friends, who were smiling broadly at him. He didn't have to think about it long. Perhaps not trusting himself to speak, he nodded firmly.

'In that case, say your goodbyes and come with us,' said Julien with a warm smile. 'Your new life starts now.'

Boyce turned to face Joey and gave him a strong hug that lasted a long time. When he pulled away he said, 'JP, at first meeting you was like hell. Everything went wrong. My boat was destroyed, I aquaplaned a car off a cliff, swam across a freezing lake. But meeting you was also the best thing that ever happened to me. Thank you for everything.'

Joey couldn't hide the smile that engulfed his face.

Tears rolling down her face, Marie also hugged Boyce goodbye and the teen climbed into the backseat of Julien's SUV.

The general opened his door but paused before getting in.

'Joey, my friend, it has been a pleasure.' He rummaged inside the car then handed Joey a photo. 'Best of luck to you.'

Julien flashed a *Mona Lisa* smile. Then he climbed into the vehicle and they set off, the two choppers following as if he were the President of the United States.

Chapter 73

Standing there alone with Marie as the dust cloud subsided, Joey glanced at the photo Julien had given him. A smile dawned on his face when he saw it, and then he laughed.

'What's so funny?' asked Marie.

'I can't believe it,' said Joey.

'What?'

'He's the spitting image of my father,' said Joey.

'I thought your father died.'

'He did.'

Just when Joey thought his family's history couldn't get any more complicated, he had been thrown a curve ball. 'They look like they might be related,' said Joey. 'I did wonder why Julien would give me a picture of the man. It seemed a little odd. Now I know why – the resemblance is uncanny. I might need to do some digging when I get home, to get to the bottom of this.'

After a week in Cyprus, getting some much-needed sleep, relaxation and alone time, not to mention the vacation they had hoped to have in the first place, Joey and Marie decided it was time to head back home to the United States. The trip to Paris and Cyprus would be one neither of them would ever forget, but it was a story they could never tell, if they cherished their lives.

Joey woke at dawn and went out onto his penthouse balcony, the place where it had all begun, to watch the Santa Monica sunrise.

Marie lay fast asleep in bed.

Joey thought about his great-grandfather, his grandmother and his father, and the secrets they had kept hidden throughout their lives. As he peered out over the ocean, he wondered about the mysterious man who resembled his father. Could he have an uncle he didn't even know existed, somewhere in Egypt? If so, who was he and why hadn't he ever been mentioned? Had his father even known about him? And who knew what other skeletons were in his family's closet?

In due time that secret would also be revealed, but for now he was going to enjoy his freedom in a world where no one was trying to kill him. He closed his eyes, enjoyed the warm sun that hit his face, and smiled as he rested his hands on the glass balustrade.

One thing was undeniable, he thought.

He certainly came from a family of amazing people.

Chapter 74

Months had passed. The water shone like a molten mirror as the summer sun beat down upon a young man who stepped out of a gondola. The smell of Venice was in the air. This was a place built on water, bridges and narrow canals that twisted around each other in an intricate knot. There was nowhere in the world remotely like it.

The man wore dark-brown jeans and a black t-shirt. His boots were Italian, expensive, dark and pointy. He strode along the canal with confidence, his face framed by his dark sunglasses. The tattoo on his wrist pictured a lion with wings and a symbol of the sun.

His old friends would hardly have recognized Boyce. He had begun his new role as an operative in Julien's organization, while finishing his schooling via correspondence alongside his training. Today was going to be a special day, though, so Julien had let him tag along, given his previous involvement in this case.

The youth walked into the square where hundreds of pigeons massed over the entire site, and some flew over his head. He turned to the eastern end of the Piazza San Marco to face the impressive entrance to the basilica, one of the most famous churches in Italy, and one of the best known of Italo-Byzantine architecture, as Boyce's history lessons had recently taught him. Its opulent design, ground-gold mosaics and its statues were a symbol of Venetian wealth and power.

Boyce peered up at the Horses of St Mark, which had been installed on the balcony above the portal of the basilica in the thirteenth century. Then he lifted his gaze to the gilded winged lion: St Mark's symbol and that of Venice.

Today the church doors were shut; no lines of tourists waited to enter. Two heavily armed soldiers, wearing the same winged lion tattoo on their wrist as now appeared on Boyce's, saw Boyce and gave him a nod, letting him enter. Boyce quickly shut the doors behind him and turned his attention to the gorgeous interior, based on the shape of a Greek cross.

As he walked across the twelfth-century marbled floor, he scanned the upper levels, which were completely covered with bright mosaics. The interior of San Marco was aglow with golden light, caused by the gilded mosaic tiles and the sunshine that streamed in during the day.

Up on the high altar was the famous Golden Pala. Boyce stood in wonder, taking in the hundreds of pieces of enamel and all kinds of precious stones stuck onto gold leaf.

Boyce continued to the end of the walkway, hearing his own footsteps echo in the wondrous space. He scanned the high altar, where the relics of St Mark were supposed to have been laid to rest. He approached a set of stairs that led him to the upper balcony level, where another tattoo-wearing soldier told him he was an hour early.

'I know I am,' replied Boyce. 'I just wanted to get the best seat in the house for the main event.'

An hour later, the church's walls were lined with military men in uniform. When the church's doors opened, cheering could be heard from the people outside, as the traditional Medici blue, red and yellow colors of the Swiss Guard entered the church. The Pope of Rome, Jorge Mario Bergoglio, followed behind them. He was accompanied by the Archbishop of Greece, as well as cardinals, patriarchs, priests and deacons.

It was evident that today was no ordinary day. Also accompanying the men of the cloth were scientists, and the Priory of Sion representative and DGSE general Julien Bonnet.

At the altar, Pope Bergoglio dug into his pocket and extracted a gold key. He handed it to Julien, who in turn bowed his head as a gesture of respect and passed it to a man wearing a white coat and glasses, clearly a scientist.

The scientist approached the box that supposedly held the crushed-up remains of St Mark and carefully unlocked it.

Pope Bergoglio spoke in Italian, holding his sky-blue rosary beads in his hand. He said, 'Forgive me, Father,' and rubbed his thumb on the cross connected to the beads.

The nerdy-looking scientist scraped a small sample from the broken bones and placed it into a sealed vial, ready to be analyzed. He then shut the box, locked it and handed the key back to the general. In turn, Julien handed it back to the Pope.

The scientist stepped over to a portable table he had set up earlier with his expensive scientific equipment and laptop for analysis. A genetic profile for Alexander the Great's father, King Philip of Macedonia, had already been created, Boyce knew. Today's test would determine if the bones showed a familial relationship to the king's profile.

Boyce watched on from above the shrine as the scientist began his testing. He glanced at the clergymen in the pews below, who were fidgeting anxiously, waiting for what was going to be revealed. If a match was found and the truth leaked, the consequences could be monumental for the church. St Mark was the people's saint, the man this amazing building had been built for, and in a few seconds, it could be proved that St Mark had never even been there.

The scientist showed no emotion as he worked. Whatever the finding, the scientist had promised to keep the news a secret.

After a long, twenty-minute diagnostic, the results were in.

The white-coated scientist turned the laptop around and the Pope stepped forward. From his vantage point, Boyce could just make out the screen. Two simple graphs overlapped each other from the two DNA samples.

Pope Bergoglio took in a breath but did not react to the results. He nodded his head to the DGSE French general and glanced up to a statue of Jesus on a cross. His gaze lasted a full minute. He then turned around to his brothers of the cloth and headed for the door, his head bowed.

Julien immediately shut the lid of the laptop and

took it with him, following His Holiness down the long corridor.

'Is it true, padre?' Boyce heard the gray-bearded archbishop ask.

Silence fell as all inside the cathedral stopped to listen to his answer.

Pope Bergoglio turned back to face the impressive basilica, but he did not say a word. He made the sign of the cross with his hands and left the building, his personal guards leading the way. As the doors opened a loud cheer from the men, women and children outside met the leader of the Catholic Church as he was ushered onto a large ship waiting among the gondolas.

At the entrance to the basilica, Julien was instantly bombarded by priests wanting to know the truth. He ignored them and looked up at the second floor and winked at Boyce.

'Quiet please,' he said, raising his arms in a gesture to calm everyone down. 'You are men of God. It doesn't matter whose bones were left in that box. Go and fulfill your duties. All that matters is that whoever was buried here was a *great* man.'

Boyce smiled at this, and slowly returned his gaze to the shrine. But this time he froze. He didn't want to look away. How had he missed it? There, in the marble on the ground, was a symbol. It was yellow in color, with sixteen separate pieces forming rays that each extruded outward to a sharp point. It was the sun symbol of the greatest general who ever lived, positioned directly below the altar that was said to have held the saint's relics. It was unmistakable. The truth had been in plain sight, staring everyone in the face all along.

MONA LISA'S SECRET

ACKNOWLEDGMENTS

I want to thank my beautiful wife Marie, and my two boys Alexander and Leonardo who supported me and put up with me, throughout this amazing journey.

A big thank you to my extended family, parents and friends for their loving support and always believing in me.

A special thank you goes out to Ian Townsend, Renos Georgiou and Nicky Aghabi for being my beta readers, who read the novel in its infant stages.

A huge thank you, to my genius editor Brianne Collins for giving this book life and making it the best it could possibly be. Brianne, who also edits Matthew Reilly's books was a pleasure to work with, I can't thank her enough. I'm looking forward to our next project together.

I also want to thank Alexandra Nahlous, for doing a fantastic job with the proofreading.

Last of all to you, my dear reader, for picking up my book. I truly hope you have as much fun reading it as I did writing it. I would love to hear from you. I can be contacted via social media, or on my website **www.philphilips.com**

ONE MORE THING ...

If you loved the book and have a moment to spare, I would really appreciate a short review where you bought the book. Your help in spreading the word is gratefully appreciated, as it helps other readers discover the story.

Fortune in Blood

A NOVEL OF MURDER, THEFT, BETRAYAL AND MONEY ... LOTS OF IT ...

Joey used to be a carefree surfer kid on Venice Beach. But as the youngest son of a notorious gangster, it seems he can't escape the life. Soon he's forced to prove himself by leading a team in the heist of the century. Will he be able to pull it off?

Vince was always worried about getting to lectures on time ... and spending time with his hot girlfriend. But everything changes when he's embroiled in his detective father's world. Now he's on the run for his life from the mob.

FBI Agent Monica is smart, beautiful, tough and unyielding. Caught in the middle of the mob and the police, her loyalty is being questioned by both sides. But Monica seems to have her own agenda ... In a world where corruption is rife, she will be tested to the limit.

Who can be trusted and who will be left standing? And who will ultimately escape with all the money? A showdown is set in motion and no one will be left unscathed.

In this elaborately plotted, fast-paced thriller, Phil Philips takes you on a roller coaster ride that will keep you guessing until the very last page.

MORE FICTION FROM PHIL PHILIPS

Last Secret Chamber

A Joey Peruggia Adventure Series Book 2

Where is ancient Egypt's last secret chamber, and what is concealed within?

When an archaeologist is murdered in his Cairo apartment, an ancient artefact is stolen from his safe – one believed to hold the clue to the last secret chamber.

When Joey Peruggia discovers that the dead man was his long-lost uncle, he travels with his girlfriend, Marie, and his friend Boyce, who works for the French intelligence, to Egypt, on a mission to find answers.

But once they arrive, they are lured into a trap and become hostages to a crazed man and his gang of thieves. This is a man who will stop at nothing to discover what lies in the last secret chamber.

All bets are off, and only the cleverest will survive this deadliest of adventures.

In this elaborately plotted, fast-paced thriller, Phil Philips takes you on a roller-coaster ride through Egypt's most prized structures on the Giza plateau, to uncover a secret hidden for thousands of years …

MORE FICTION FROM PHIL PHILIPS

Last Secret Keystone

A Joey Peruggia Adventure Series Book 3

When a cargo plane carrying an ancient vase crashes into the Atlantic, the DGSE – otherwise known as the French CIA – immediately suspect it's deliberate. The vase is believed to hold a key that gives entrance to a hidden cave on Easter Island: a site connected with ancient Egypt and an otherworldly portal discovered deep beneath the Great Pyramid of Giza.

Joey, Marie, and Boyce are once again caught up in a dangerous adventure, forced on them by a trained assassin who is on his own spiritual quest for answers ... A ruthless man who will stop at nothing to get what he wants.

His objective: to find the last secret keystone, and with it activate the portal once again. Joey and his friends must stop him – at any cost.

In this fast-paced thriller, Book 3 in the Joey Peruggia Adventure Series, Phil Philips takes you on a roller-coaster ride from the giant Moai statues of Easter Island to the Greek island of Santorini and back to Egypt, where the fate of humankind once again rests with the most unlikely of heroes.

MORE FICTION FROM PHIL PHILIPS

Guardians of Egypt

Short Story - Prequel to the
Joey Peruggia Adventure Series

When Julien Bonnet finds the remains of an ancient city under the Red Sea, he unleashes the might of the Guardians of Egypt. They carry the burden of destroying ancient sites – and anyone who discovers them – to keep their secret safe.

Only this time, they messed with the wrong guy. Killing him will not be as simple as it seems

Get a **FREE** copy when you sign up to my mailing list. You also will be notified on giveaways and upcoming new releases. www.philphilips.com

Lightning Source UK Ltd.
Milton Keynes UK
UKHW011827141120
373340UK00001B/104

9 780992 534554